KEEPERS
OF
Blackbird Hill

KEEPERS
OF
Blackbird Hill

LAEL LITTKE

SHADOW
MOUNTAIN

SALT LAKE CITY, UTAH

Visit us at ShadowMountain.com

This is a work of fiction. Characters and events in this book are products of the author's imagination or are represented fictitiously.

Library of Congress Cataloging-in-Publication Data
Littke, Lael, author.
    Keepers of Blackbird Hill / Lael Littke.
        pages   cm
    Summary: After sixteen years in Hollywood, Jayda returns to Blackbird Hill determined to save her childhood home and protect her inheritance of the family property. Orphaned as a young girl, Jayda stands alone against her extended family, who wants to sell the land to real estate developers. But the developers want all of the property or nothing, and Jayda is convinced that the old house is a powerful symbol of the past and should be preserved.
    ISBN 978-1-60908-744-9 (paperbound)
 1. Homecoming—Fiction.   2. Real estate development—Fiction.   3. American fiction.
I. Title.
    PS3612.I874K44 2011

    813'.6—dc22   2011019713

Printed in the United States of America
Publishers Printing, Salt Lake City, UT

10   9   8   7   6   5   4   3   2   1

For Peggy, just because

Acknowledgments

When I need bits of information for a manuscript I'm working on, I've found that asking a friend or relative who has expertise in a subject is even better than Googling. For this book, Peggy Gyllenskog happily supplied family history information. Sue Vogel answered my real estate questions. Tom Shanahan satisfied my queries about military procedures. And when I needed a snippet of Danish, there was Melissa Malan who is fluent in the language and knows all about Denmark. I greatly appreciate the contributions of these people as well as the constant support and advice of my incredible Tuesday writing group, known simply as Lunch Bunch. Thank you all.

Chapter One

THE FIRST THING JAYDA SAW as she crested the last rise in her car and looked out over the valley was a person moving along the side of the old red barn on Blackbird Hill. It wasn't the fact that someone was there that caught her attention—it was the way the person skulked close to the side of the barn, as if not wanting to be seen. *Furtive* was the word that came to her mind. She pulled her little car off the highway and stopped so she could see better.

She was too far away to see if the figure was a man or a woman. As she watched, the person looked behind himself or herself and then crept around the corner of the barn and disappeared.

"Who do you suppose that could be, Tarzan?" she murmured.

The dog in the cramped space of the backseat scrambled to his feet and poked his brown snout through the open window. "*Woof,*" he said.

Jayda thought of phoning ahead to ask Aunt Leora if she knew someone was sneaking around her property. But she and Tarzan would be there at the house in five or six minutes. She could check things out herself. Besides, it could very well just be kids playing hide-and-seek as she and her cousins had done when they were young. No reason to alarm Aunt Leora. But Jayda had been apprehensive from the first about returning to this place where she'd lived as a child, and seeing the lurker only increased that feeling.

Before starting up again, she took a moment to scope out the familiar valley she'd left sixteen years earlier. In the bright June sunlight, the sheltering mountains still hovered in the background—mountains she'd found so oppressive at eighteen. Well, maybe not so much oppressive as demanding. Stern. Stalwart. Inflexible. Just like her family, the indomitable Jorgensens. Did she really want to deal with them again?

Buck up, she told herself. You're thirty-four now. Give it a try. Aloud, she said, "We're home, Tarzan."

The dog brought his head back into the car. "*Woof*," he said again.

"Right." As Jayda drove the little blue Mini Cooper down the hill, she took a good look at the valley floor and saw how many new houses there were. Thirty, and more to come, Aunt Leora had said. They stood in orderly rows, a distance back from Blackbird Hill and the Jorgensen house, as if not daring to challenge its dominance. It had always been the biggest house and landholding in the valley, which was appropriate since it had been the home of the founder of Blackbird, Asa Jorgensen.

Danish immigrant in the last quarter of the nineteenth century. Pioneer. Empire builder. Long gone by the time Jayda was born. But his influence had lingered on. Stalwart. Inflexible. Demanding.

The late-afternoon sun glinted on the house's array of dormer windows, giving it a secretive look, like someone wearing reflecting shades. When she'd lived there, Jayda had fancied those dormers were watching her, pricked forward like the ears of a horse. Passing judgment. Cautioning her always to remember the family adage: "If the pioneers could do it, so can we."

She felt Tarzan's hot breath on the back of her neck as she crossed the valley and turned left onto the long driveway leading to the house on Blackbird Hill, the house Aunt Leora was expecting her to save somehow from a date with the wrecker's ball. Aunt Leora hadn't explained exactly how she was supposed to do that, but Jayda had come anyway. There wasn't much reason to stay in California. Not since her movie career had fizzled. Not since Ethan had ended their marriage.

There was no sign of a lurker by the barn now that she was up close. It looked good—aged and rickety but with a fresh coat of red paint. A horse, equally aged and rickety, stood in the adjacent corral. With delight, Jayda realized it was Twister, an old gray bag of bones she'd expected to be long since gone to whatever reward old rodeo horses go to. He was the only sign of life on the place, except for a kid who seemed to be digging a hole under one of the apple trees remaining from the old orchard. Maybe the kid had been the person by the barn a few minutes before. Nope. Too small.

Tarzan shifted restlessly in the backseat. It had been a couple of hours since they'd made a rest stop. Besides, Jayda suspected that the big dog, all seventy-five pounds of him, might be getting a bit claustrophobic in the limited space. Probably warm, too, with all that dense brown fur.

"Okay, okay." Jayda braked the car and got out, allowing the travel-weary dog to scramble free. He headed immediately to the corral where Twister stood watching them, his ears pricked forward, for all the world like the dormer windows of the old house.

Tail wagging, Tarzan trotted to the fence. Twister dipped his head down, nickering softly, and when the friendly dog came within reaching distance, he nipped him sharply on the behind. Startled, Tarzan froze while the old horse turned his back and ambled nonchalantly toward the barn, trailing rude noises as he went.

"Never mind," Jayda said. "Come on, Tarzan. I'll introduce you to the rest of the family."

She was picking up her purse from the front seat when she saw Aunt Leora come out of the back door, arms loaded with boxes. Jayda hadn't seen her for several years and was amazed at how much she'd aged. Her hair, graying when Jayda had last seen her, was now snow-white. She'd always carried herself as straight as a flagpole, but now she was slightly bent. She had to be in her mid-eighties since she'd been almost seventy when Jayda had left. She was actually Jayda's great-aunt—sister of her grandfather. She'd seemed old even way back when Jayda had come to live with her at the age of four, after the terrible accident left Jayda an orphan.

Aunt Leora wore glasses now, something she'd never needed before. Peering over the rims, she called, "Jane! I'm so glad you made it before I left." Stacking the boxes in the back of her old red pickup, the same one Jayda remembered, she walked briskly forward, arms outstretched. "Oh, my dear, my dear," she murmured as she hugged Jayda. "Thank you for coming. I told everybody I knew Jane would come home."

Jayda returned the hug enthusiastically and then stepped back. "I'm Jayda now, Aunt Leora," she said. "*Jayda.*"

Aunt Leora shrugged. "You'll always be Jane to me. I never could figure out why you changed it—a good, honest name like that."

"Randy said *Jayda* Jorgensen would look more, more . . ." Jayda searched for the right word. "More glitzy or whatever, on theater marquees. That was back in the days when I was going to be a big star of the silver screen."

Aunt Leora acknowledged that with a terse nod. "Randy," she said. "He was the one who convinced you to run off to Hollywood in the first place, wasn't he?" Not waiting for Jayda to answer, she went on. "Didn't last long, as I recall. Whatever became of him?"

Jayda reached down to give Tarzan a reassuring pat. He watched Aunt Leora closely, apparently wary after his greeting from Twister. "Randy disappeared into the Hollywood scene right after he could see I wasn't going to be his meal ticket. I think I wrote about how his movie producer uncle wouldn't even let us date. I was supposed to be the innocent ingénue both on screen and off." She shrugged. "And now Ethan is gone, too." Ethan, her husband of eight years.

She pulled the dog forward by his collar. "This is the only guy I trust anymore. Name's Tarzan. My protector."

Aunt Leora made a humphing noise. "Kind of a 'Me Tarzan, you Jane' thing?"

"You got it." Jayda turned her gaze to the old red truck. "How come you're loading up all by yourself? Where is everybody?" She had expected the uncles and the aunts and the cousins by the dozens to be there to send Aunt Leora off to the new life she'd chosen. Even maybe to welcome herself, Jane/Jayda, home.

"Boise," Aunt Leora said. "Seattle. North Carolina. South Dakota. West Virginia. You name it. Lucas is the only one who still lives here, although Belinda comes every summer to stay a few months. The two of them bought out all the others. You're on your own for the time being, Jane. *Jayda*. You and this worthy male you brought along." She reached forward to rub Tarzan's head.

"But who's going to drive you to Ogden and get you settled at the—" Jayda hesitated. She didn't know what to call the place where Aunt Leora had chosen to live.

"The retirement village?" Aunt Leora laughed. "I'm driving myself. I'm allowed to have a vehicle." She eyed the truck. "Although they might not like having this old wreck parked on their fancy landscape."

Feisty as ever, Aunt Leora was. She'd been a highly successful psychologist in private practice for all her working years, but she'd insisted on driving battered pickup trucks right down to their last gasp. Jayda wasn't surprised that she was still doing it "her way," which was what the relatives had always accused her of. "Might as well back off and let Leora do it her way," they'd said after every confrontation Jayda could remember. Maybe that's why there hadn't been much flak—yet—about how she was leaving the old house and its fate to Jayda.

But, Jayda wondered, what kind of artillery would the cousins bring in once she was gone? Aunt Leora had said a developer wanted to buy the Jorgensen property, including where the house stood. She was offered a huge price, so Jayda had been told.

"Well, let's go bring out the rest of my stuff," Aunt Leora said now. "I want to get to Ogden before dark. My eyes aren't what they used to be."

She was leaving *now*? "But . . . but . . . but . . ." Jayda sputtered. "You can't go yet. I need you to brief me on what I'm supposed to do. About where things are. About what arrangements have been made."

Aunt Leora raised her eyebrows. "For what?"

"For my taking over. For my fending off the developers."

"It's just Lucas and Belinda you'll have to fend off," Aunt Leora said. "They're all for taking the money and running. They think the investors might decide now is not the time to be paying high prices for real estate if you don't sell right away."

"So can't they sell what's theirs and get on with it?"

Aunt Leora shook her head. "The developers want all or nothing. A package. They have big plans for the land the house sits on and the orchard and the rest of the hilltop." She snorted. "Dave Bradbury calls it 'the crowning glory,' for whatever it is they want to put here." She started toward the house. "All or nothing," she repeated.

She didn't say who Dave Bradbury was.

Jayda trotted after her. "Aunt Leora," she said, "I saw someone out by the barn when I came over the last rise. Did you notice anybody there?"

"No," Aunt Leora said over her shoulder. "Probably kids."

"That's what I thought." Jayda didn't mention the furtiveness. The *skulkiness*. What was the point? Apparently it was Jayda's problem now.

She followed Aunt Leora inside the kitchen, which looked much the same as it used to, except for new cherrywood cupboards and granite countertops. Very much in keeping with the vintage and style of the house.

Aunt Leora gestured toward two plastic clothing bags draped over the big round kitchen table. "Will you take those out? They're the last things to go. The rest is yours—do with it whatever you want."

Numbly, Jayda picked up the bags. "Can't you at least stay long enough for us to have dinner together? Or until tomorrow morning? I was young when I lived here with you. I don't know the history of the house. I remember you always talked about our legacy from the past, but who cares about stuff like that when you're eight or twelve or seventeen? I need to know all about it if I'm going to battle for the survival of the old family manse."

Aunt Leora smiled at the term. "You don't have to battle for it if you don't want to. But I'm betting you will. After you get to know it." Plucking her purse from a chair, she went outside and walked toward her old truck. "Things will work out, Jayda."

"But aren't you going to give me any instructions?" Jayda wailed.

"Yup," Aunt Leora said. "Don't forget to feed the old horse." She twitched her head toward the barn.

"I mean about the *house*." Jayda stumbled after her, the long clothing bags tangling her feet. "How can I get to know it if you don't tell me about it?" she pleaded.

"Let *it* tell you," Aunt Leora said over her shoulder.

"Yeah, right." Jayda couldn't believe what she was hearing. "As if the walls have voices."

"Exactly," Aunt Leora said.

Later, after the old red truck had rattled off, leaving behind Aunt Leora's final instructions not to bother her with phone calls unless someone died, Jayda brought her belongings in from the Mini. She didn't have a whole lot of baggage. Not the external kind, anyway. Just enough suitcases and old playbooks and computer equipment to fill her small car. Her baggage was mostly internal, and she had a truckload of that. Maybe that's why Aunt Leora had left the house and all its history to her. Some kind of therapy. She'd always said you could never know who you *are* until you found out who you *were*. So was it her theory that if Jayda communed with all the old ghosts who lingered around the house, somehow it would add up to who *she* was as well as what *it* was? That kind of thing had always seemed like psychobabble to Jayda.

She really didn't have a clue as to how to go about saving the old house. Couldn't Aunt Leora have said more than just to let *it* tell her?

She looked at the nearest wall. "Speak," she commanded.

Tarzan's ears raised to full alert. "*Woof,*" he said.

Chapter Two

AFTER JAYDA DEPOSITED ALL of her stuff upstairs in the east-facing room that had been hers when she was young, she realized she was hungry. She hadn't bothered to stop at the local supermarket when she came through the one-stoplight main part of town. Surely Aunt Leora would have left some canned chili or tuna fish or something in the cupboards.

With Tarzan at her heels, she returned to the kitchen. She fed him first from the provisions she'd brought with her. She might have forgotten to pick up food for herself, but she'd thought ahead for his needs.

It was when she went to the refrigerator that she found a note from Aunt Leora taped to the door. "I've made a stack of meals for you," it said in her handwriting. "Things you used to like. The quit-claim deed and other papers you'll need, along with a check that should cover expenses for a while, are in a plastic file box next to the computer desk in the Remembering Room. By the way, I told Smoot Ferguson he could come by once you get settled. You'll like him."

Jayda whuffed. Trust dear auntie to supply her with a man as well as a stack of meals. She didn't recognize the name. There hadn't been any Fergusons around when she'd left town. Well, she'd make short work of him. One thing she didn't need was another man.

The note was signed, "Love and best wishes, Aunt Leora."

Jayda smiled as she opened the freezing compartment of the refrigerator. It was so like Aunt Leora to leave a fridge full of food. She'd portioned it out into what looked like dozens of small individual plastic containers. Neatly labeled. *Danish chicken dumpling soup. Ham and lima beans. Beef stew* as well as *Beef stew, curried. Navy bean soup. Minestrone.*

Selecting Danish chicken dumpling soup, a traditional family favorite for as long as she could remember, Jayda carried the container to the microwave, which she set on "defrost." While it thawed, she sat down at the table, feeling disoriented and out of place. She didn't belong here. But she didn't belong in California either. Not anymore. Now that Ethan was no longer part of her life. She still missed him. She *could* call. Tell him she'd arrived safely. Would he care?

No, she couldn't call. And she knew he wouldn't be calling her. Not now that the divorce was final. It had been simple and quick, since they didn't own any property to speak of that needed to be legally divided.

Ethan was the one who'd ended things. "It's over, Jayda,"

he'd said. "Finished. The credits have run, the curtains are closed, the lights are out."

Show business metaphors. She'd wondered if he'd rehearsed the lines.

She'd moved out and rented a bleak little apartment until she got Aunt Leora's letter, asking her to come home and save the old family home. She'd wondered then and she wondered now why she should care. She'd more or less run away from the "old family home" sixteen years ago. What difference did it make to her if it was sold to developers?

After nuking her meal, she ate quickly and then took Tarzan with her to the barn to make sure the old horse had been fed. There was hay in the outside manger by the watering trough. Perhaps that's what the lurker had been doing earlier.

Feeling somewhat reassured, she called Tarzan, who had refused to go near the corral, and headed back to the house, stopping just a moment for a look. The house was big, but of indeterminate style—its two stories and a windowed attic added up to three stories. At one end was a round tower, as tall as the house and with a witch-hat roof and a balcony. The tower had been a favorite place to play for her and the cousins when she was a child. Later, when she was a teen, she'd seen it as just one more place to clean.

♦ ♦ ♦

Jayda woke the next morning to the ringing of the telephone. She'd stayed up late the night before, prowling through the old house, looking at pictures, touching furniture, trying to re-acquaint herself.

She hadn't gone into the Remembering Room. That was something you needed to prepare yourself for. She wasn't ready yet.

The ringing of the phone was loud and insistent. Used to having her cell phone as her only means of communication, she hadn't thought about the old house having a land line. Opening an eye, she glared at the clock on the bedside table. Seven o'clock. Which meant six in California. That's when Ethan always got up to do his morning run.

Jayda reached out to pull the phone into bed with her. Could he be missing her? How did he get this number? "Hello?" she asked softly.

"Jane! Heard you were here!" Lucas didn't have to identify himself. His booming voice was his credential.

Jayda sat up. She cleared her throat silently so he couldn't tell she'd just come out of a deep sleep. Lucas was the early-to-bed, early-to-rise type and scornful of anyone who wasn't. Lucas was cousin-in-chief of the clan and keeper of the motto ("If the pioneers could do it, so can we"). Lucas was the mover and shaker of the family. She didn't bother to tell him she was Jayda now, had been for years. "Good morning, Lucas," she said. "Who told you I was here?"

"Well," Lucas boomed, "Velda Klippert was the first. Called last night. Saw you drive past her shop. Then Bill Arden happened to mention it when he came to pick up eggs this morning, and . . ."

Jayda laughed. "I guess I've forgotten how the tell-a-person works around here. How are you, Lucas, and how are Leila and the kids?"

"Tell you when I come over," Lucas said. "Are you up and around?"

He wanted to come *now*? "Oh, sure I am, Lucas. Want me to fix you some breakfast?"

"Already ate. The day's half gone, Jane. I'll be over at 7:30. There are things we need to discuss." He hung up.

"I'm not ready for this," Jayda said aloud. Tarzan stretched himself on the braided rug at the side of her bed, then sat up and yawned as if to say he wasn't ready either. "Maybe we'll catch a nap later," she told the sleepy dog.

She'd been too tired to shower the night before when she'd finally gone to bed, so she did now. Quickly. And hurriedly combed her hair, long and dark blonde now—its natural color—after years of being whatever hues were right for the characters she played. She chose jeans and a conservative, short-sleeved, blue plaid shirt to put on. She was back home in Blackbird now. She didn't want to give Lucas the opportunity to comment on how "Hollywood-y" she'd become, the way he'd done when she'd come home briefly for Aunt Etheline's funeral a few years previous. It had been one of two visits here—both for funerals—since she'd gone away and, yes, she had indeed dressed Hollywood-y at the time, in funky finery from a second-hand shop.

Morning sun lit her way downstairs to the bright kitchen where the old windup wall clock tocked cheerfully, telling her it was 7:20. No time to eat before Lucas came. But he'd notice the absence of cooking smells. "Can't do a good day's work without a good breakfast," he'd inform her.

Oh, well.

She let Tarzan out the back door so he could take care of necessities. He ran onto the porch but then stopped stock-still. Turning his head from side to side, he gazed at the landscape before him. The lawn. The trees and bushes. The flower beds. The orchard beyond. It must have been overwhelming to his doggy mind, accustomed as he was to the tiny backyard in California with three potted plants and a few square feet of grass. He looked questioningly at Jayda as if asking where he should do his business.

She waved a hand. "It's all yours," she told him.

Barking happily, he bounced down the five stairs and ran madly over the grass, circling a flower bed, racing around a garden bench, and finally stopping to sniff a tree before he began marking his territory.

Lucas arrived promptly at 7:30 in a shiny black Hummer. Jayda could have predicted his car would be big and impressive. As he got out, he stared at her little blue Mini Cooper as if it were some kind of noxious bug. To forestall any nasty comments, she hurried over to him. The uniform he wore reminded her that he was the lone lawman in town, part of the county sheriff's department. Blackbird was too small to have its own police department.

"Lucas," she said with fake enthusiasm, adding a homespun

twang that seemed to return naturally now that she was back where she'd grown up. "It's really nice of you to come see me."

"Thought we might as well get things taken care of right off," he said, "so you can be on the road again."

"On the road?" she repeated.

"Yeah. Back to civilization. Back to that Edward, or whatever this one's name is."

His tone implied that she'd been married as many times as some movie stars, when it had actually been only once. "Ethan," she said. "And he's history."

He nodded. "Figures. Now let's go on in and get the necessary papers. The Summertree Meadows people are anxious to line things up so they can get started."

He took her arm to guide her into the house, but she shook it free, not moving. "And who, may I ask, are the Summertree Meadows people?"

"The developers," he said. "You should see the plans they have for the hill here, where the house is. They're going to keep the creek, of course. Everyone loves the sound of a creek."

"I'm partial to it myself," she said. "I really don't think I'm up to discussing this right now, Lucas. I'm still tired from my trip. I've got stuff to think through."

An annoyed look crossed Lucas's face, but his voice was bland as he said, "Not much to think through, as I see it. Just sign the papers and Dave Bradbury will take care of the rest."

Dave Bradbury again. Aunt Leora had mentioned him. Jayda guessed he was part of "the Summertree Meadows people." She could picture him. Big belly hanging over his belt. Unctuous. Smooth. She knew the type.

Lucas was still speaking. "We really need to get this settled so we can tell the rest of the family where we'll have our reunion this year since the house will be long gone by then."

"And the reunion is when?"

"Last week in August. You know that, Jane. That's always been when we have the family reunion. You haven't been a part of it for so long you've forgotten all of our traditions."

"Like returning to the ancestral home," she said. "Like reliving memories in the old house."

Lucas leaned back against his Hummer. "Yup. That too. But, Jane, we don't need this crumbling old house to relive our memories. And we can build new ones for ourselves if we sell now. Did Aunt Leora tell you what the Summertree Meadows folks are offering?"

"No," she said. "Lucas, I haven't decided what I'm going to do. I need time. So there really isn't anything to talk about right now."

"You're too much like Aunt Leora," he said bitterly. "She never would listen to reason either." Opening the door of his vehicle, he got in. "The deal is nixed without your property. What is it you plan to do with it? Have you saved a couple of million bucks for its upkeep?"

"Good-bye, Lucas," she said. "Nice to see you."

He was about to start the car when Tarzan came bounding around the house, stopping a couple of times to mark yet another tree. "Well, hello," Lucas said to Tarzan. Turning back to Jayda, he asked, "Did he come with you?"

She nodded. "Name's Tarzan."

"That's one fine mutt. Funny, I would have thought you'd have one of those scrawny little Hollywood designer dogs."

She remembered how Lucas had always been a defender of mutthood. It was something she'd liked about him when they were kids. They both watched as Tarzan gazed off toward the barn where the ancient horse dangled his head over the corral fence. "Old Twister greeted him yesterday with a nip on the rump."

"Oh, yeah, that's another thing," Lucas said. "What are your plans for that old hay burner? He's getting a bit long in the tooth."

Jayda glanced at the corral where Twister watched them. "Is he part of what's mine?"

Lucas nodded. "I believe he is."

"Then he'll live out his life where he is."

"Or as long as you own the property." Lucas turned the key, and the engine purred to life. Before he went, he worked up a smile. "It's nice to see you, Jane. Guess you'll be out to church on Sunday. Everybody will be looking to see you. You're Blackbird's only claim to fame."

"Yeah, right. Yes, I'll probably be there. I wonder how many people I'll still know."

"Quite a few," he said. "Lot of new families, too." He waved a hand at the new houses in the distance.

"Aunt Leora mentioned that," she said. "Do you know some-one named Smoot Ferguson?"

"Oh, yeah. Everybody knows Smoot. I'm sure he'll be com-ing by soon. You'll like him."

So was it a conspiracy involving everybody in town to get her together with this Smoot guy?

Lucas slammed the door and started to drive off, circling her little car to head downhill. Jayda was puzzled when he stopped and got out again. "Did you know you've got a flat tire?"

"Flat tire?" she ran around the Mini to take a look. The front right tire was totally pancaked.

"Prob'ly picked up a nail yesterday," Lucas said. "Well, we'll get 'er changed in a blink, if you'll open up the trunk."

It was when she came back from getting her keys that Jayda saw the folded note under the windshield wiper. She picked it off and peered at it, while Lucas opened the trunk and pulled out the spare tire. It was a page from a small spiral-bound notebook. There was a crude drawing of a car with a black circle around it and a broad black diagonal slash from the top left to the bottom right. Like the signs that warn you not to do something.

Underneath was printed:

Go back to Hollywood.

"Lucas," she said. "Somebody purposely flattened my tire."

"Naw," he said, already jacking up the car. "Nobody here does stuff like that."

He changed his tune when she showed him the note. "Well,"

he said, sitting back on his haunches, "there are a lot of folks who stand to benefit from a bunch of new people moving in. Prob'ly someone is just expressing an opinion."

"Lucas," Jayda said, "this is malicious mischief." She told him about the lurking figure by the barn she'd seen when she first arrived. "Somebody is trying to scare me away."

"Maybe," Lucas said. "But nobody around here would hurt you. Don't worry about it. I'll keep an eye on things."

She had to be satisfied with that.

She thanked Lucas profusely when he finished putting on the spare tire and promised she'd take the car down to Bill Flinders's garage later to have the damaged tire fixed and replaced on the rim. When he left, she dropped the offensive circle-and-slash note on the kitchen counter where Aunt Leora had always stacked messages. She then took Tarzan back upstairs for the promised nap. After all, she wanted to be well rested when the everybody-likes-him Smoot made his predicted visit.

Perhaps he might have an idea about who flattened her tire and warned her to get out of town.

Chapter Three

THIS TIME IT WAS NOT THE phone but a car horn that wakened Jayda. It blasted a beep-ba-ba-beep-beep rhythm that was right out of her teenage years. Only one person honked like that.

"Emmylu!" Leaping up, she raced down the stairs and out into the yard, arms outstretched to embrace her old best friend from their childhood days.

Kids spilled out of the SUV, with Emmylu emerging after them. They whirled off in every direction, and Tarzan was there, barking happily and accepting pats and kisses from what seemed like an entire school.

"Hope you don't mind that I brought my brood," Emmylu yelled above the din after she and Jayda had hugged and squealed and hugged again. "Thought you'd like to see what I have to show for the passing years. There are two more at home. The older ones."

"These are all *yours*?" Jayda asked and then hoped she hadn't offended Emmylu by her incredulous tone.

Emmylu laughed joyously. "Only five of them. The rest belong to neighbors. We mix them together in the summer and try to get them all sorted out when it's time for school to start."

"Well, come up on the porch and rest while you can." Jayda took Emmylu's hand and led her to adjoining Adirondack chairs. When they were settled, she said, "You look happy, my friend. Mass motherhood agrees with you."

"It's all I ever wanted to do," Emmylu said. "I never did have big dreams of fame and fortune, like you did." She reached out to pat Jayda's hand. "Was it fun?"

Jayda smiled. "Yes, it was. I loved being a star, even if it was just in a few cheesy beach musicals."

"I'm glad," Emmylu said.

"Even the last few years have been fun," Jayda said. "I've had some bit parts in movies, but playing in community theater productions has been my main thing recently."

Emmylu took time to yell a warning at an overly rambunctious child who was climbing up the porch railing. Then she said, "What parts? Remember how you always wanted to do Nelly Forbush in *South Pacific*?"

Jayda nodded. "Did it. More than once. And remember how we used to love *Bye Bye Birdie*? I did Kim McAfee when I was still young enough to do it, and then a couple of years ago I played Rosie. I guess this is the right time to leave—before I'm asked to do Mamma Peterson."

They laughed together.

"So you think you'll be staying here?" Emmylu asked.

"Don't know yet. Not much to go back to California for, now that Ethan's out of my life."

Emmylu put on a sympathetic face. "I was sorry to hear about that." She snagged a passing child. "This is Annie, from the show of the same name."

The little girl gave Jayda a gap-toothed smile before wiggling free.

"Remember," Emmylu went on, "how we always said we'd name our kids after the heroines of our favorite musical productions? I remember you were going to have a Brunhilda because you liked Wagner operas."

Jayda didn't answer because Emmylu had left her chair to separate two boys who were having a disagreement. She didn't want to talk about it, anyway. Brunhilda had never come into being. It had been a sore spot between her and Ethan. She'd wanted babies. "Not yet," Ethan had said. "Not until I get my big break." He'd looked around their small apartment. "Where would we put a baby?"

"Look," Emmylu said to Jayda, "we can't visit with this mob churning around. Come over for lunch soon. I'll chain them up or something."

Jayda passed out hugs as the children got back into the car. One of the boys tried to pull Tarzan in too, but apparently decided there wasn't room. Tarzan had been willing to go. Probably figured it would be lots more fun at their house than here alone with her.

She waved as Emmylu drove away with what she had to show

for the passing years. It was a whole lot more than a pile of yellowing scrapbooks. "A stack of empty yesterdays is what *I* have to show," Jayda muttered. It came from a line in *The Music Man*, something said by Professor Harold Hill to Marian the Librarian. Jayda had played that part in a dinner theater production just before she left California, as well as here in Blackbird. She and Lee Spencer had been the leads in their high school production. She wondered what had happened to Lee in the intervening years.

The next thing on her schedule was to get her flat tire fixed at Bill Flinders's garage. Bill had been at Blackbird High when she was there, and as he worked, he entertained her with tales of the pranks he and his buddies had perpetrated in "the old days."

"Remember when . . . ," he'd say and then go off into yet another story. It made her think perhaps Lucas was right about the flat tire and nasty note on her windshield being just a prank.

But then Bill asked her how long she was going to be around. "Indefinitely," she said.

He frowned. "Lot of folks are looking forward to having the town grow when this new development gets built," he said. "We're hoping you'll sell out in a hurry so it can get started." *And go back to Hollywood where you belong,* she thought. He didn't say that, but she got the message.

So, she went back to wondering. Maybe he would know who'd played a prank on her. Very likely he wouldn't confess even if he did, so she didn't say anything.

After her tire was taken care of, Jayda took the opportunity to reacquaint herself with the little town. She walked down Main Street, recognizing some features and noting that others were new, like the Back Porch Café. Peering through the big front window, she saw several customers and assumed the food was good. She made a mental note to try it soon.

Looking south, Jayda saw the high school in the distance, and along the way was Velda Klippert's Hair Affair. Velda was an institution all by herself. Jayda looked forward to seeing her again. It was time to have her hair trimmed anyway.

The hardware store looked much the same as it had sixteen years ago. It was while she was admiring its window display—not nuts and bolts and hammers, but decorated baskets and handwork she assumed to be local—that a man she knew stopped at her side. It was Jake Sterry, who had been there in Blackbird as long as the rocks in the ground. Or at least that's what he always told the kids.

"Heard you was back, Janey," he said. "Nice to have you here."

She smiled. "Good to *be* back, Jake."

"Heard you'd be leaving again as soon as you sell that old house on the hill," he said.

"Don't believe everything you hear, Jake. I'll be around for a while." She looked up the street behind him. "Is Madge with you today?"

"No, she ain't, Janey," he said. "She's in the cemetery."

She chided herself for not catching up on the news before blurting out personal questions. "I'm so sorry. When did she pass away?"

Jake grinned. "Oh, she ain't dead. Just up in the cemetery

planting petunias on her ancestors' graves. You remember she was always big on family history and all that."

Jayda punched him lightly on the arm. "Well, you sure got me that time, Jake. I can tell you haven't changed a whole lot."

He laughed, apparently delighted that she'd fallen for his joke. "Neither have you, Janey," he said. "Still the purtiest girl in town."

She didn't correct him on the Janey thing, nor the "purtiest girl," although she wondered if she still qualified as a girl. "Why, thank you, Jake," she said sincerely. "That's right nice of you to say."

He tipped his hat, a battered Stetson, to her and went off down the street chuckling.

It truly was good to be back, Jayda decided. For a while.

She spent the rest of the day getting settled in. She was warming up another of Aunt Leora's little containers of food for an early dinner when she heard a firm knock at the door. Perhaps this was the promised Smoot coming to call, the man apparently everybody knew she'd like. She did like his firm hand on the door. It spoke of a man who had confidence in himself.

She patted her hair, glancing into the oval mirror beside the door before she opened it—and looked expectantly into vacant air.

Chapter Four

SHE HAD SUPPOSED SHE'D SEE someone as tall as she, or taller, but she had to drop her gaze to see her visitor. It was a boy, dressed in shorts and a scruffy blue T-shirt. Blond hair, with a newly cut buzz. Maybe seven. She'd worked with elementary school theatricals, so she was familiar with kids. Second grade, Jayda guessed.

"Well, hi." She wondered if he was one of Emmylu's brood, perhaps wandering back to play with Tarzan. "This is a pleasant surprise," she said.

The boy raised his eyebrows. "Didn't Aunt Leora tell you I was coming? I'm Smoot."

This was Smoot Ferguson? "Yes, of course she did," Jayda recovered quickly. "Come on in." She couldn't help but smile at crafty old Aunt Leora, setting her up to expect a man. No, it was she herself who'd done that. Was she so eager for a new male interest that she saw fix-ups where none existed?

Smoot walked inside as if totally familiar with the house, which he undoubtedly was. "Is it okay if I leave my game here in the vestibule until we're ready to play? Me and Aunt Leora always play Monopoly on Friday, after we watch *Wheel of Fortune*."

Jayda was so charmed by his use of "vestibule"—Aunt Leora's term for the entryway—that she scarcely noticed what else he said. He was expecting her to play Monopoly? How was she going to tell him that she really wasn't in the mood to buy and sell railroads and build houses and hotels? He seemed to take for granted that life would go on as before, with her as a substitute for Aunt Leora.

She opened her mouth, searching for words to put in it, but just then Tarzan came bounding in from wherever he'd been outside. Smoot's eyes lit up. "A *dog*!" he exclaimed.

"*Woof!*" Tarzan barked, his tail whipping back and forth in greeting.

Smoot fell to his knees, wrapping his arms around the big brown mutt. Kids always loved Tarzan. Those in Jayda's California neighborhood had stopped in frequently to ask if he could come out and play.

"His name is Tarzan," she said.

"Aunt Leora didn't mention him," Smoot said amidst hugs and face lickings.

"There are quite a few things she didn't mention," Jayda muttered, then aloud said, "She didn't know about him ahead of time, that's why. By the way, Smoot, are you *related* to Aunt Leora?"

Smoot got to his feet, shaking his head. "She just told me to call her that."

It figured. Back when Jayda had lived there, Leora had been called Aunt Leora by half the county. She'd earned it. Never having had children herself, she'd "adopted" every one she encountered, sending homemade cookies on birthdays and flowers to the girls when they graduated from high school. She also dispensed free counseling to them, even though she charged other people large fees.

"Well, you know what, Smoot? It was probably okay with your parents for you to come here and play Monopoly with Aunt Leora on Fridays, but now that I'm here we'd better check it out with your mom."

Smoot looked down at Tarzan. "My mom's dead."

"Oh, I'm sorry. Well, then we should tell your dad."

Now he looked up at her. "He's in the Marines in Af-ghan-i-stan. I live with L. G., and he doesn't care if I'm here."

"Elgie?" Jayda asked. She couldn't remember anyone by that name in town.

Smoot nodded. He sniffed the air. "Something smells good."

So Jayda fed him, letting him pick out one of the little containers from the stash in the freezer. She made a fresh salad and sliced off crusty bread from a loaf Aunt Leora had apparently made just before she left. They ate at the kitchen table, with Tarzan sprawled at Smoot's feet. Smoot kept up a steady stream of chatter about the house, the horse, and the town.

Lucas called just as they were finishing. "Be home tomorrow morning at nine, Jane," he boomed as if this were the eleventh

commandment. "Dave Bradbury wants to talk to you. He repre-
sents the developer and has some renderings he wants to show
you."

"I'll be here," Jayda said, hanging up. She turned to Smoot.
"Okay, buddy, let's go to your house so I can talk to this Elgie
you live with, and we'll ask about your staying to watch *Wheel of
Fortune* and play Monopoly." She could phone, but she wanted to
see this guy in person.

Smoot chewed a last bite of bread. "He might not be home."

So did he just leave Smoot to his own devices? "We'll find
out," she said.

"If we go out past the orchard," Smoot said, "we can look
down and see if his truck's there." He led the way out the
back door. She noticed that he sidled past the doorway of the
Remembering Room, pressing himself against the opposite wall.
"That's where Aunt Leora talks to people who aren't there, but
used to be," he said in a low voice, as if he didn't want anybody
to hear.

He was clearly spooked by the room. Its main feature was a
wall of drawers at one end. Ten drawers high and twenty drawers
wide. Jayda remembered that they contained pictures and letters
and papers from the past one hundred years of the family's history, which was why it was called the Remembering Room.

Jayda had never been all that interested in the room when
she'd lived there, preferring playbooks and stage sets to musty
drawers full of faded papers. She wasn't sure what Smoot meant
by Aunt Leora talking to people who weren't there.

She followed him, trying to keep pace, wondering why kids

never walked if they could run. As they approached the orchard, Jayda thought back to the day she and Tarzan had arrived. "Smoot," she said, "I saw somebody digging a hole out under an apple tree a couple of days ago. Was that you?"

"Yup," he said. "I was having a funeral."

"Oh, I'm sorry. Did something . . . die?" She hoped it wasn't a favorite pet.

"L. G.'s computer mouse," Smoot said. "Somebody dug a hole there so I used it for a grave."

Jayda put a hand up to her mouth to hide a smile and then followed the boy as he led her along a path through the raspberry patch, where he stopped long enough to pick a handful of berries for them to taste. "I'll bring more later," he declared.

The patch was overgrown, as if Aunt Leora hadn't cleaned it out last fall, the first sign Jayda had seen that the old lady, like the old horse, was no longer up to full steam. The June grass hadn't been cut, and it grew tall and luxurious all around the patch. And braided. Someone had separated it into sections and braided it.

"Did you do this, Smoot?" she asked, pointing at the neat plaits.

He shook his head. "Bug does that."

"Bug?"

Smoot nodded. "She's a girl. She's older than me and she bosses me a lot."

"Do you know why she braids the grass?"

He shrugged.

Actually, it was a thing Jayda had done when she'd lived

there. Not for any good reason. Just because the grass was there. And long. Aunt Leora had told her once that she, too, had braided June grass. And she'd learned how from her grandmother. Jayda had a moment of seeing the grand sweep of generations, in something as inane as braiding June grass. She resisted the feeling of being part of it, not wanting to be too firmly bound to this place before she decided what she was going to do.

She wanted to ask more about Bug, but Smoot skipped on ahead with Tarzan at his heels. "We're almost there," he said. "See that old cabin down there by the poplar trees?"

The Bride's House. That's what it had been called for as long as Jayda could remember. The little log cabin Asa Jorgensen had built for his bride when they first came to this land. Well over one hundred years old, it was shabby but still sturdy, still home to somebody. To Smoot and this Elgie, whoever he was, who didn't take adequate care of the boy in his charge.

"His truck isn't there, so he's still gone," Smoot said. "He goes somewhere most afternoons."

So did he just leave Smoot to his own devices when he went? Jayda was appalled that he wasn't more concerned with the boy's welfare. And what about the community? Things in Blackbird seemed to be a bit loosey-goosey, to use an old term of Aunt Leora's, what with people lurking about and flattening tires and letting small boys wander at will.

Well, she'd take it up with Lucas later, Jayda decided. For the moment she said, "Okay, Smoot. Let's go back. I'll talk with him later."

Smoot took her back to the house by a different route, past

the little spring that bubbled out of a hillside. "I like to stop here for a drink," he said, kneeling down to inhale a few swallows of water. Jayda thought she would do the same thing, until Tarzan interrupted his delighted running about and sniffing to drink from the little pool beneath the spring with noisy slups and slurps, drooling into it as he drank. After that, she thought better of tasting it. At least for the moment.

As Smoot escorted her across a meadow toward the barn, Jayda had a feeling of déjà vu. The things he commented on were things she'd liked as a child. Of course, there was no mystery about it. Aunt Leora had coached both of them about how to see the wonders of their world—wonders which would be paved over if the developers had their way.

When they got to the barn, Tarzan barked at Twister holding vigil at the corral fence. For his part, the old horse raised his head high and pulled back his thick lips in the sneer he'd been famous for as a rodeo personality. "I love that guy," Smoot whispered as if he didn't want the horse to hear.

"Me too," Jayda whispered back. She was glad that although the bony old animal had lost his physical prowess, his spirit remained intact.

She watched as Smoot climbed the rails of the fence so he could rub the horse's face. "Don't let him bite you," she warned.

"He doesn't bite people he likes," Smoot said. He picked something off the top rail and jumped down, a puzzled look on his face. "What's this?" He held out a scrap of paper, torn from a small spiral-bound notebook. Drawn on it with a heavy marker was a black circle with a slash down through it.

"It's nothing," Jayda said. Taking the scrap, she crumpled it in her hand. "Somebody was a litterbug."

"But it was thumbtacked to the rail," Smoot said, showing her the tack.

"Well, that's a mystery, isn't it!" Jayda said lightly. "Race you back to the house."

But it was no mystery. The "prankster" was at it again. A reminder that she wasn't wanted here in her own home.

It worried her a little that she was now thinking of it as home. She'd been here only two days, but she already felt drawn into more lives than she cared to be. It was as if she was supposed to instantly morph into being Aunt Leora, weaving the varied strands of other people's lives into her own fabric. It wasn't anything she'd planned for. But she had to do something about Smoot's situation, didn't she? And find out what was going on with this Elgie guy. And meet with Dave Bradbury, the developer's representative, so she could make a decision about what she wanted to do with the old house. And watch for the barn lurker and tire flattener. And somewhere along the way meet Bug, the girl who had a penchant for braiding June grass.

Chapter Five

BACK AT THE HOUSE, Jayda put the note from the corral railing on the kitchen counter along with the one that had been on her car. She had the uneasy feeling there would probably be more.

Smoot turned out to be an astute Monopoly player, despite his scant seven years. He bankrupted Jayda by building hotels all along the green properties—Pacific, North Carolina, and Pennsylvania—where she inevitably landed on every turn around the board.

They were stacking the game pieces back in the box when the telephone rang.

"Ms. Jorgensen?" a polite male voice asked.

"Yes?"

"I understand Smoot is there with you."

"Yes. With whom am I speaking?"

"L. G. He lives with me. Is it all right if he stays there with you tonight?"

Jayda sucked in air while she framed words to tell this guy what she thought of him as a caregiver, but he went right on without waiting for her to respond.

"He's used to staying there," he said. "Please send him home in the morning. I'll be back then."

He hung up.

Jayda removed the handpiece from her ear and stared at it. "Just like that!" she said aloud.

Smoot looked up curiously. "Was that L. G.?"

"Yes." She refrained from saying more. She should be careful what she said until after she'd talked with Smoot's so-called guardian.

"Am I staying here tonight?" Smoot's voice held a hopeful note.

"You sure are, buddy," Jayda said. "Which room do you want to sleep in?"

He got to his feet. "Generally I take turns with the rooms. Tonight I'd like to sleep in the Good Morning, Sun room. That's where I keep my pajamas."

Jayda added that to her arsenal of facts about Smoot. Apparently sleeping overnight was a common occurrence. After he was tucked into bed in the Good Morning, Sun room with a happy Tarzan curled up beside him, he smiled at her and said, "Aunt Leora always sang a sleepy song to me."

A sleepy song. Jayda searched her memory to find a file of "sleepy songs." She located the term, but it was tenuously connected to her mother—and just out of reach. She'd been only four when her mother died, and when Aunt Leora had tried singing lullabies to her, she remembered covering her ears and saying she couldn't listen.

"How about this one?" she said now, perching on the edge of the bed. With an arm around Smoot's shoulders, she sang "My Favorite Things" from *The Sound of Music.* She'd played the part of Maria in community theaters several times.

When she finished the song, Smoot sighed. "You sing nice," he said and closed his eyes.

Jayda sat upright in her own bed for a long time, wondering what role she was auditioning for in the drama of Smoot's life.

◆ ◆ ◆

Dave Bradbury, the Summertree Meadows developer's representative, came promptly at nine the next morning. He wasn't what Jayda had been expecting. He could have come right out of central casting. He was a tall, late thirtysomething, dressed in sharply creased gray pants and a cobalt blue shirt with a patterned tie, and had a smile that was wide and beguiling. He had a dog biscuit for Tarzan, and he presented Jayda with a cheerful "Good morning, Ms. Jorgensen," along with a small basket of red apples.

"'Comfort me with apples,'" she murmured as she took it.

"Song of Solomon, chapter 2, verse 5," he said.

His knowledge of the Bible surprised Jayda, although she wasn't sure why. She decided to go along with it. "Seems to me there's an apple in Genesis, too," she said. "Had to do with enticement. And a serpent."

Dave quirked an eyebrow. "And the one in Song of Solomon had to do with love."

At seventeen, she would have blushed. But she was way past that. "It's beautiful literature, Mr. Bradbury."

He nodded. "You're right, Ms. Jorgensen. Please call me Dave. May I call you Jayda?"

Now it was her turn to raise an eyebrow. "Yes. But why not Jane? That's how I'm known around here."

"Prime rule of making an impression," Dave said. "Know as much as you can about the person you're dealing with. I Googled you. Found out about your alter ego and that you retained the name Jorgensen after you were married."

"Not much ego left," she said. "I fizzled in Hollywood." She motioned toward a chair beside the kitchen table. "Sit down, Dave Bradbury, and say what you came to say."

He sat, after motioning for her to be seated first.

He was good at what he did, which was to spread out large sheets of paper with houses and trees drawn in, and roadways winding through what he called elevations, which were indicated by curving lines. He hitched his chair closer so he could point out various features. She was aware of the cologne he wore, a compelling fragrance that made her senses sit up and take notice. She wondered if that was another prime rule of making an impression on clients.

"You can see from this rendering how attractive Summertree Meadows will be when it's all built," Dave said.

She interrupted. "Not nearly as attractive as the natural meadows that are here right now."

"We'll try to retain as much of them as possible," Dave said smoothly. "Green space, or common land, is always an asset to a development. And the quaking aspen—those will definitely remain. Some of the little irrigation ditches may have to be altered, but we'll try to retain the existing ambiance."

Jayda thought of the bubbly spring where Smoot had knelt to drink. How would they alter it? Would a shiny steel drinking fountain have the same "ambiance"?

Dave continued on, pointing out the way the houses would be positioned so that windows looked out at the surrounding mountains. And how the "crowning glory" of the area would be the recreation center which would be where Jayda's house now stood. "Everybody will be able to take advantage of the center," he said. "The swimming pool, covered and heated, will be right out there where your deck is now."

"You speak as if it's a done deal."

"Isn't it?"

"Not at all. My cousins may be eager to sell, but I obviously have final say about my own property, and I'm not convinced that tearing up the scenery and 'altering' the ditches is something I want done. You can build an attractive development without including my place."

She was not used to saying "my place." It felt good on her tongue. And it *was* hers. Legally and lawfully deeded to her by Aunt Leora.

"The investors want it *all*," Dave said. "All or nothing."

Jayda remembered Aunt Leora saying the same thing.

"But," she said, "why does your development have to be *here?*

There is plenty of vacant land in the area. Why do you have to take over where there is already a town?"

"Economics," Dave said smoothly. "The infrastructure is already here, for the most part. We don't have to start from scratch. It's also a low-crime area, which makes it very attractive. And the market for homes with common land attached is huge. Need any more reasons?"

At that moment, Smoot came clumping down the stairs, followed by Tarzan. He was dressed in the shorts from yesterday but a different T-shirt. Green stripes today. *So he keeps clothes here as well as pajamas,* Jayda noted to herself. And then she had the thought that turning over this land to a developer would be more or less like opting out of taking proper care of a little boy who loved the landscape just as it was.

"Hi, Mr. Bradbury," Smoot said, waving a hand. "Hi, Jane. I hafta take Tarzan outside before he busts." He headed toward the back door.

"Town pet," Dave commented as he watched Smoot go. "I see he's added you to his list of admirers."

"He's a delight," Jayda said. Under the guise of looking closer at the rendering she stood up, managing to move her chair a few inches to the right, away from Dave's overpowering cologne. "Mr. Bradbury," she began.

"Dave," he prompted.

"Mr. Dave Bradbury, if my cousins indicated that I was an easy sell, they were mistaken. I don't know yet what I'm going to do with my property. I have to think about it. And right now I have an urgent appointment, so if you'll excuse me, perhaps we can talk again later."

He gave her a sly, sideways glance. "We haven't even discussed the price yet, Jayda."

"Later, Dave. Later."

He was cheerful enough about leaving, exuding confidence that she would come around to his way of thinking eventually and that Summertree Meadows was just over the horizon. She got the impression that he thought it was just a matter of dangling a big enough carrot.

He commented pleasantly while he slowly gathered up his renderings, first remarking on the sunny kitchen and then slipping in an aside that though he could understand why it might be hard to give up the house, with the money Mr. Yoshida was offering, she could custom build a place—or two, he smilingly added—for herself. He was on his way out of the house when he spotted the circle-and-slash notes on the counter.

"Hmmm," he said, picking them up, "what's this?"

"Harassment," Jayda said. "I hope they aren't from you?"

"Believe me, Jayda," he said, "if I wanted to annoy you it would be something a little more sophisticated than these sophomoric notes. Probably some town joker with too much time on his hands. I'll check around and see if I can put a stop to them."

"I'd appreciate it," Jayda said.

Tossing the notes back on the counter, Dave left.

Jayda fed Smoot before they set off for his home. This Elgie guy didn't know it yet, but her "urgent appointment" was with him. But the fire behind her resolve to scorch the guy for neglecting Smoot cooled slightly as she followed the boy and Tarzan along the path that led to the Bride's House. Smoot seemed perfectly happy to return to his sorry excuse for a guardian. He skipped and sang and stopped to show Tarzan a large ground squirrel burrow, into which the dog immediately thrust his snout. After a few snuffles and snorts, he pulled it out and began to dig enthusiastically, although he came up with nothing but a nose full of dirt.

"I know that guy," Smoot told Tarzan. Pointing to a flat rock beside the burrow, he said, "Sometimes he comes out and sits there on his porch and chatters at me when I pass."

The dog sneezed as they continued their way along the path.

There was a blue pickup parked beside the poplar trees at the Bride's House. "That's L. G.'s," Smoot informed Jayda. "Sometimes me and him go in it to the city and see a movie."

"Do you like movies, Smoot?" Jayda asked.

"Oh, yeaaaah." Smoot drew the word out to indicate how much. "Especially *Ratatouille* and stuff like that. I don't like the war movies L. G. gets sometimes from Netflix."

The fire of indignation within Jayda flared again. Why would the guy let a little kid like Smoot watch war movies? Especially when his dad was in a war zone?

When they were within a few yards of the house, a man came from the door. When he saw who was there he put out his arms. No. His *arm*. Jayda was shocked to see that he had only one. The left arm ended just below the elbow with a hook at the end of an extension. The left side of his face, which was toward

Jayda, was scarred as if it had been burned. There was a spot on his temple where no hair grew.

"L. G.!" Smoot sang out, running into his one-armed embrace.

"Smoo-teeee," the man cried, equally as enthusiastic. "How are ya, buddy? How much did you miss me?"

"From here to Plymouth Rock," Smoot said, pointing at the huge rock on the hill behind the house.

So they still called it that. Jayda remembered that she'd been the one who'd given it that name years ago. She'd told the younger kids that it was where the Pilgrims had landed, which perplexed them no end because they couldn't figure out how ships had sailed up to it. She and Emmylu had snickered at their confusion.

She brought herself back from her memories to see the man gazing at her. "Hello, Jayda," he said. "Nice to see you again."

It wasn't until then that she recognized him. "Lee?" she whispered. "Lee Spencer?"

He bowed grandly, making a sweeping gesture with his right arm. "The same. I wondered if you'd know me. You didn't recognize my voice on the phone last night."

"You said your name was Elgie," Jayda scolded.

"L. G. That's the special name Smoot calls me. My middle name is Grover, remember? L. G. Spencer?"

"L. G.," Jayda said with a laugh. "I thought Smoot was saying 'Elgie.' I just figured it was someone new in town."

He laughed with her and then looked a little sheepish. "I'm sorry I dumped Smoot on you like that. I went into the city for my therapy session. I'm learning to use a prosthesis that resembles a hand." He held up his left arm with the hook. "And then there was a student performance I wanted to attend at the university."

Jayda's fire fizzled out, as if water had been thrown on it. This was her old friend Lee, the only one in town who'd understood her wild ambitions to be an actress. He'd had ambitions himself. He had played the part of Professor Harold Hill to her Marian the Librarian in their high school production of *The Music Man,* and Petruchio to her Katherine in *Kiss Me, Kate.* The two of them had shared their dreams of being on Broadway, or in pictures, or something equally grand.

"I'm sorry, Lee," she stammered. "Nobody told me about—" She hesitated and then finished, "anything." Lame, lame, lame. She could feel her face reddening and was embarrassed that she couldn't control it. But this was Lee, who'd been her leading man in more ways than one in high school. She had shared her first kiss with him. Not just a stage kiss, but a *real* one, as they stood under a blossoming apple tree in the orchard.

Lee smiled sadly at her. "Don't be embarrassed, Jayda. I know I look different. I *am* different."

"So am I," she said.

He nodded and then leaned down to speak to Smoot, who stood close beside him. "Who's the grand dog that followed you home? Do we get to keep him?"

A brief hope flashed across Smoot's face, but then he shook his head. Leaning close to Lee, he put his hand to one side of

45

his mouth and behind it whispered, "She needs him. She doesn't have anybody else."

Lee nodded solemnly, but over Smoot's head he gave Jayda a brief smile. "Well, buddy," he said, "I don't think Jayda minds sharing him with you."

A puzzled look crossed Smoot's face. "How come you keep calling her Jayda? She's Jane. Aunt Leora called her *Jane* when she talked about her."

"She used to be Jane. She changed her name to Jayda when she was in the movies."

Jayda was surprised that he knew that. He'd kept better track of her than she had of him.

Smoot seemed to mull that over and then abandoned it.

Turning to Jayda, he said, "Is it okay if I take Tarzan behind the house to see our chicken coop?"

"He'd love to see it." She touched the top of the boy's sun-warmed head as she spoke.

"Yay!" Smoot shouted. "Come on, Tarzan. I'll show you Ethel and Dolly and Phyllis and all our other hens." They ran together down the path.

"Smoot *needs* a special playmate," Lee said. "Looks like Tarzan gets the honor." He gestured toward the house. "Come on in and sit down. I'll make raspberry tea and we'll talk about why you've come back. I assume Dave Bradbury has been to see you already with his rolled-up renderings of Summertree Meadows under his arm."

"Yes." She followed him inside the cozy cabin where a fire crackled cheerfully in an old black woodstove, not because the

June day was chilly but apparently to keep a pot of fragrant soup simmering slowly on a back burner. At a gesture from him, she sat on the sofa that faced the stove. There were things she'd prefer to talk about rather than Dave Bradbury. Like Lee's family. She'd heard that his parents had died. But he'd had a sister.

"Where's Lynette these days?" Jayda asked, watching Lee spoon something from a tin into a teapot and then pour in water from a kettle that sat on the back of the stove.

Without looking around, Lee said, "She's dead. Smoot is her son."

Jayda wished fervently that she could start this whole visit all over again, armed with knowledge of what had happened here in Blackbird during the sixteen years she'd been gone. Neither she nor Aunt Leora had been big on correspondence, and Emmylu had been too busy with her large family to write very often. Jayda had not been interested, anyway, in what went on back in the village she'd escaped from. That's how she'd thought about it at the time. Escape.

"I'm so sorry," she said.

He shrugged, his back still to her. "Water under the bridge."

To change the subject, Jayda said, "You mentioned the university." She knew he meant the one in the city, thirty miles away. "Are you taking classes?"

"Teaching," he said. "Part time in the music department." And then, as if he didn't want to say any more about that, he shifted to what he obviously did want to talk about. "What's your plan for saving the old Jorgensen place from the wolves?"

"What plan? I have no plan, Lee," she said. "I don't know

why Aunt Leora deeded it to me. I wasn't in on any of the back story. I don't know what I'm doing here. I don't know how I'm going to stand up against my cousins. Apparently they want to sell everything."

He turned his head to look at her. "But you *are* going to stand."

"I don't know," she said miserably. "What do you think I should do?"

He put the teapot and two cups onto a tray, which he brought over to the sofa table. "Have you seen Dave's renderings?"

"Yes."

"Do you need to ask what I think you should do?"

The Lee she'd known had always had a deep love for their mountain village. It all sat well with him. But he hadn't belonged to the Jorgensen family where the pressure was strong to be like the early pioneers and achieve the impossible. The "If our ancestors could do it, so can we" mentality. Not that she hadn't loved the area, too—at least the mountains and meadows and streams. But she'd felt smothered and had grabbed the opportunity when Randy with the movie producer uncle had convinced her she could have a career on the screen.

"No, you don't have to tell me," she said. "I think I know."

"It feels like a losing battle." He poured hot raspberry tea into the two cups and handed one to her, then sat down beside her. "Those who favor the development regard it as progress. I can see how it probably is. But they don't have to destroy *everything*. The old house should stay." He took a sip of tea. "So kids like Smoot can know there was once a Camelot." He smiled at her.

The last show she'd been in here had been a community production of *Camelot*, with Lee as King Arthur and her as Guinevere.

Apparently in his mind Blackbird was—or at least had been—something great and good and magical. "So how are you involved in it all?" Jayda asked.

He shook his head slowly from side to side. "I'm not. I'm the local bogeyman, Jane. Jayda," he corrected. He touched the scarred side of his face. "I suspect people probably warn their kids to be good or Lee will get them. They're not sure how to deal with me. I'm a recluse. I keep to myself."

"So who will help me?" Jayda asked.

Lee put down his cup. "I'd recommend you go have your hair done."

"Do *what*?" She touched her hair as if to fix whatever he thought was wrong with it.

"You remember Velda Klippert," he said.

"You mean at The Hair Affair?"

He nodded. "You can't have forgotten she's the town encyclopedia. She knows everything. Knows how everybody stands on every subject. Make an appointment. She'll fill you in without your even asking."

"I'll do that," Jayda said, grateful for a clue as to how to get a start on this project.

It wasn't until she and Tarzan were ready to go home that Jayda remembered she'd come there ready to reprimand Smoot's guardian for his neglect of the boy. Even though he turned out to be her old friend, she still felt compelled to at least mention her concern.

"Lee," she said, "maybe it's because I've been in the city too long or something, but I worry about Smoot wandering around by himself so much."

Lee nodded, his face troubled. "That's the way his dad wants it. Colonel Chad Ferguson wants him to be strong and self-sufficient. I worry sometimes, too, but I know nobody here in Blackbird would hurt him, so I honor the Colonel's wishes."

Lucas had said the same thing about the good people of Blackbird. Certainly it had been safe enough when she was a child for kids to run about largely unsupervised. She'd have to trust it was still true now.

But when she got home, she found another page out of a small spiral-bound notebook lying on the driveway near the porch steps, as if the wind had brought it there. This one was blank. But she got the message.

Chapter Six

JAYDA PUT THE BLANK PAGE ALONG with the first and second notes in a folder. If there were more to come, she'd collect them and perhaps convince Lucas by sheer volume that he should post a watch on her place. Which he probably couldn't do because he was the only lawman in town. She'd just have to hope he and Lee were right about people in Blackbird not being the kind who would do any real harm.

As soon as she got back to the house, she called Velda Klippert to make an appointment.

"If you can get here in about half an hour, I can work on you," Velda said enthusiastically. "Been wondering how long it would take you to come see me. Remember, I was the one that gave you that spiffy 'do you set off for California with. No wonder they put you in the movies. You looked grrrrreat, girl. Why, that was more than fifteen, sixteen years ago, wasn't it? I was always so proud when I'd see you up there on the big screen, and

I'd tell people how it was me who made you look like a movie star even before you was one."

Jayda went on listening while Velda went on talking. She didn't tell her that the 'do she'd left town with hadn't even lasted all the way to California, nor that the studio people had changed everything about her hair, even the color, for the six movies she'd starred in. The flow of Velda's words was soothing and familiar, like sitting in a warm, pleasant stream, and Jayda let it just go on. And on. Until Jayda heard a bell in the background, and Velda said, "Nice talking with you, Jane. Gotta go now and finish up Grace Taysom's perm. She said she saw you going over to Lee's this morning with Smoot, so I guess you know all about his sad story. I'm really looking forward to seeing you. Isn't it the pits what that development company wants to do with your old house? Ta ta." She hung up.

Jayda felt breathless, as if she'd been running a marathon. She sat there by the phone for a few minutes, actually puffing a little. She liked Velda and was glad she hadn't changed in all the years she'd been away.

Tarzan, who'd been sprawled at her feet, sprang to his feet when she stood up, gazing eagerly at her, tail swinging, feet dancing.

"We've had our walk," she told him. But when she looked down at his pleading face and churning tail, she relented. "Okay, but you can do your own walks here, you know. Just this once we'll go out again, and then I've got to get busy."

Busy doing what? She had no plan for saving the old house.

She wasn't even sure she wanted to go to the effort and she had no idea how to support it even if she could save it.

As she and Tarzan headed for the back door, she paused at the entrance to the Remembering Room—where Smoot said Aunt Leora talked to people who weren't there but used to be. Maybe that was the first thing to do. Have a conversation with all those ancestors whose histories and letters and receipts and old report cards were in the wall of drawers. Maybe they could tell her what the house wanted her to do.

Yeah, right.

Outside, the first thing Jayda saw was the old horse, Twister, sagging against the corral fence. As soon as he saw her and Tarzan, he straightened, threw up his head, and gave a little buck. Probably as much as he could do these days.

Tarzan watched him. He undoubtedly remembered the humiliation of being nipped on the rear by that arrogant old bag of bones on the day they'd arrived. A volley of barks burst from his throat as the horse glanced over his shoulder and then flung out his back legs in a maneuver that made him stagger.

What would happen to him if she decided to go along with Dave Bradbury's plans for Summertree Meadows? While Tarzan made a stiff-legged approach to the corral fence, Jayda gazed off down the hill to the cluster of houses already built. They seemed like an advancing army, crawling slowly up the slope. Was there really any way to stop them? People needed good places to live—places to bring up their children away from the fumes and noise of the cities.

But what would happen when all the meadows and green places were paved over? When Camelot was just a memory?

Jayda was surprised when she looked back toward the corral to see Twister hanging his head over the top rail and Tarzan reaching up to touch noses with him. Had they already reached a truce? *Watch out,* Jayda whispered under her breath. And even as she thought it, the villainous old horse bared his enormous yellow teeth and delivered a nip to Tarzan's shoulder. The dog yipped and backed away, barking. Challenging. *This isn't over,* he seemed to say.

Just then a girl came around the corner of the barn. A black-haired, gypsy-looking girl, dressed in tattered jeans and a flouncy orange and gold striped blouse. She looked about fourteen going on thirty.

"There are two things you can't trust around here," she said without preliminary. "Old Twister and Dave Bradbury."

"Hi," Jayda said. "I'm Jayda, and that's Tarzan." She gestured toward the dog.

The girl nodded. "I'm Bug."

Bug. The girl who braided the June grass in the orchard.

"I've come to help you save the old house," Bug said. "I'll put you in touch with your relatives and let them tell you how."

Jayda gave a short chuckle. "Oh, Lucas has already been here, and we don't see eye to eye at all. He wants me to sell."

Bug stared solemnly at her. "I'm not talking about the living ones," she said. "What I'll do is help you talk to the dead."

If the girl's remark was designed to get Jayda's attention, she had it. But of course she didn't mean it literally. Or did she?

"Well, that would be interesting," Jayda said slowly. "So when shall we get started?"

It apparently wasn't what Bug wanted to hear. She stared at Jayda, her Maybellined eyes curious. "Did you hear what I said? I talk with dead people."

Jayda had been in Hollywood environs long enough not to be shocked by anything, which was obviously the effect Bug wanted to achieve. Why else the dead-black dyed hair and black holes for eyes? What was she rebelling against? Did her relatives push her to be like long-suffering pioneer ancestors, too?

"I heard." Jayda remembered a movie from a few years back in which a boy talked with dead people. She wondered if the girl had seen it but decided not to ask. Who was *she*, anyway, to say people couldn't play out a part they'd seen somewhere?

"Well," she said, "I'd really like to talk with my great-great-grandpa Asa and find out if he has any suggestions as to what I should do about the old house. Do you think you could locate him?"

"Maybe," Bug said. "I could try."

Jayda nodded. "Do you have your appointment book with you?"

Bug shifted the position of her head and pursed her lips, clearly implying that she knew she was being put on. "Forget it," she said. "I just wanted to help."

Jayda chided herself for forgetting how sensitive fourteen-year-old girls could be. "I'm sorry," she said. "I just meant we should set a time. I'm about to go to Velda Klippert's place to get my hair done. Can you come to my house later? I need all the help I can get." That was true enough, although Jayda was not counting on any ghostly advice.

Bug regarded her skeptically for a moment and then lowered her mascara-encrusted lashes. "Okay," she said. She walked off toward the orchard.

Jayda was sorry to see her go. A strange girl, but interesting. And puzzling. Jayda felt an affinity toward her. "I used to braid the June grass too," she called.

Bug kept on walking.

Tarzan, who'd been lying chin on paws watching Twister munch hay from the manger inside the corral, got to his feet. The old horse ignored him.

"Let's go, pal," Jayda said. "You can't win 'em all, you know."

Yet she felt she'd made some kind of progress. It was like a casting call, with people showing up to audition for whatever parts they would play in the coming drama. At least she had some allies now. Lee. Emmylu. Smoot, for sure. And now Bug.

As she walked toward the old house, Jayda tried to see it as a stage set. It was impressive enough, sporting dormers and balconies and the round tower with the witch-hat roof. A lot of life had been played here during several generations of family. People had been born here. And died. Those who had gone on must have left something of themselves behind. What secrets might it hold within its walls? And when were those walls going to speak to her, as Aunt Leora had said?

It might be interesting to see how Bug planned to contact the dead. Not that Jayda believed for an instant that she actually could.

The first thing Velda said when Jayda walked through the door of The Hair Affair was, "Hear the news?" No greeting. No "Nice to see you again."

Velda hadn't changed a bit in sixteen years, Jayda decided. She raised her eyebrows in response to the question. "You mean *my* arrival in town has already been superseded?"

"Belinda's back for the summer," Velda stated. "Lives in New York City the rest of the year, in the fancy apartment one of her husbands left her. Although rumor has it she's having a hard time paying the rent. Likely she needs money." She slanted a look at Jayda to make sure she got the significance of that. Then, the gossip delivered, she pulled a towel from the cabinet beside her hair-washing sink and motioned toward her shampoo chair. "Sit," she said.

Jayda sat. "Belinda," she repeated. Visions of the cousin she hadn't seen since she was about eight years old filled her head. Belinda had come home for Grandma Martha's funeral, as had all the uncles and the aunts and the dozens of cousins. Jayda had been puzzled by all the whispering behind hands that had followed Belinda's entrance into any room. "Prances in like she owns the place," Jayda had heard someone say at the meal prepared by the church ladies after the services were over and Grandma was buried in the graveyard up the hill.

"Pranced" was a good description of how Belinda had walked. As if she owned the place. At eight, Jayda had been impressed by the pretty lady with the big hair and flashing legs. In fact, for several days afterward, she'd practiced prancing herself. She wondered now if memories of Belinda had had anything to do with her own running off to Hollywood. She'd have to be careful not to prance when she went to church on Sunday.

Velda flipped a lever, which made the shampoo chair lay back. Jayda remembered that chair. It was about the only thing Velda had salvaged from a shop she'd had up in Pocatello before her marriage went sour and she'd come back to Blackbird. Jayda stretched her neck across the support that she'd always thought had been created by the designer of a torture chamber.

"Not a man in town will be safe with her around," Velda said morosely, "swinging those windshield-wiper hips all over the place." Turning on her spray hose, she began wetting Jayda's hair without once inquiring what Jayda wanted done. If you came for Velda's services, there was the implicit understanding that she had the last word in how you wanted to look.

Jayda weighed the pros and cons of telling Velda that the water was too hot and her brain was solidifying like a boiled egg. But the memory was there that if you said anything like that, Velda was programmed to flip into a litany of apologies and by the time she'd finished, she'd sold you a piece of Tupperware for half price to make up for her blunder.

Jayda wondered if she still sold Tupperware on the side. She knew better than to ask. So she waited until her hair was shampooed and conditioned and the spray hose turned off, and then, scalp tingling from Velda's vigorous scrubbing, she said, "Any idea as to *why* Belinda's back?"

Velda was only too eager to continue the tale. After she'd escorted Jayda to the antique hydraulic chair in front of a big mirror, she went on. "Heard her fifth husband died, the one who didn't have any money, the one she married for L-O-O-ve, so she's probably here to get what she can out of the sale of your old homestead. I'm sure she's ready to sell her part of the package, and I'm sure it will all go for top price because the way I hear it the Summertree Meadows folks want it real bad. Leora said you were coming back to call a halt to it all."

Jayda's head jerked as Velda attacked her hair with a comb, but she didn't attempt to break into the stream of words with a complaint.

"Some of the business folks," Velda went on, "think a big development like that would bring money to town, and who wouldn't like a little more of that? But the rest of us think we'll lose more than we'll gain, what with trees and creeks being torn out to make room for it all. And your old Jorgensen place being gone with the wind."

Jayda was pleased to learn that Velda was another ally, but she said nothing. She almost broke into the recital when Velda picked up her scissors and began snapping it at sections of her hair. She was relieved to see that the result was just a few split ends on the floor.

When Velda applied the blower, Jayda had a few moments to think of questions. She decided not to ask anything but rather just let Velda go on. Which she did, as soon as she turned off the blower.

"That Dave Bradbury," Velda said, "is a slick one. Nice as the day is long, but always with a purpose. Single man. Might try to date you. Unless Belinda gets to him first. Never mind that she's my age. Robbing the cradle is no matter to her, as long as he has

59

money. Think Dave has money? Well, he will if this deal goes through. What you got in mind to stop it?"

"I don't have a clue, yet," Jayda managed to say before Velda started up again.

"Let the house tell you," Velda said, and Jayda noted to herself that this was the second person to say that.

"Dig out its secrets," Velda continued. "Might be some reason to have it declared a historical treasure or something like that. Locate the skeletons in the closets. Get something on Lucas. He seems to be the most eager to let it go. Or find out why Belinda left town when she was seventeen. Nobody ever knew for sure, far as I know."

If Velda didn't know, it had to be a secret buried as deep as Grandma Martha. Velda had given her some paths to follow. Although she wasn't sure she'd go so far as blackmail. Or maybe she would. Wasn't the old house worth anything she could do to save it, even something underhanded?

Jayda debated that question inwardly as she watched Velda survey her, apparently deciding what kind of 'do she needed at the moment. What she did was begin to plait it into a long French braid. Like the June grass in the orchard.

When she was finished, Velda handed Jayda a mirror and turned the chair so she could see the back of her head. "How do you like it?"

Jayda had been skeptical about the wisdom of the French braid, which was how she'd worn her hair a lot when she was a teenager. But Velda had pulled a few tendrils out to frame her face and the effect was becoming.

"You look good, so young they'll think you never left town," Velda said, "and nobody will wonder about what went on down there in Hollywood. Good to see you, Jane. Let me know if I can help you make that old house give up its secrets."

Jayda was so caught up with gazing at her French-braided self in the big mirror by the door that she scarcely heard what Velda said. Her mind was occupied with wondering if Dave Bradbury would be coming up to the house again before the becoming hairdo fell apart.

Chapter Seven

JAYDA CHIDED HERSELF ALL THE way home for thinking she'd like Dave Bradbury to see her new hairdo. What was she—seventeen and frantic for a date? What possessed her to think such a thing? The last thing she needed right now was another man. She was irked with herself, especially since Velda's remark about secrets had gone right past her.

She thought about driving back to The Hair Affair and asking Velda what secrets she was referring to. But she knew Velda would say that if she knew *what* secrets, then they wouldn't be secrets, would they?

Disgusted with herself, she drove home, parked in the side yard, and entered the house where a nervous Tarzan greeted her. He seemed to want to tell her something. Had the house been whispering its secrets to *him*? Whining, he paced across the kitchen, turning his head to gaze down the hall that led to the back door.

"Need to go out?" Jayda asked. "Or just having a little separation anxiety?" This was the first time she'd been out of his presence for any length of time since they'd left California. She'd put him in the house so he wouldn't be going out to challenge that crazy old horse Twister while she was gone. Very likely he'd been lonesome.

When he stopped at the doorway to the hall and barked, Jayda experienced a chill. *Someone* was there.

"Smoot?" she called. Who else would come into her house without an invitation?

She heard footsteps, and then Lucas appeared in the doorway of the Remembering Room. "Oh, hi, Jane," he said. He offered no explanation as to why he was there.

"Lucas!" she said reprovingly. "What are you doing here?"

He put on a bewildered look. "Why the burr under your saddle? I just wanted to talk to you. You weren't home so I came in. Anything wrong with that?"

"Well, yeah," she said. "People don't generally wander around other people's homes while they're away."

He chuckled. "You been down there in L.A. too long, Jane. This is Blackbird, where nobody locks their doors. And this is the old family home, so I got a right to come in if I want to."

Jayda put her hands on her hips. "It may be the old family home, but it belongs to *me* at the present time and I don't like to come home and find somebody snooping around. Especially since I *did* lock the door. How did you get in?"

He shrugged. "I've got a key. Aunt Leora gave it to me, just in case I ever needed it."

She held out her hand. "I'd like it back."

Obligingly, he fished the key out of his pocket and laid it on her palm.

"Okay, now," she said, "what were you snooping around for?"

She had the thought that he could have been looking for new places to plant the little circle-and-slash notes. He could easily have left the first one on her car, and the one on the corral fence. And the blank scrap. He wanted her to sell the house and go back to Hollywood.

He grinned amiably. "Maybe I just came to talk. What would I be snooping for?"

Jayda wished she knew. Did he know the old house had secrets? Was he trying to uncover them before she did?

"Did you barge into the house when Aunt Leora lived here?" she asked. "With or without a key?"

"Aw, Jane, you know how Aunt Leora was. Strictly by the book."

"And in her book," Jayda said, "people didn't trespass on other people's property."

Lucas put up his hands. "Okay, okay. I won't do it again. I just thought things might be a little looser around here with Auntie gone."

"Well, they won't be," Jayda said crankily. "You made Tarzan nervous in addition to trespassing, you know."

Lucas looked contrite. "I didn't think he was going to let me come in. Barked up a storm. Good watchdog." He reached down to pat Tarzan's head. The dog's tail moved in an almost imperceptible wag. He watched Lucas suspiciously.

"Too bad you didn't take the hint," Jayda muttered. "What was it you wanted to talk to me about?"

"Belinda's back in town," he said.

Jayda nodded. "Velda told me."

Lucas shrugged his shoulders. "Figures."

"So why has she come back?"

"*That's* what I came to talk about." Lucas made a gesture toward the kitchen. "Can we sit down and maybe have a bite to eat while we talk? I had breakfast at six, and it's wearing thin."

Jayda made toast while she thawed one of Aunt Leora's little containers of soup in the microwave. Setting the finished products on the kitchen table in front of Lucas, she sat opposite him. "Okay," she said. "Talk."

Lucas savored the soup for a moment before saying, "Belinda's been talking to Dave Bradbury."

So much for Dave Bradbury, Jayda thought. He'd not be seeing *her* again, new French braid or not, after being caught in Belinda's dazzle. That's what they'd called it when they were kids. Belinda's *dazzle*.

"About what?" she asked.

"Huh!" Lucas said. "What do you think? She's hoping to up the price for the whole package of land so she can grab her cut and vamoose to scope out the next rich husband. She didn't say so, but that's my guess." Hitching his chair forward, he looked Jayda full in the face. "So, Jane," he said, "how much would it take for you to agree to give up this old shack?"

"Not for sale," Jayda said shortly.

Lucas sat back, and Jayda saw various emotions warring on

his face. Should he start yelling, or should he be gentle and placating, or should he exercise his authority as senior cousin and just lay down the rules?

Eventually he merely shrugged and said, "Belinda will be over to see you."

"Is that a threat?" Jayda asked.

"More like a promise." Lucas finished his soup and got up to go.

"Lucas," Jayda said as she and Tarzan walked him to the door. "What *were* you doing in the Remembering Room?"

His face flushed slightly, tattling that he'd been there for a purpose. But all he said was, "Talking to the relatives."

"Sure," Jayda muttered as he headed for his Hummer.

After Lucas drove away, Jayda went down the hall to the Remembering Room to see if anything had been disturbed there. She'd been awed by the room when she was a child. Awed by the wall of drawers and what was in them. "If our pioneer ancestors could do it, so can we," Jayda whispered, which made Tarzan look curiously up at her.

She patted his head. "It's okay, buddy," she reassured him as she gazed around. It certainly was not an unattractive room. There were two multi-paned windows which let in abundant light. A large oval braided rug, faded and threadbare but still beautiful, covered most of the floor. Jayda wasn't sure which ancestor had made it, but the story was that she'd used every scrap of discarded clothing she'd saved over the course of several years, so it was a veritable treasure trove of family history. Against one wall stood the vast cabinet made up of two hundred drawers

(Jayda had counted them once), much the same as the file cabinets that libraries used before computers came along, except that the drawers were bigger. One of the ancestors had made it. Jayda didn't know which one. When she'd lived here before, she hadn't been interested in that kind of thing. In fact, she'd resisted knowing family history. She'd felt oppressed, weighed down by it. She'd left town to get away from it, hadn't she?

She walked across the room to open a drawer of the cabinet. Had Lucas thought there was something here that would convince her to sell the old house to the developers? Or had he just been idly curious as he waited for her to come home?

Her thoughts were interrupted by a knock at the front door, followed by a bark from Tarzan. Could this be Belinda already?

Jayda tried to marshal her thoughts as she walked to the door. It had been almost twenty years since she'd seen Belinda, but she remembered her as being overpowering in her effect on people. Not only was she beautiful, but she was also charming. And smart. And calculating.

But it wasn't Belinda at the door. It was Bug—her dead-black hair partially hidden by a multicolored scarf that covered the top of her head, tied gypsylike in the back. Opening burgundy-lipsticked lips, she spoke. "I've come to help you. Like I said I would."

The girl was almost a caricature, costumed for the part of talking to the dead.

"Come in." Jayda opened the door wide, and Bug came in, stopping to scratch Tarzan behind the ears. He rewarded her with wide wags of his tail, unlike his lukewarm acceptance of

Lucas's pat. Which said something about the two people. Tarzan was a good judge of character.

"I was in the Remembering Room," Jayda said. "Looking through some drawers."

Bug nodded. "That's where Aunt Leora used to talk to them."

"Them?"

"Ancestors."

"Oh, yes, that's what Smoot said. Did they talk back to her?"

Bug slanted a scornful look at Jayda. "She'd get out her family history stuff, and she'd say, 'So when was it you signed the homesteading papers?' and then she'd look through a bunch of papers and find the right one and she'd say, 'Oh, that's when it was.'"

Jayda almost laughed. Was that what Bug meant about talking to the dead? Talking *to*, not *with*.

"So that's how you're going to help me?" Jayda asked.

"Sure," Bug said. "What did you think?" And then suddenly she stiffened. "Somebody's been here."

Jayda felt a little thrill of something. Maybe the girl *was* psychic after all. "How can you tell?" she asked.

"There's a hat over there that doesn't belong here." Bug pointed at a dark blue billed cap lying beside the lamp on a small table.

"Oh," Jayda said, "that probably belongs to Lucas. He was here while I was gone."

Bug's eyes narrowed. "What was he looking for?"

"I don't know," Jayda confessed.

"Maybe you'd better find out," Bug said ominously.

"Right," Jayda agreed. "Shall we get started?"

But what were they going to start? Talking *to* the dead? Digging the secrets out of this old house and saving it from destruction?

Maybe . . . giving purpose to her own life?

Chapter Eight

JAYDA STEPPED BACK TO SURVEY the wall of drawers. For the first time it occurred to her that perhaps Aunt Leora had meant *literally* her statement about letting the walls tell the story of the old house. *This* wall, these two hundred drawers, must contain vast amounts of information.

Of course she hadn't been totally incurious about the drawers when she was young and lived there in the house. She'd pulled a lot of them out to see what was inside. But mostly it had just been papers, which she wasn't interested in. Occasionally she'd happened upon what Aunt Leora called a "trinket." A small china doll that had belonged to a little girl sometime in the past. She remembered a hard rubber ball. A notebook full of jump-rope rhymes. *Down in the meadow where the green grass grows, there sat Merna as pretty as a rose. Along came Eddie and kissed her on the nose. How many kisses did she receive?*

She remembered that notebook, but she'd never asked who Merna was. Or Eddie. She hadn't cared. Then.

"Okay," she said to Bug, "where do we start?"

Bug raised her eyebrows. "Where do you *want* to start?"

"I don't know. How exactly did Aunt Leora go about talking to the dead?"

"Well," Bug said, "what do you want to know?"

What did she want to know? Just about everything. "How about any secrets the house might be hiding," she said.

Bug frowned. "That's kind of . . . of—"

She seemed to be searching for a word, so Jayda supplied it. "Non-specific?"

"Non-specific," Bug said, and then repeated it, as if trying it on her tongue. Jayda could almost see her filing it away for future use. Then she said, "I mean, who do you want to ask about what?"

"I get the idea." Jayda paused to consider. "For starters, I'd like to know who built this wall of drawers."

"Now we're getting somewhere." Bug looked up and down the rows of drawers. "Do you know how old it is? The wall of drawers, I mean?"

"No."

Bug flicked her a curious glance. "Didn't you ever wonder?"

"I'm ashamed to say I didn't."

"Boy," Bug said, "you sure passed up a lot of neat stuff."

"Yeah, I know," Jayda said.

Bug reached up to touch a drawer high up on the left side. "Let's try way back. With your great-great-grandpa Asa." She pulled the drawer all the way out and handed it to Jayda. "You say, 'Asa, I'd like to know who built these drawers.' Then you look through this drawer and see if there are any clues."

Jayda smiled to herself. But it was worth a try.

The drawer was full of papers. Single slips. Fat letters, or what appeared to be letters anyway. Yellowed newspaper clippings.

Jayda picked up a faded sheet of paper. The date at the top was July 7, 1901. She looked at the sign-off at the bottom. "Papa," it said.

Jayda took the drawer and letter over to the sofa, where there was enough light to read the faded ink, only to discover it was written in Danish.

"Well, this isn't going to help," she said, laughing.

Bug came close and peered over Jayda's shoulder. "What's so funny?"

Jayda showed her the Danish letter. "Can't learn much from this," she said.

Bug took the sheet of paper. After a moment she said, "This must have something to do with the wall of drawers. Look, here's the number 200. There are two hundred drawers." Jayda saw other dimensions listed, probably drawer sizes.

On a hunch, she stood up and walked over to the shelf where Aunt Leora had the volume she called her "Book of Remembrance." Flipping through it, she located Asa Jorgensen and saw that his father was Jens Jorgensen. Flipping to the previous page she found where Jens Jorgensen was listed as the father of the family that included Asa. A note at the bottom said Jens was a carpenter. "Bingo," Jayda said. "Asa's father must have built the drawers," Jayda said. "Asa led the company of pioneers who settled Blackbird, but I remember Aunt Leora saying his father had been part of the group."

Bug grinned triumphantly when Jayda showed her the note. "Okay, now do you understand about talking to the dead?"

Jayda nodded slowly.

"You could learn a lot from these drawers," Bug said. "Why didn't you go through them when you lived here?"

Jayda considered the question. Why hadn't she? "I guess it was because the pioneers were always held up as superpeople, and we were supposed to measure up to them. It griped me."

"Huh!" Bug said a bit scornfully. "You sure gripe easy. Is that why you ran away to be in the movies?"

"I guess so," Jayda admitted.

"Huh!" Bug said again. "You could probably write better movies from the stories in the drawers than the ones you were in."

"I don't write movies," Jayda said.

"You must know somebody who does."

"I know someone who writes musical scores for movies," Jayda said. "My ex."

Bug shrugged. "So there's a start. Take it from there. Think outside the box. Don't you have any imagination?" She turned abruptly and left, patting Tarzan's head before she exited.

"Apparently not," Jayda said at her retreating back. Bug sounded as if she were forty-five, not fourteen. Jayda wished she hadn't thought about Ethan. It still hurt, the breakup. At one time she'd loved him so much, had wanted to be with him forever, had even wished to raise children with him. But all she'd gotten was Tarzan. An anniversary gift from Ethan three years ago.

She pulled out the drawer she'd been going through and took it over to the sofa where she began shuffling through it. Underneath a stack of yellowed receipts she came to a slip near the bottom of the drawer. A note. "Have gone to visit Mildred," it said. "Be back for supper. Don't worry." It was signed, "Arvilla."

Bug's comment about a movie now intrigued her. If Ethan had been there, he would have seen possibilities for a movie in that simple note. How about *Visiting Mildred* for a title? Or *Be Back for Supper*? He would have immediately started composing a musical score for the background.

In a flight of fancy, Jayda saw herself calling Ethan. "I've got an idea for a movie," she'd say. "Title it *Don't Worry*." Ethan would be intrigued, and he'd come up there to Blackbird to do the research himself. And he'd be there, all six feet two inches of him, and Tarzan would wag himself into hysteria. And Jayda? She would give him the smile he used to love so much, the one that showed her almost-dimple in the left cheek, and he'd admire the French braid Velda had done for her and say how she looked just like the Jayda he'd married.

She leaped off the sofa so swiftly that Tarzan sat up and barked. "Idiot," she told herself. She hurried over to the wall and slammed the drawer back into place. "He's gone," she told Tarzan. "Gone and forgotten." But she wasn't sure even Tarzan believed that.

Chapter Nine

LEE CALLED EARLY SUNDAY MORNING to ask if Jayda would take Smoot with her to church. "I assume you're going," he said.

"Yes," she said. "But why don't you take him yourself?"

"I told you, Jayda. I'm the town bogeyman now. I frighten little children."

"Lee, that can't be true. You grew up here in Blackbird. People love you. Besides, you're a war hero."

He snorted. "Not so. I was injured by a roadside bomb. Nothing heroic about that."

"Lee," Jayda began, but he interrupted.

"So can you take Smoot with you? If you can't, I'll drop him off as usual."

"Of course I can take him," she said.

Smoot chattered happily as they drove along the creek route to the pretty chapel on another of the several local "elevations," as Dave Bradbury called them. Jayda wondered cynically if he and his investors had tried to buy that site for their fancy development. What would they care if the church was so closely tied to the history of the early settlers?

Had *she* cared when she was eighteen?

On the other hand, she'd always loved the red brick building that she'd fancied watched protectively over the residents of Blackbird, welcoming them to the various activities that took place there, and then providing a final resting place in the sunny green cemetery farther up the hill behind it, with only a tree-filled ravine separating it from the Jorgensen property.

There were a number of cars already in the parking lot when Jayda and Smoot arrived. She saw Emmylu's van and knew there would be at least one friendly face. She wondered about the others. Would they point fingers and whisper that she was the one who was keeping them from becoming rich from the potential new residents of the Summertree Meadows Estates?

"Jayda." Smoot broke into her thoughts. "Jayda, will you take me to talk to my mom after church?"

"Talk to your mom?" But hadn't Lee told her Lynette was dead?

"In the cemetery," Smoot said softly.

"Sure I'll take you, Smoot," Jayda said.

Smoot visibly relaxed. "I like to go there," he said. "I tell her all about what I've been doing. Aunt Leora used to take me sometimes." He paused while he kicked a stone across the pavement, and then confided, "L. G. doesn't like to go there."

That didn't surprise Jayda. Lee probably had a thing about cemeteries at the moment. "I need to visit my mom and dad, too," she said. "I haven't talked to them in a long time." Actually, she'd never talked to them. She'd avoided the cemetery when she'd lived in Blackbird.

"Did you know I used to be friends with your mom?" Jayda asked. "Back when she and I and Lee—" She stopped and then changed her wording to say, "when she and I and L. G. were young?"

"Really?"

"For sure."

Smoot skipped happily beside her. "She'll be glad to see you," he said.

Jayda reached out and took his hand. "We'll go there right after the service."

Heads turned as the two of them entered the chapel. There was no fingerpointing, although there was some whispering behind hands, and one woman she didn't recognize gave her a look so venomous that Jayda almost flinched. But most people smiled and came over to shake her hand or hug her and say how nice it was to see her again.

She was surprised at how many in the congregation she still knew. The families with the old Scandinavian names—Olsen and Petersen and Sorensen and Rasmussen—were well represented. They were descendants of the band of settlers Asa Jorgensen had brought. There were others she knew—Bradley and Palmer and Meacham families who'd lived there for a long time too. They sat encircled by batches of new little descendants who wore the same faces as the kids she'd grown up with. And there was Christine Hatch playing the organ, just as she had when Jayda lived there. She must be as old as Aunt Leora, Jayda reflected, but her hands were still steady and sure on the keys.

The organ prelude ended. The opening song was "There Is Sunshine in My Soul Today," which Smoot sang enthusiastically.

There were good voices in the congregation, especially a young, clear soprano that soared out above everybody else. Jayda located the source, a dark-haired girl of probably sixteen years. She sang as if it were the thing she loved most in the world, re-minding Jayda of herself at that age.

She found herself filled with contentment as she sat there with the sunlight streaming through the tall windows and babies crying and teenage girls giggling softly as they sneaked glances at the teenage boys who ignored them, for all the world like the teenagers she'd been part of twenty years before.

The only troubling thing was the woman of the nasty look, who sent a couple more barbed glances her way. Maybe she should go up to her afterward and explain that she truly hadn't yet decided what she was going to do about the old house.

Or maybe she should just keep her mouth shut.

As the service proceeded, Smoot stretched up to whisper in her ear. "I like having somebody to sit by," he said, hitching him-self a little closer.

Jayda put an arm around him. She liked having somebody to sit by too.

Later, at the cemetery, she saw repeated on the headstones the same last names as the people she'd just been with. She made a realization. The history of Blackbird didn't involve just Jorgensens. All of these other families had crossed oceans and prairies and mountains to get here too, some of them with Asa. The old house was a monument to them as well as to him. Aunt Leora had spoken of it having served as a school when the original schoolhouse burned down. And as a place for parties and dances, even up to Jayda's day. It had been the site of an outdoor show—a pageant—about Blackbird's history when Jayda was fifteen, and she remembered that she and Lee had sung a spirited duet from the top of the tower, their voices amplified for the large audience. There'd been other shows on the grounds after she left.

Somehow she felt that she'd taken a step forward in saving the old house, just to be realizing how closely the townspeople were tied to it.

Smoot looked around the cemetery with satisfaction. "I know most of the people here," he said, making a broad gesture that included all the graves. "I like to go around and look at the headstones."

Jayda was uncomfortable being there, but she allowed him to take her to an attractive marker with mountains and trees carved into its granite face, along with the name Lynette Spencer Ferguson.

"Hi, Mom," Smoot said.

Jayda stood beside him as he told his mom how Jayda was there to say hello, what a great dog Tarzan was, and how the dog and Old Twister were going to be friends. Eventually. "Pretty soon," he said. "But maybe not."

While he talked, Jayda found her thoughts drifting back to the woman in church who apparently disliked her. She hadn't considered that the tire flattener and note leaver might be a woman. But why not? Did the woman own a business that would suffer if Jayda obstructed the new housing development? How many other people in town were going to actively object?

She reined in her thoughts when Smoot, after running a finger over his mother's name, said, "Jayda, did you know my name's on here, too?" Taking her hand, he pulled her to the back of the monument where he read aloud, "Beloved son." Under that was carved "Smoot."

"I like it to be there," he said. "It makes me feel like I'm still close to my mom."

Jayda felt a jolt. She had tried never to think about it, but her name, like Smoot's, was chiseled on the back of her parents' headstone, a local custom. Almost all the stones had children's names listed. But Jayda remembered being frightened when she'd seen her name there. Her parents had died together in an accident that she'd survived when she was four. She'd been firmly strapped into a child restraint seat and hadn't even been hurt. But seeing her name on the stone had made her feel she should be there with them in the deep, dark grave. It was soon after the burial that she'd started slipping out of herself into fictional characters and roles in plays. Even last year Ethan had commented that he wasn't sure if he knew the real Jayda or not.

Shaking herself like Tarzan flinging water off himself, she walked up the roadway, knowing where she was headed but reluctant to get there. On the way she passed a monument she vaguely remembered from the few times she'd been to the cemetery. The gray granite bore the name Sgt. Boyd Jorgensen, and the inscription, "Died on foreign shores, July 17, 1918."

Embedded in the granite was a bronze marker that told his rank and again listed his death date. She recalled asking Aunt Leora at one time where "foreign shores" were, but couldn't remember what she'd said. Perhaps there would be something about him in the wall of drawers.

Continuing on, she came to her destination, the grave where her parents were buried side by side with a single stone marking the spot. Like Smoot, she leaned over and traced their names with a finger. Thomas Asa and Diane Smith Jorgensen. Born. Died. She hated that word. She remembered hating it on the day they were buried. It was about the only thing she remembered about that terrible time—except for one more thing. That her name was on the back of the monument, just like Smoot's name was on his mother's headstone.

Forcing herself to step around to the back, she stared at the carving there: Beloved daughter. Underneath that, Jane. With horror she saw that the words were surrounded by a large circle of black spray paint, with a thick black slash running diagonally down through the middle of it, almost obliterating the letters.

Chapter Ten

NOT WANTING SMOOT TO COME OVER and see the ugly vandalism on the back of her parents' headstone, Jayda walked swiftly toward a tall obelisk before pulling out her cell phone. Quickly she thumbed in Lucas's number.

"Lucas," she said tersely when he answered. "Meet me in the cemetery in twenty minutes. At my parents' gravesite. I have to run Smoot home, but then I'll be back here."

"Aw, shoot, Jane, give me a break," he complained. "I barely got home from checking out an accident."

"Lucas," she said. "Please come."

Closing her phone, she stared briefly at the obelisk. The name on it, as she well remembered, was Asa Jorgensen. Born. Died. She flashed briefly on herself as a small child hiding behind the monument during a game of hide-and-seek with her cousins. When she squatted behind it, she was completely concealed from anyone approaching.

Now she reached out and patted the cold shaft. "Good to see you again," she said, and then called Smoot and told him it was time to go.

Lucas arrived in a bad temper, shortly after she returned. "What's so dang important that you have to drag me away from my Sunday nap?" he groused.

Silently Jayda positioned him behind her parents' desecrated stone.

"Hmm," he said as he gazed at it. "Looks like the work of vandals."

"Looks like the work of whoever is trying to scare me away," she said. She wanted to add, "you ninny," but thought better of it. "It's not a random act of vandalism. Somebody is targeting *me*."

"Okay, Jane. You're right." He pushed his billed cap forward and scratched the back of his head. "I'll report it in this week's crime column in the *Blackbird Clarion*."

"Along with the criminals who returned a library book late and jaywalked?"

There wasn't a lot of crime in Blackbird. Which, as Dave Bradbury had said, was one of the things that had attracted the Summertree Meadows folks to this particular little valley.

"Well," Lucas said, "maybe somebody will come forward with information about who's doing this stuff."

Jayda huffed. "And maybe they won't. What else are you going to do about it?"

"Scrub it off. Maybe have to sandblast it."

"What else?"

Lucas took in a deep breath and let it out. "Well, I'm gonna believe you when you say somebody is seriously trying to encourage you to sell the house and go back to California. Happy now?"

"No," Jayda stated. "I want you to appoint some deputies to keep a watch on who comes and goes around my place."

"Aw, Jane, there's no budget for that kind of stuff."

He looked concerned enough that Jayda softened her tone. "Okay, but I'd really appreciate it if you'd do a little investigating."

"You watch too much TV," Lucas growled, but he made notes in the little pad he carried before going to his Hummer.

The first thing Jayda did when she got home was check to make sure that all of the doors and windows were securely locked. The vandalism of the gravestone had all the aspects of a direct threat. To make herself feel safer, she propped chairs against all the doors, with Tarzan as an interested observer.

Tired from the tensions of the day, she read for a while, trying to forget the desecration of her parents' headstone, and then, in an attempt to get the ugly image out of her head, she went to the Remembering Room to see what she could find about Sergeant Boyd Jorgensen. She opened drawers until she found some papers dated 1918. Taking that drawer to a table, she shuffled down through it, finding receipts for the sale of hay and wheat back in 1918 and 1919, as well as an elaborate drawing, artist not identified, of a quilt pattern entitled "Ages Past," depicting what were apparently Jorgensen historical scenes, including the building of the house. One of the blocks puzzled

Jayda. It unmistakably showed the house on fire. Flames shot from the tower, and a group of men in front frantically pumped a manually operated fire truck. She set the drawing aside as something she needed to look into. Perhaps it would lead her to a family story that might be good for a movie, as Bug had suggested.

Before she could dig any farther into the drawer, there was a knock at the door. Smoot maybe?

With Tarzan at her heels, she hurried to answer the knock, removing the propped chair and opening the door enough to peer out. It was Smoot, all right, but he wasn't alone. A slender woman with smooth blonde hair and creamy smooth skin, dressed in an unwrinkled beige pantsuit stood there on the porch with him.

Belinda.

"This lady wants to see you," Smoot said. "So I showed her the way."

Oh, sure. Already she had Smoot snagged firmly in her web. As if she needed directions to the old house that she'd been in countless times when all of the cousins were young. Velda had good reason to worry about the single men of the community when Belinda was around. Even Tarzan wagged his way straight to her side, gazing up at her with doggy devotion.

"Hello, Belinda," Jayda said.

Belinda laughed, a charming, tinkly little sound. "I'm surprised you recognized me, Jayda," she said. "It's been so many years."

Jayda put on a smile. "And I'm surprised you called me Jayda. Lucas insists on Jane."

"Oh, honey," Belinda said, "Lucas does that out of sheer contrariness, if nothing else. You know how he is. May we come in?"

Jayda was embarrassed that she'd forgotten her manners. She stepped aside and gestured for Belinda and Smoot to enter. "I'm happy to see you," she said. "Both of you. I was just thinking of having a bite to eat. Would you like to join me?"

"Yes," Smoot said.

Belinda laughed again. "Smootie, sweetie," she said, "you're a bottomless pit." To Jayda she said, "We just had fried chicken at Lee's place."

So she'd already swept Lee into her wake, Jayda thought. Poor, wounded Lee. Belinda hadn't changed over the years. She had to have every male in town flocking around her. Whatever age, whatever condition. Whatever *species*, she thought, watching Tarzan gaze at her with eyes of love. If they went out to the corral, even old Twister would probably whinny and snort and paw the ground in abject adoration.

"Sit down, Smoot," Jayda said. "I'll nuke something for you."

"Okay," he said contentedly. He sat down at the kitchen table.

Belinda sat, too. "While he eats, we can talk about how we might convince Lucas that it would be a mistake to sell this old house."

Jayda's amazement must have shown on her face because Belinda, smiling sweetly, said, "You thought I came here to join him in baying for its demise, didn't you." A statement, not a question.

Jayda could only nod dumbly.

86

"Jayda, dear, I'm here to help you save it," Belinda said. "And as soon as Smootie finishes eating, we'll all go to the Remembering Room and see what we can dig up that will help us."

If she hadn't mentioned the Remembering Room, Jayda would have totally believed she was there to help protect the old house. They could have sat in the parlor to talk about it. But the mention of that room alerted Jayda to the fact that Belinda was, in the past, famous for using any means necessary to get what she wanted.

Even deception.

Chapter Eleven

BELINDA LED THE WAY INTO the Remembering Room, her spiky heels clicking on the polished hardwood floor. She chattered all the way. "Lucas and I used to play a lot in here," she said. "We called those drawers the Wall of Wisdom. We thought all the knowledge of the world must be in there. Whenever we needed something special for school, Grandpa opened a drawer and pulled out a battered old notebook or a picture or a book we could use."

Jayda followed her, watching as Belinda approached the drawers and reached up to touch one in the third row from the right. "I barely remember Grandpa," Jayda said. "He died when I was about five."

Belinda nodded. "I was sixteen, so I got to know him pretty well. He said all the family was in this wall. Lucas used to spook the little kids by saying that everybody was in here, all shriveled up and stashed in the drawers."

Jayda remembered that. Maybe that was why she'd never explored it much.

"Figuratively speaking, I guess that's true," Jayda said. "I mean, that everybody is in here. They're listed on family group sheets in Aunt Leora's Book of Remembrance." She thought again that this was what Aunt Leora meant when she said the walls could speak.

Belinda nodded. Pulling out the drawer she'd been touching, she carried it to a table and sat down. "This was my drawer when I was a kid. I could put anything I liked inside."

Jayda walked over and stood beside her, curious as to what Belinda would have liked when she was a child. Looking over her cousin's shoulder she saw a dried and faded rose which Belinda picked up gingerly with thumb and forefinger, her other three long-nailed fingers extended as if to make sure they didn't touch it. She dropped the ancient rose into a wastebasket beside the table.

"About time I got rid of that," she said, offering no explanation why.

Next she picked up what appeared to be a report card. Jayda saw a row of A grades. That surprised her. She'd always thought of Belinda as an airhead.

"Not too shabby," Belinda said. "Considering all that was going on my senior year." No further comments on that item either.

She shuffled through other scraps of paper and pulled out a snapshot of a pretty teenage girl standing in front of a tall, somewhat handsome, well-built guy. He had a twisted smile due, Jayda guessed, to the scar that crossed his right cheek and pulled down that corner of his mouth. She had a faint memory of him, but no name came to mind. His arms surrounded Belinda, pulling her close to him.

Belinda drew in a sharp breath as she looked at the picture. "Grandpa would spin in his grave if he knew I still had this," she said softly.

Jayda couldn't stop herself from asking, "Who is he?"

For a moment she thought Belinda wasn't going to answer. But then she said, "Bracken. Bracken Morehead."

At the name, Smoot rose from the floor where he and Tarzan had been sprawled, Smoot's head resting on Tarzan's belly. He'd been so quiet Jayda had forgotten he was there. "Bracken?" he said, coming over to stand next to Belinda. He peered at the picture. "I've seen that guy."

Belinda shot Jayda a startled glance, although Jayda was puzzled as to what she wished to convey. "Are you sure, Smootie?" Belinda said.

Smoot nodded. "He looked different, but he had a scar like that. And his name was Bracken."

"He was only eighteen when the picture was taken. He got the scar in a rodeo when a horse threw him and then stepped on his face." Belinda put an arm around the boy and drew him to her. "Tell me," she said coaxingly, "where did you see him?"

Smoot's eyes practically glazed over, being that close to the dazzling Belinda. Tarzan heaved himself to his feet and came over to crowd close to the two of them, putting a paw up on Belinda's knee as if asking her to notice him too.

Fickle, both of them. Well, let them beg food from Belinda

that night. Jayda was disgusted that they acted like every other male on the planet in Belinda's company.

"I saw him in the orchard," Smoot said. "Under the Jonathan tree. The one that has those good apples."

"What was he doing?" Belinda asked gently.

Smoot shrugged. "Nothing. He was just standing there when I saw him."

Belinda looked at Jayda. "That's where we used to meet," she half-whispered. "Bracken and I. Under that tree."

Jayda wondered if that was when the Jonathan apple tree began to be a favorite trysting place. That's where Lee Spencer had first kissed her. Turning to look at Smoot, she asked, "He told you his name was Bracken?"

Smoot reached across his body to scratch the opposite shoulder. "He didn't say nothing. When he saw me, he disappeared."

"Disappeared?" Belinda repeated. "You mean like POOF?" She snapped her fingers. "And he wasn't there anymore?"

Smoot shook his head. "No. He just went around the gooseberry bushes, and I didn't see him again."

Belinda put a long fingernail alongside Smoot's chin and turned his face so she could look into his eyes. "When was this, Smoot?"

Smoot's brow furrowed. "About a few days after school let out."

"About three weeks ago," Belinda murmured, counting under her breath to herself. To Smoot she asked, "How did you know his name was Bracken if he didn't tell you?"

Smoot was beginning to look a little worried, probably

because Belinda's tone was so serious. "Aunt Leora said that's who it was," he said. "I told her I saw a guy under the Jonathan tree, and her eyebrows went way up on her forehead and she said, 'Oh? What did he look like?' And I told her about the scar, and she said, 'Sounds like Bracken. I wonder why he's ghosting around the orchard.' And then she didn't say any more and neither did I."

"It's okay, Smootie." Belinda gave him a little hug, which made Tarzan move in a little closer.

"Smoot," Jayda said, "why don't you and Tarzan scoot out to the kitchen and find the cookies Aunt Leora left. They're in the freezer, next to the soups."

Smoot looked reluctant to leave Belinda's warm embrace, but he said, "Come on, Tarzan." The two of them left.

"So what's going on?" Jayda asked. "Who is Bracken?"

"Bracken Morehead. You don't remember him?"

"The picture stirs up some memory, but I don't know who he is."

"Was," Belinda said. "He's dead. Or supposed to be. He went away. Grandpa didn't approve of him. Said he was no good for me. Grandpa told me he was dead and that I should forget about him."

Jayda sat down in the chair opposite Belinda. "Okay. Why don't you tell me the whole story? What was it about him that would make Grandpa spin in his grave if he knew you still had the picture?" She gestured at the photo Belinda still held.

Belinda's eyebrows went way up, like Smoot had said

about Aunt Leora's. "You don't remember how it was with the Jorgensens and the Moreheads?"

"No. The Moreheads moved away when I was in elementary school. Megan Morehead was in my class. She used to break my pencil lead and call me names. I didn't know why."

Belinda nodded. "Think Hatfields and McCoys."

"A feud? You mean between the Jorgensens and Moreheads?"

"Yes. Something about a disputed deed. I never did know the full story."

"But you liked Bracken."

Belinda smiled. "I lo-o-o-o-oved Bracken. He used to come over to ride Old Twister during the winter months to keep in practice. Summers he rodeoed, traveling the circuit as Twister's escort. Used to win bronc-riding purses. He was handsome and manly and totally fascinating to me. I used to sneak out under the Jonathan tree to meet him."

Abruptly she put the picture back in the drawer, stood up, and walked over to the wall to put the drawer back into its slot. "I have to go. If it really was him ghosting around the orchard, like Aunt Leora said, I need to find out what's going on. Did Grandpa lie about him being dead?" She gave Jayda a grin. "Or is he one of the undead out of the *Twilight* movies?"

She walked swiftly to the kitchen where she kissed the top of Smoot's head, patted Tarzan on the rump, and then was gone.

Dazed, Smoot and Tarzan followed her to the front door and watched her get into a little lavender convertible and drive away.

"She's beauteous," Smoot breathed. "She smells like lilacs."

"Yup," Jayda said. "She always has. And I'm an old hag. And I smell like warts."

Smoot looked up at her. "No. You smell like clean sheets."

She put an arm around his shoulders. "I'll consider that a compliment, pal. Want to come with me out to take a look at the Jonathan apple tree?"

"Yes," he said. "Do you want to see if that Bracken guy might be there again?"

"No," she said. "Those Jonathan apples are mighty fine when they're green. We'll take a salt shaker with us and have dessert there."

The apple tree was much the same as she remembered it. A little skimpy, compared to the other apple trees, a little gnarly. But it was in a corner, next to the gooseberry bushes, and thus somewhat secluded. She'd liked to play there when she was a child. She'd braid the June grass all around it and pretend it was her own little kingdom.

And then there was that first kiss. From Lee Spencer.

But she didn't dwell on that. Instead, under the guise of checking for fallen green apples, she looked for footprints. If there were footprints, a very real man had been there for Smoot to see. If there were not . . .

There were no prints. But there was fresh dirt that indicated someone had been digging there.

"Is this where you buried the computer mouse, Smoot?" she asked.

"Yup," he said. "There was a hole so I used it."

"I wonder who dug the hole."

"I guess that guy Bracken did," Smoot said. "He had a little shovel when I saw him. Like L. G. has, that he says is to dig foxholes when you're in a war. So I dug a little more to see if anything was there."

"Find anything?"

"Yeah."

"What?"

He grinned. "Two angleworms and a potato bug."

She rubbed his bristly hair. "Smoot, you're a comedian."

"Yeah," he admitted. "After that I buried the mouse."

Jayda laughed as she handed him the salt, and while he picked a green apple and began eating, she pondered the significance of Bracken having been there with a shovel. She kicked at the dirt, and was surprised when she saw something roll out onto the grass. A button. Picking it up, she held it in the hollow of her hand. It seemed to be brass and had a military insignia. She couldn't recall having seen one quite like it before.

"Smoot," she said, "did you see this when you were digging?"

"No." He picked it from her hand and turned it over. "Cool. Can I have it?"

She took it back. "I think we'll just file it in the wall of drawers."

Shoving it into a pocket, she picked a green apple and joined Smoot.

The only thing she knew for sure was that if Bracken had carried a shovel, he hadn't been a ghost. Unless he'd used it to dig himself out of his own grave.

Jayda and Smoot sat under the Jonathan tree for a good ten

minutes, pouring salt onto green apples and munching them contentedly. The taste brought back memories, one of which was of bellyaches. "Don't eat too many," she cautioned Smoot. "There are consequences."

He rolled his eyes. "I know!"

Every country kid knew. Would they still know such pleasures and possible consequences if Lucas and the other cousins had their way and this land was sold for development? Which brought another thought: Did Lucas know that Belinda was on *her* side? Did *she* herself know for sure?

She was pondering that question when she saw a silver Lexus glide smoothly up the hill and turn into her driveway. She recognized the car. It was Dave Bradbury's.

Almost automatically, she reached up to smooth her hair— the gesture of a girl who wanted to look her best for a man.

But she wasn't a girl anymore. And Dave Bradbury was not a fella-come-a-calling. He was the representative of the developer.

The enemy.

Chapter Twelve

DAVE BRADBURY'S SMILE WAS WIDE and friendly. "Hello, Jayda," he said. "Hi, Smoot."

Smoot waved a hand, and Jayda responded with, "Hello, Dave. Did we have an appointment?"

"No. I'm sorry for dropping by unannounced. But I just picked up something at the post office that I'd like to show you. Can we go to the house where I can spread it out?" He held up a mailing tube with a rolled-up document sticking out of the top, as if he'd been so excited he hadn't bothered to push it all the way in.

Jayda considered saying no, she wasn't interested in what he had in the tube. But the fact was, she *was* interested in what his next ploy would be. It was like a game, and she'd always liked games.

"Yes, we can do that, Mr. Bradbury," she said.

"Dave," he reminded her.

"Dave," she repeated.

He walked with her and Smoot to the house where Jayda took him to the Remembering Room for some reason she couldn't identify. *Maybe the ancestors need to get a look at this guy who is trying to take over what they'd built up over four generations,* she thought. Maybe the walls there could see and listen as well as speak.

Yeah, right. But she had come to like the room and figured she'd make it the center of operations for saving the house.

"Sit down." She indicated the table she and Belinda had so recently used. "Would you like something to drink?"

"Ice water would be appreciated," he said. "I've been on the run since early morning, and I've worked up quite a thirst."

She went to the kitchen and brought back two glasses and a pitcher of ice water on a tray. She put it on the table next to him, and as he gratefully drank, she pulled the button she'd found under the tree from her pocket and dropped it into a drawer. It was unlikely she'd find any history on it, but she didn't want to just throw it away.

"Wait till you see this," Dave said when she sat down beside him. He drew a large document from the tube and spread it across the table, pushing the tray precariously close to the edge. It was another rendering of the same territory as the first one he'd showed her. But there was a difference. On this one, the old house still capped the hill. And there were subtle differences in the homes that crept up the slopes—they resembled the style of the old house without seeming old-fashioned. Whoever did it had a flair for design.

But the barn was still gone. And there was still a parking lot where the Bride's House and the orchard stood. And the creek was still altered.

"I told the head office how you wanted to preserve the house," Dave said. "They understood. So they're willing to change the concept of the development. The chief investor thinks the others will go for it. He's Japanese, but he loves Old West movies and thinks it would be nice to give the development a Western feel."

Jayda studied the rendering. "So what would the house be used for if they don't demolish it?"

"Same as what they'd planned before: administrative offices and a recreation center. Can't you see people coming here to this room for games and just sitting around the fireplace in the winter?" He looked around the room, at the two hundred drawers full of dead ancestors and their stories. "I'm sure they'd retain that wall."

"For what?"

"Well, to store games," he said. "CDs. DVDs. Whatever." For the first time he seemed at a loss for words. The wall was overwhelming.

"And what would they do with all the stuff that's in those drawers?"

"Well, it's yours, right? What are *you* going to do with it? You could donate it to the library," he said. "Or the historical society, maybe."

"Wouldn't that be something like desecrating a cemetery?" she asked. "I mean, those drawers are full of family history."

He recovered quickly. "You won't be throwing out family history, just relocating it." He gave her his best smile.

"No," Jayda said.

"No?"

"No deal."

"Not even if we save the house?"

"Not even."

Dave looked down at the rendering, smoothing it with a hand so that it would lie flat, as if that would make it more acceptable. He was silent, but Jayda could almost hear the gears of his brain grinding out a new argument.

"You love this valley, I can tell. Don't you think that others might appreciate it the way you do? Think how many families would be able to get away from the city and live closer to nature."

"Huh!" she said. "Nature paved over. Nature altered." She pointed at the parking lot on the rendering, and the creek. Squinting at him, she said, "What would these houses be selling for?"

The amount he named made her gasp.

"These are high-end houses, Jayda. People will pay a lot to live in a place like this."

"Paved over," she repeated. "Altered."

"Better than living in city fumes."

She stared silently at him.

Finally he said, "What are *you* going to do with the house? Bed and breakfast maybe?"

"Maybe." That was something of a hoot. She could manage the beds, but what did she know about breakfast? Cooking had never been among her major talents. In fact, too many frozen dinners had been one of the strikes against her in Ethan's eyes.

"Mr. Bradbury," she began.

"Dave," he reminded her.

"Dave," she said, "I don't know what I'm going to do with the house. That's a fact. But I do know one thing I'm *not* going to do, and that's sell it to your company. Once they own it, what would keep them from going back to their original plans to tear it down?"

Straightening up, he looked her directly in the eyes and said, "Nothing. Unless it is written into the contract. And they won't sign off if that clause is in it."

She shrugged. "Well, at least you're honest."

"I am, Jayda," he said.

She nodded. "So am I. And I'm not selling."

It was his turn to nod. "Mrs. Nordland said you wouldn't."

Mrs. Nordland. Belinda. Why the formality? Was he telling her he hadn't fallen for her charms as she'd expected him to? Was there one male on the planet who wasn't swept up in Belinda's wake?

"That's interesting," she said.

"Why?"

"Thank you for coming," she said.

"My pleasure." He rolled up the rendering and inserted it into the long tube.

After his Lexus glided down the hill, Jayda went back to the Remembering Room and began pulling out drawers. Looking for what? Anything that would give her a clue as to why she shouldn't sell the house, take the money, and return to her own life. Which wasn't her life anymore without Ethan.

In one drawer she found a stack of letters dating from the World War I years. The return address showed the writer as Sergeant Boyd Jorgensen who was apparently overseas at the time. In foreign lands. She saw in her mind the inscription on his tombstone. He'd died far from home. She made a mental note of which drawer held the letters. She wanted to read them later. Maybe connect them somehow with the button she'd found.

In the same drawer she found a divorce decree for Constance Savage and Jeremy Jorgensen. Dated 1919. Then there was a faded program from what was identified as a "pioneer pageant," listing Leora Jorgensen among the cast. Dated 1947. There seemed to be no rhyme nor reason to how things were filed. Jayda sighed. Was she going to have to go through each one of the two hundred drawers to find something she could use?

Looking at the program for the pioneer pageant gave her an idea. She couldn't do a movie about the Jorgensens, but something more modest might be possible.

"Aunt Leora," she said aloud, "you're going to have to help me with this." She took out her cell phone and punched in the number of the retirement village.

"Who died?" Aunt Leora asked as soon as Jayda identified herself.

"Nobody," Jayda assured her. "But *I* might if you don't help me with the house."

"Your problem," Aunt Leora said. "I'm late for a hot date."

"Come again?" Jayda said.

"Is that so hard to believe?" Aunt Leora said. "There are gentlemen here at the retirement village, you know. And I'm having dinner with one of them."

Jayda chuckled silently to herself. Now that she had time on her hands, Aunt Leora had a boyfriend! "Aunt Leora," Jayda said, "I've learned a lot in the few days I've been here. The main thing is that I wish I had paid attention to the family stories when I was a kid."

Aunt Leora humphed. "Well, that's a step forward. I never did know where your head was back in those days, but it sure wasn't with the family. You just didn't care."

"I do now." Jayda gripped her phone. "Can you tell me anything about how all the family history is organized in the wall of drawers?"

"It isn't. Organization never was my strong suit. Or anybody else's, for that matter. People would take things out and then not bother to put them back in the same place. But it's all there if you can dig it out."

"What I just dug out was an old pioneer pageant program that you were in. Was that something that happened regularly?"

"No," Aunt Leora said. "Maybe every five years or so in the beginning. Those were a lot of work. But Grandpa Asa thought we should do it to remind everybody of what our ancestors had done—the progenitors of the whole town, not just Jorgensens. It was kind of a celebration of what they had all done."

What they had done. What she was expected to do. That was what had made her turn off her listening ears when she was young. Young and *foolish*, she thought now.

"It made us care," Aunt Leora said.

Jayda almost missed those few words, being caught up in the old feelings of rebellion. But when she actually heard them and let them sink into her mind, she had a feeling of elation. Maybe that was the secret. To make the cousins and the townspeople care. Could a visual, dramatized presentation of what the house symbolized do that?

"Remember those old Judy Garland–Mickey Rooney movie tapes you used to like to watch?" Jayda asked. "Where they'd put on a show and save the farm?"

"Better than doing nothing," Aunt Leora said.

"There's not enough time," Jayda protested.

"It's not like it has to be Cleopatra's entry into Rome. Go for it."

For the first time since she had arrived, Jayda felt a glimmer of hope. "Thanks, Aunt Leora. I'd better get started reading all those drawers."

"Talk to your friend Emmylu. She helped with the last pageant we did, maybe seven, eight years ago. She knows how to get things going."

"Aunt Leora, I could kiss you."

"Too far away. Dinner is calling, Jane dear. Good-bye."

Jayda's excitement lasted only as long as it took for common sense to kick in. She couldn't pull off a pageant. Judy Garland and Mickey Rooney had all the resources of Hollywood to help them do a show, and it was fiction anyway. What did *she* have?

And then she had one of those "Aha!" moment. She had Ethan. She had described him to Bug as someone who just wrote musical scores for movies. Actually, Ethan was kind of a jack-of-all-trades when it came to anything that had to do with show business—in addition to being quite adept at composing background music. He was good—not quite good enough to make it really big in Hollywood—but he was good enough to be a perennial hanger-on. He was always looking for a new assignment where he could showcase his creativity and build his portfolio.

Before she could rethink whether this was a good idea or not, she had punched in his cell phone number.

Chapter Thirteen

JAYDA LISTENED TO THE PHONE RING, seeing in her mind's eye the sunny little apartment she and Ethan had shared, imagining his cell phone vibrating on the counter next to the jars of unsalted peanuts and pots of Creeping Charlies she'd kept there just because he'd liked them. He was the one who'd kept them alive, talking to them, watering them on cold days with slightly warm water so as not to shock the roots, all the while teasing her about being a farmer's daughter who didn't know squat about growing plants successfully.

By the third ring, she was ready to hang up, reluctant to leave her message on his voice mail. When he suddenly picked up, she still considered hanging up. She had no right to think Ethan would drop everything to fly up to write and produce a show that would save her old family home from destruction. What was in it for him?

"Yo," Ethan said. "Speak."

His voice was strong and deep and full of energy, as always. Had she expected him to be pining away to a splinter because she was gone?

"Ethan?"

There was a small silence. She was sure he was going to hang up on her. But then he said, "Jayda?" All warm and welcoming. "Jayda! How nice to hear you."

"Great to hear you, too, Ethan," she said. "How are you?" Inane question, a useless formality because who ever wanted to know how anybody really was?

"Top of the world," he said. "And yourself?"

"Same," she said.

"And Tarzan?"

"Loves his new territory." Ethan adored Tarzan, and when their marriage disintegrated, she figured Ethan would miss the dog much more than he did her. But Tarzan had been given to her by Ethan on their fifth anniversary. It was only fair that he would be on her list of divided property.

"Well, give the old rascal a scratch behind the ears for me," Ethan said.

"Will do." Now that she was speaking to Ethan, she wasn't sure how she should approach the project she had in mind. Or didn't have in mind. What was it she wanted him to do?

"Ethan, are you working on anything right now?"

"Just finished the music for a documentary. Looking for whatever might bring in the next dollar. Got something in mind?"

She should have found out what arrangements could be

made to pay for a pageant before calling him. The check Aunt Leora had left wasn't big enough to cover much. Ethan got paid well when he worked. She should have sketched out a budget of some kind. And how to get some up-front money. She had no idea what kind of profits there might be in doing what she was proposing. Limply, she said, "Well, maybe."

She explained as well as she could what she'd been considering.

The stakes.

The conflicts.

The problems.

The possibilities.

There was a long silence when she stopped talking. She felt sure he was going to tell her to forget it, that he didn't want to be involved. Instead, he said, "And you say this show, or pageant, or whatever, would be presented right there with the house as a background? An outdoor thing?"

"Yes," she said. "You know the way the house sits near the top of a hill with the orchard on a slightly higher rise to the left? There's kind of a natural amphitheater. They've done pageants here before."

"No," he said quietly. "I don't know. You never took me there, Jayda."

That had been one of his resentments, that she'd never taken him home, never introduced him to her vast, pioneer-minded family. He had no family of his own to speak of, and certainly no traditions to guide him, or, as in her case, to rebel against. He'd always said, "How can I know who you really are, Jayda, if

I don't know where you fit?" And then he'd looked at her piercingly and said, "And how can *you* know who you are if you've rejected everything you've been?"

She'd considered it a fair question. She'd always answered it, saying, "I *don't* know who I am, Ethan. That's what I'm trying to find out."

She was still trying.

"Ethan," she said, "forget I called. I think I overdosed on Aunt Leora's collection of old put-on-a-show-and-save-the-farm movies. But I can't save this farm by putting on a show."

"Come on, Jayda, you're slip-sliding away from the hard stuff again. Let's give this thing a try. I'll think about what we might do. Is there enough talent in Blackbird to pull off something like this?"

"I'm sure there is. There's also a broken-down old rodeo horse that is a town treasure."

He chuckled. "I'll keep him in mind." He paused and then said, "You'd be the leading lady, of course. Strong pioneer woman." His voice was contemplative. His *creating* voice. She could tell that he was getting into it already. "Is there a leading-man-type guy around or would I have to bring one from here?"

She thought of Lee. Poor, wounded Lee. And there was Dave Bradbury whose deep voice *sounded* as if he could sing.

No, forget that.

"Yes," she said. "War veteran. Lost an arm in Iraq. He used to star with me in all the local musicals, but I don't know how he'd feel about going onstage again. He has a great voice."

"Time frame for this extravaganza?" Ethan asked.

She repeated what Aunt Leora had said about it not having to be Cleopatra's entry into Rome, which brought another chuckle from Ethan. Remembering that Lucas had said the annual family reunion would be the end of August, she had the thought that this would be a good time. If she could make them care, they might support the idea of saving the house. And even offer a bit of monetary support.

"End of August," she said, "before the kids go back to school."

She waited for him to say it took a whole lot more than two and a half months to produce a musical show, even for a guy like him who made his living doing such things on demand.

He didn't. He was silent for so long she thought they'd lost their connection. But then he said, "Western trails music. Conquering the land." His voice was soft, but then his creative energy kicked in and he said, "Gotta go, Jayda. I feel a song coming on. Great to talk with you, babe."

He hung up.

She sat there at the table for at least ten minutes, wondering what she'd started by calling him. Did she really want to open up all the old wounds by seeing Ethan again?

Another of the family aphorisms came up from somewhere deep in her mind: What's done is done. Pull up your socks and go on.

She spent a few minutes randomly pulling out drawers, finding nothing more compelling than a couple of school report cards from back in the days when each class was marked as Satisfactory or Unsatisfactory. No As, Bs, or Cs. "Satisfactory" didn't tell much about how smart her ancestors had been. Did it matter? Smart didn't make a show. But accomplishments might.

Tired of thinking about it all, she took Tarzan out for a late walk and then went upstairs to bed.

◆ ◆ ◆

She was just finishing a quick breakfast of toast and orange juice the next morning when she heard the rattle of a vehicle out front. She didn't recognize it by the sound, so with her toast still in her hand, she hurried to the window to see who was there. Tarzan came with her and put his paws on the windowsill so he could see too. A rusted pickup sat just beyond the porch steps. She was surprised to see Belinda open the passenger door and step out. A man whom Jayda didn't recognize got out the driver's side and came around to join Belinda. The Beauteous Belinda, as Smoot had called her.

Belinda was dressed in skinny blue jeans and a bright blue shirt—more informal than the other times Jayda had seen her. And, of course, the spiky heels. Her companion was also dressed in jeans, but his were faded and out at the knee. Stylish for the younger set, on him they just looked ratty.

Jayda hurried to the door to open it before they knocked. "Well, hi, Belinda," she said. "Nice to see you again."

Belinda's smile made Tarzan bark with joy. "You remember Bracken, don't you, Jayda?" Belinda said, gesturing prettily toward the man by her side.

Bracken Morehead, the man Smoot had seen lurking under the Jonathan apple tree. Apparently he wasn't dead after all. Up to no good, Jayda was sure, if Grandpa had been so eager to have Belinda forget him that he'd lied about his death.

So what had he been doing under the apple tree when Smoot saw him? Not there to savor the green apples, that was for sure.

Now that she was looking at his sour, scarred face, Jayda remembered him a little better. He'd always been cranky around her and the younger cousins. Belinda had defended him, saying he was grouchy because of being a part-time rodeo cowboy. Riding broncs like Old Twister would scramble anybody's brains and make them snarly.

"Hello, Bracken," Jayda said.

He acknowledged her with a nod. "Jane," he said, "I heard you're going to sell the house. I've come to do a search of that wall of drawers to find the deed. It has to be in there somewhere."

Jayda was bewildered. "What deed?"

"Now, Bracken," Belinda said, "you don't know for sure."

"Oh, yes, I do," Bracken growled. "I've gone through all my family records, and it's not there. I even dug under the Jonathan apple tree in your orchard because there's an old family story that somebody might have buried it there." He stopped long enough to give a derisive snort and then went on.

Jayda took the opportunity to ask, "And who might that have been who buried it there?"

Bracken shrugged. "It's just a story. Old Asa probably told it to throw my family off track. He had to have hidden it in those drawers. And I intend to find it." He headed for the door, then stopped and put up a warning finger. "And, Jane, when you sell the house, I'm taking my share of the money. Get used to the idea."

Jayda positioned herself in the doorway, a hand on either side of the framework. "Now wait a minute," she said. "I don't have a clue what you're talking about."

"Bracken says there's a deed that shows his family owns half of the property here," Belinda twittered. "He wants to look for it, Jayda."

"Well," Jayda said, "he's not going to barge in and start ransacking the place. I'm going through the drawers myself right now. If I find a . . . ," she hesitated, and then said, "a *deed*, I'll let you know."

"I'm going to look for myself," Bracken said nastily. He tried to push past her.

Tarzan growled as Jayda stood her ground. "You're not coming into my house, Bracken. This is my property, and I want you *off it*." She was surprised by her own forcefulness. She'd never had occasion to play a scene quite like this before, but she definitely felt as though she was in an old-fashioned melodrama.

"And who's going to stop me?" Bracken snarled.

"I am," Jayda said calmly. "And maybe my saber-toothed tiger, here." She gestured toward Tarzan, whose lip was lifted to show his teeth.

Bracken retreated a step. "Now look, Jane."

"The name's Jayda," she informed him.

"Jayda, shmayda," he said. "I'm going to look through those drawers myself. I don't trust you any more than my great-great-granddaddy trusted Asa." He glared at her. "I'll get a warrant if I have to. Whatever it takes."

"Do that," Jayda said. "In the meantime, get yourself off my land."

He turned to go. "I'll be back," he said. "Come on, Belinda, let's get out of here."

Belinda tapped across the porch behind him on her strappy little sandals. "I don't believe I will, Bracken darlin'," she said. "I think I'll stay and visit my cousin for a while."

"Talk some sense into her," Bracken spat out as he got into his old truck. The truck sprayed gravel as he gunned out of the yard. Tarzan shot a volley of barks after him.

"Bracken's not so bad," Belinda said as she stood beside Jayda watching the truck disappear in a cloud of dust. "He just doesn't know how to behave in polite company. His bark is worse than his bite."

Jayda wasn't so sure about that. Bracken was going to be trouble.

And then, suddenly, she knew who had been leaving the notes with the circle-and-slash. It had to be Bracken.

She amended her first thought. Bracken was going to be more than trouble. He was going to be *big* trouble, especially if that deed actually existed.

Chapter Fourteen

"BELINDA," JAYDA SAID. And then stopped.

"Yes?" Belinda tipped her head like a cute puppy and gave Jayda a quizzical look.

But Jayda thought better of what she'd been about to say, which was to ask if Belinda knew if Bracken had been leaving threatening notes around the place. Belinda would be sure to give out more bark-worse-than-bite garbage and would tell Bracken Jayda was on to him. He'd up the ante a notch and pretty soon he'd be burning down the house or something equally drastic.

And who was to say Belinda herself hadn't left the notes?

"Never mind," she said. "Would you like some lunch or something?"

"It's barely past breakfast, dear one," Belinda said. "No, I figured you'd be going through more drawers to see if there really is something about a deed there, so I thought I'd stay and help. Two can go through more drawers than one."

And two could make sure one didn't find the deed and destroy it, Jayda thought nastily. Belinda might insist she was on Jayda's side, but who ever knew about Belinda?

But what excuse should she give her for not wanting to start going through the wall of drawers right now?

"I was just going to ask," she said, "where Bracken has been all these years when he was supposed to be dead?"

"Trying to get by," Belinda said. "Grandpa obviously lied about him being dead. When he heard that Blackbird Hill might be sold, he came back to get his share. Or what he thinks is his share." She headed toward the Remembering Room, where she opened one of the drawers near the left-hand side and began riffling through it. "What do you suppose a deed would look like?"

"An official-looking document, I assume. Old. Faded perhaps." Jayda opened a bottom drawer, fourth row from the left, and knelt to look through it. "Why does Bracken think it exists, anyway? And what is it supposed to say?"

"Just what he said." Belinda paused as she pulled something out of her drawer and stared at it. "Well, will you look at this!"

Jayda thought for a moment that she'd found the deed, but when Belinda handed it to her, she saw it was a picture of a young girl striding across a brick courtyard, her dress swirling about her slim legs as she smiled flirtatiously at the photographer.

"That's when I was modeling," Belinda said. "In New York. I'm surprised the family kept it. I heard Uncle Len wanted to fly out and drag me back home by the scruff of the neck. He wanted me to stay here and become a teacher."

Jayda stared at the picture—Uncle Len had been the patriarch of the family during her growing-up years. She then said, "He told me my assignment was to be a nurse." It occurred to her that she and Belinda had more in common than she'd ever imagined.

"Uncle Len was a tyrant," Belinda said. "But I think he just wanted to keep the family together. We were starting to scatter, and some had even sold part of Old Asa's holdings already."

Jayda, being fourteen years younger than Belinda, hadn't been aware of all the currents that had flowed around her as a child. Her mind had been so filled with singing and acting and stories and escaping from the terrible memories of her parents' deaths that she'd simply not paid attention to what was going on. And then she, like Belinda, had left to pursue a frivolous fantasy, or at least that's how Uncle Len had regarded it.

She took another look at the photograph before she handed it back to Belinda. "You were way cute," she said.

"Yes, I was," Belinda said, and they giggled together.

Jayda went back to pulling papers from the bottom drawer—a crayon drawing of a misshapen dog (his legs sprouting from the middle of his belly), a recipe torn from a magazine (titled "No Peekie Stew"), an old *Reader's Digest* dated November 1957, and a sheet of typing paper with a black circle and a thick slash across it.

She was so startled to see the familiar circle-and-slash that she gasped.

Belinda glanced down at her. "Something wrong?"

Jayda slid the sheet back into the drawer and held up the dog drawing. "Just feeling sorry for this poor mutt," she said, not really understanding why she didn't just say somebody—Bracken maybe—had planted another nasty threat. But she hadn't told Belinda about them yet. Perhaps it was wise to keep it all to herself.

Jayda closed the drawer and stood up. "Belinda," she said. "I just remembered I'm supposed to have lunch with Emmylu. Could we continue this another time?"

"I can stay here and keep looking," Belinda said. "I didn't have much of anything planned today."

"Oh," Jayda said lightly, "I'd like to be here to share in the discoveries. How about coming back tomorrow or the next day?"

Belinda gave her a shrewd look, which said she knew Jayda didn't trust her there alone to look for the deed. But she shrugged prettily and said, "Sure, darlin', I'll do that. Can you drop me off on the way? Bracken left me without transportation."

"Sure thing," Jayda said. She'd have to run Belinda home and then return to the house to call Emmylu, who wasn't aware that she was about to have a lunch guest.

It wasn't until she stopped her little Mini Cooper in front of the gingerbread Victorian Belinda had inherited from her parents that she remembered Belinda never had got around to telling her how Bracken had come back from the dead or how she had managed to locate him in such short order.

Smoot was at the house when she returned to call Emmylu. Jayda was beginning to believe the boy had some kind of antennae that told him when something interesting was going on.

"L. G. said I could do whatever I want to today," he said. "I decided to hang out with you and Tarzan." He hugged the dog, who flapped his tail joyously.

Jayda couldn't help but feel annoyed once again at Lee's lack of responsibility for this child who was in his care. Even if Smoot's dad, Colonel Chad Ferguson, wanted him to be independent, Lee could place some kind of restrictions on him, just for his own safety. She didn't want to complain to Smoot and dim his sunny assumption that he was welcome at any time, but she was going to have to have another talk with Lee.

"I was going to visit my friend Emmylu," Jayda said. She wondered if Lee might have laid down any rules about getting into other people's cars. Apparently not, because Smoot grinned happily. "I'll go with you," he said. "I like being with all those kids," he said.

Jayda couldn't remember the rules for child restraints in a car, but she needn't have worried because Smoot was up on everything. "I'm supposed to ride in the back until I weigh more," he said. "I'd rather be in the back with Tarzan anyway."

He and the dog clambered into the backseat and he buckled up while Jayda pondered the legalities of taking Smoot with her. Would Lee sue her if she got into an accident and the boy was injured? But perhaps that thought came from living for so long in southern California, where a cross-eyed look could bring on a lawsuit. She got in and started the car, then remembering she'd better call Emmylu before showing up on her doorstep with

Smoot, she pulled out her cell phone. She needn't have worried about her welcome. Emmylu merely said, "There are plenty of peanut butter sandwiches."

Smoot talked the whole time they were driving. He sat there in the backseat with his arm around Tarzan and spoke about Old Twister, who sneered, as usual, as they went by ("Did you know he has a cavity in one of his big front teeth?"), about Velda ("Did you know she has a new guy?"), about dinosaurs ("Did you know . . . ?"). And then he broke into one of his own comments to say, "I almost forgot to tell you. Bug is going away."

Jayda wondered why Bug hadn't mentioned it to her. "Where is she going?"

Smoot leaned forward into the space between the seats. "She goes away every summer. She stays with her Aunt Polly while her mom is in re-, re-, re-something. Then they come home and her mom is okay. For a while. Her dad ran away a long time ago," he added.

Re-something? Rehab, maybe? Jayda didn't want to jump to conclusions, but she wondered if this was why Bug hid behind dyed black hair and mascara. "If you see her, tell her I'd like her to come to lunch before she goes," she said.

"Me too?" Smoot asked.

"You too," Jayda assured him.

Their welcome at Emmylu's house was pandemonium personified. After a lunch of peanut butter sandwiches and milk, the seven little Carters plus a clutch of neighborhood kids hauled Smoot and Tarzan outside, leaving Jayda and Emmylu free to talk.

"So how are things shaping up?" Emmylu asked as she led Jayda into her toy-strewn family room. "Are you getting anywhere with Lucas?"

"Nowhere!" Jayda said. "It's a case of irresistible force meeting up with immovable object, I think. I'm wondering if I can actually become that irresistible force." She pondered telling Emmylu about the circle-and-slash notes, but decided this wasn't the time.

Emmylu pushed a fat orange cat off a leather recliner chair. "Put your feet up, and we'll talk about it," she said. "There are a lot of people in town who will stand with you."

Jayda sat, adjusting the lever on the recliner so that she could lie back with her feet high. The displaced cat eyed her lap for only a moment before jumping up to sniff up and down her pant legs, apparently checking out the cafeteria of Tarzan scents. She must have passed inspection because he settled himself comfortably and began to purr.

"I hope there's a whole army ready to stand with me," she said, "because that's what I'll need, in more ways than one."

Emmylu headed for the kitchen, bringing back two frosty glasses of lemonade. She handed one to Jayda and then sat in a matching recliner nearby. "Don and I spend a lot of time in these," she said, "after the kids are in bed. Sometimes we don't wake up until morning." She sighed as she settled back. "So you must have figured out some strategies."

"One, at least." Briefly Jayda rambled around about Mickey Rooney and doing a show and what Ethan's response had been when she'd called him. "Knowing him, I figure he's got half the show written already, music and all," she said. "He'll probably be up here in a week, script in hand and ready to cast it. So what I need to know is how do we pay for it all. I'm sure he'll wait to be paid from the ticket sales, but I'm wondering if there is someone who usually fronts the cost of costumes and props and all that."

Emmylu stared at her as if she'd taken leave of her senses. "Jayda, dear," she said. "This is Blackbird, not Hollywood. There are no ticket sales. The pageants we've done in the past have been free to all attendees. Costumes and props have come out of people's attics. We do have some covered wagon frames and canvases somebody made for the show we did a few years ago. We figured the settlers of Blackbird came here in covered wagons even if they didn't cross the plains. I think the frames are stored in Jake Sterry's barn." She took a long sip of lemonade. "Our shows have always been nonprofit, just-for-the-fun-of-it, some-thing-to-keep-the-kids-busy-in-the-summertime affairs. If Ethan is expecting to be paid, you'd better call him right now and tell him the facts of life in Blackbird."

Jayda's heart sank. How could she have forgotten that in small rural communities there was no money to pay for some-thing as big as what Ethan was undoubtedly already putting to-gether?

Well, scrap that possibility. Scrap the show. It probably wouldn't have been enough to keep the old house standing any-way.

Perhaps worst of all, as far as Jayda was concerned, scrap ever seeing Ethan again.

Disgusted with herself, she flipped the lever on the recliner and jerked upright. "I'm living in a dream world," she said. "It's time I get real."

Emmylu gave her a puzzled look. "About what?"

"About putting on a show and saving the world. Happens only in feel-good movies from the forties." She stood up. "Nice to visit with you, old pal, but I gotta go."

Emmylu got to her feet and blocked her way. "Go where?"

Jayda gave her a rueful smile. "Somewhere to soak my head. Maybe I'll call Dave Bradbury and tell him to bring back his renderings. Maybe it's time I signed on to pave over the landscape."

"In other words, run away again." Emmylu stood firm, despite Jayda's efforts to go around her.

Jayda blinked. This was a different Emmylu from the easy-going one who'd been her best bud sixteen years ago. This one had birthed seven babies and was well on the way to raising them to adulthood. She'd taken the road that Blackbird girls were expected to choose. It was a hard road, but Emmylu apparently thrived on it.

"I didn't run away," Jayda said. "I was just looking for—"

Emmylu looked her straight in the eye. "For what? An easier life? Something less challenging than living up to family expectations here in Blackbird?"

"No. I was looking for what I really want to do with my life. Randy encouraged me. He said I was just the type his uncle was looking for to star in some movies he had in mind. And I was." Jayda could hear how lame she sounded.

"Yes, you were, for a while," Emmylu said. "And what did

you do when you couldn't play those parts anymore, when things became difficult?"

Jayda planted her hands on her hips and stared back at her old friend. "I stayed and faced them."

Well, she'd stayed, at least. Stayed and taken the path of least resistance. Had taken whatever roles she could get in whatever movie or theater production. And then she'd found Ethan. She'd been sure he was going places in Hollywood, and she had wanted to go along with him. She'd loved him deeply, but suddenly she saw herself as no better than Randy, looking for a meal ticket. Jutting out her chin, she said, "I did a lot of community and dinner theater work. That's not exactly nothing. I waitressed a lot. I went to school, too."

"And got a degree?"

"Yes," Jayda said firmly. "In music and dramatic arts therapy. That's something I stuck with. I was planning ahead for the time when nobody would call me with parts anymore."

Emmylu's face softened and she put an arm around Jayda's shoulders. "And now you're going to quit again because doing something for a good cause turns out to be a whole lot harder than you expected."

"Slip-sliding away is what Ethan calls it," Jayda said.

Emmylu nodded soberly. "Yeah, it's from an old Simon and Garfunkel song. But Jayda, you've got it in you to make a difference. Aunt Leora believes that, and so do I."

Jayda stood back and straightened her shoulders. "You mean, 'if our pioneer ancestors could do it, so can we'?"

They both collapsed in giggles. When they were teenagers

they'd rolled their eyes and giggled whenever anybody made reference to the noble pioneers.

When Jayda could get her breath, she said, "I wanted to make my life mean something." Which was the wrong thing to say. As she looked at Emmylu, she realized her comment implied that Emmylu's life, filled with kids and PTA and community projects and canning a cellarful of food from her homegrown garden each year, had no real meaning.

Emmylu's face sobered, but all she said was, "I'll forgive you for that, old friend. But with a proviso: that you get off your dime and figure out some way to do what it takes to save our old town from extinction. Or at least from concrete. Let your Ethan come on up here and see what the two of you can do. Maybe reminding Lucas and Belinda of what they're all about will do it. Maybe not. But you have to try."

Jayda straightened up. "Yes," she said. "I do. Despite—" She considered all the despites, with the circle-and-slash notes as number one.

"Despite what?" Emmylu asked.

"Despite myself," Jayda said.

Chapter Fifteen

SMOOT AND TARZAN WERE NOT eager to leave. Jayda had to let them finish a raucous game of "I See a Gray Wolf" with Emmylu's brood. Where would the kids play that and "Kick the Can" and "Run, Sheep, Run" if the orchards and fields were replaced by houses?

As Emmylu waved them off, she called, "Don't worry about the money. We'll figure it out." And then she ran after Jayda's car hollering, "And go see Jake Sterry about those covered wagon frames."

Jayda nodded her thanks. Covered wagons would be a start. Despite her dismal ruminations, her spirits lifted on the way home with the thought that Emmylu believed in her. And she'd said, "We'll figure it out." Jayda didn't feel so alone anymore.

She eyed the old house as she drove past the Summertree Meadows development and on up the long lane. It was a powerful symbol of what the generations of the past had accomplished, perched there on top of its hill, gazing out at the fertile valley that had supported so many people over the past 130 years. But the valley had changed. The land grew houses now. Wasn't that the way of the future? Maybe it was time for the old house to change, too. Symbols were good. But Lucas thought money was better.

Still, going into the future didn't mean you had to abandon the past.

"Look at Twister," Smoot said as they passed the corral. "Somebody must be here. He's putting on a show."

Sure enough, the old horse was galloping stiffly around his territory, head and tail held as high as he could still lift them. His head turned arrogantly this way and that, just the way he'd done back in his rodeo days when he'd succeeded in bucking off a cowboy.

"Does he do a show only when there's someone to see it?" Jayda asked.

"Yeah. Guess he doesn't want to waste his energy." Smoot was silent for a moment and then said, "What do you need money for, Jayda?"

"Well," she said, straining her eyes to see who might be there by the corral, "maybe we'll be putting on a show of our own. But it takes money to do that."

As soon as she parked the car, Smoot opened the door so he and Tarzan could spill out. "I can loan you some," Smoot said. "I've got $17.42 in my piggy bank."

Jayda smiled to herself. "That's very nice of you, Smoot," she said. "But hang on to it until we decide what we're going to do."

Smoot and Tarzan walked back toward the barn. "Maybe Twister could be in *your* show," Smoot said over his shoulder. "He'd like that."

Jayda followed the boy and dog. "Who do you think he's showing off for right now?" she asked.

Smoot shrugged.

Jayda walked around the barn, but whoever had been there was gone now. She came back to see the old horse apparently realize there was somebody new to perform for. His milky old eyes located Smoot. With a toss of his head, he came over to greet the boy, stretching his neck over the rails. Tarzan backed away, barking. Twister sneered and gave a small buck.

I could learn something from that old bag of bones, Jayda thought. Something about spirit and fortitude and never giving up.

"Let's go, Smoot," she said, not wanting to leave him there by the barn when there might still be someone lurking nearby. "I've got work to do."

When Jayda got her cell phone out of her pocket to set it on the counter, she noticed a missed call. It was Ethan. "Hey, babe, set some extra places at the table Friday night. I'm coming up and bringing Paul and Sal with me. We've got two songs sketched out, and we need to scope the territory so we can go into rehearsals as soon as possible. We'll be driving Paul's truck with some minimal sound equipment. See ya soon."

It was so like Ethan to plunge into a project, staying up all night creating music, scratching out the notes, and planning orchestration. Sal was the script writer and lyricist he liked to work with. Paul, her husband, knew all about lighting and sound and sets. Like Ethan, the two of them lived on a shoestring between paying jobs. They needed this to be a paying job.

Smoot's $17.42 wasn't going to go very far to make it that way.

Settling Smoot and Tarzan in front of the kitchen TV with a cookie (not homemade—she'd bought a package at the supermarket) and a dog biscuit, she slipped in the *Ratatouille* DVD. "You two need to rest a while after all that activity with Emmylu's kids," she said. "I'll be in the Remembering Room."

When she got there, she stood in front of the wall of drawers, wishing Bug were present to guide her in "talking to the dead." Taking a deep breath, she said, "Okay, all my dear progenitors, I need something to help me with the project of saving this old house from the developers."

She felt silly talking to an empty room, but what could it hurt? She'd talk to a tackle box or a telephone pole if it would point her in the right direction. At the moment, she just needed enough cash to at least pay for gas for Paul's truck to bring him and Sal and Ethan up here to look things over. Friday night, Ethan had said in the message on her voice mail.

Thinking about it gave Jayda a small twinge of panic. She wasn't sure why. Was it because she had absolutely no organized thoughts to offer the trio about what she wanted them to do after coming all that way? Or was it because she wasn't sure how she'd feel when she saw Ethan again?

Don't think about it right now, she told herself. After all, as

Scarlett in *Gone with the Wind* had said, "Tomorrow is another day."

Surveying the wall of drawers, she advanced toward it, closing her eyes and reaching out a hand. Hoping some long-dead ancestor would guide her to a save-the-house idea.

Again she felt silly that she was doing something so lame.

Grasping the knob of the first drawer her hand encountered, she pulled it out. She opened her eyes. The top item was a faded notebook. In one corner of the cover was some scarcely discernible writing. Jayda carried it to a window where the light was better and she could make out "Arvilla Jorgensen." Underneath that was "Seventh Grade," followed by "Domestic Science." There was a date: September 1911.

Notes, she decided, from some hundred-years-ago class Arvilla had taken. "Okay, Arvilla," she said, "you're going to have to do better than that. How am I going to raise money with an old class notebook?"

Huh. Even Smoot had better ideas than that. He'd suggested that Old Twister could put on a show.

As if thinking about him made him appear, the ancient horse galloped into her line of vision out in the corral. If you could call it a gallop. It was more like his front legs took a hitch forward and his back ones shambled after them. But he held his head and tail high. Putting on a show. For somebody.

This time she was going to find out who was there.

Dumping the faded notebook back into the open drawer, she hurried to the kitchen where Smoot and Tarzan, both half asleep, watched the DVD she'd put in. "Smoot," she said, "would you stay here with Tarzan for a few minutes?" When he nodded, she left by the back door, locking it after her. She knew the front door was locked because she'd kept it that way since Lucas had intruded. The boy and dog would be safe.

Walking close to the house, she slid behind the hedge that separated the lawn from the vegetable garden. She wasn't sure why she felt she had to stay hidden. This was her house after all. Where did her need to be furtive come from? A warning from those dead ancestors maybe?

Yeah, right. But somehow she felt spied upon. Why didn't whoever was out there just perch on the rails of the corral to visit with the old horse? Could it be Lucas, maybe? No, he was an in-your-face kind of guy. He didn't lurk. Belinda? Jayda couldn't imagine her prancing around the barn in her little strappy shoes.

Well then, who? Dave Bradbury? What could he hope to learn from spying?

She decided it had to be Bracken visiting his old nemesis. Rude, sneaky Bracken.

Stealthily, Jayda crept past the corn patch. There was an open area between that and the orchard, and then to see the back of the corral she needed to cross the creek that flowed behind the barn. She'd have to risk being seen. Should she just stroll casually across the green and then look for stepping stones to help her over the creek? Or just make a run for it?

She'd run. Feeling like a character in a B-movie, she launched herself across the grass, skidding to a partial stop on the creek bank so she could aim at a large rock in the middle of the stream. She leaped for it, discovering too late that it was mossy, and therefore slippery. Her feet went out from under her, and she fell flat on her bottom.

It was icy cold. She tried to scramble to her knees, but the rocks in the streambed were slick and she flopped face down in the water. As she came up gasping, she heard a male voice say, "Well, Jayda, if you're trying to drown yourself, there are better ways to do it."

Peering blearily through the water in her eyes, she saw a man standing on the opposite bank. Lee. Grinning, with his hand outstretched. "If you'll crawl over here a little closer," he said, "I'll fish you out. I really don't want to get my shoes wet."

Managing to get her feet beneath her, Jayda stood up. "Well, thank you, Lee Spencer, but I'll fish myself out."

With as much dignity as she could muster, she started wading to the bank, only to slip on another mossy stone and plunge ignominiously back into the water.

This time he came striding to her, scooping her up into his arms. She looped her elbow up around his neck and was aware of the scent of his apparently newly shampooed hair. His cheek, the unscarred one, was close to her lips, and, as he carried her to dry land, she remembered other times, long ago, when he'd carried her, both onstage and off. He'd been strong and young. And whole. And she'd been . . . What *had* she been?

When he set her on her feet, she felt the coldness of the hook brush her arm. Then she felt guilty about having been snarky to him. But she knew he preferred that to pity. Besides, he'd set the tone—reminding her of their teenage relationship when he'd frequently teased her. That is, until that last year when he'd kissed her under the Jonathan apple tree. Then things had gotten more serious. That was before Randy had come and lured her to Hollywood. No, not lured. She'd left willingly, happily. And left Lee behind.

Shaking herself, Jayda shed as much water as she could, and then, dripping, she faced Lee. "What were you doing at my corral, making that poor old horse perform?" she asked.

He blinked. "I wasn't at the corral. I'm on my way to fetch Smoot."

Jayda looked toward the barn. "Well, then, who *was* there?"

Before he could answer, Jayda caught a mere glimpse of a figure slinking swiftly past the corner of the barn and disappearing behind the hedge that separated the barnyard from the orchard.

She ran a few steps forward, as if that would give her a better view of the fleeing person, but immediately realized that her legs had taken a beating in the creekbed and were not going to get her anywhere fast. Turning anxiously to Lee, she said, "Could you tell who that was?"

"No." Lee put his hand up to shade his eyes as he gazed toward where the figure had disappeared. "But it could have been almost anybody. Smoot loves to perch on the rail and watch Twister."

"Smoot's in the house. And besides, he wouldn't run away like that."

"So maybe it was just somebody who felt guilty about coming here without permission." Lee lowered his hand. "Why are you so suspicious, anyway? This is Blackbird, Jayda. Not exactly inner city L.A. Look, let's go to the house so you can put on dry clothes."

She'd almost forgotten she was dripping wet from her foray into the creek. "Okay," she agreed. "We need to talk, too."

He raised his eyebrows. "Glad to. Any particular subject you have in mind?"

She walked gingerly toward the corral, still favoring her left leg that had hit a rock in the creek. She'd spotted a sheet of white paper spiked onto a nail that was meant to hang bridles on. "Tell you later," she whispered.

He must have taken the whisper for lightheartedness because he whispered back, "I love a mystery."

"Well, here's one for you," she said, yanking the circle-and-slash sheet of paper from the nail and handing it to him.

Then she stalked a few steps toward where the furtive figure had disappeared. Something had snapped inside her. Enough was enough. If whoever it was thought she was just going to fold her tent and silently creep away, he/she/it was *wrong*. Cupping her hands around her mouth, she screeched. "Come on out and face me, whoever you are. You can stop this game now because *you're not going to get the best of me*."

Chapter Sixteen

"SHADES OF ANNIE OAKLEY," Jayda heard Lee comment behind her.

She whirled on him, still angry at the disappearing intruder. "What do you mean by that?"

He put up his hand, as if to hold her back. "You know, the song about 'Anything you can do, I can do better.' You must have played in *Annie Get Your Gun* sometime in your career."

"I did." She managed to replace the scowl on her face with a grin. It wasn't Lee she was angry with. "And, yes, I do intend to out-do whoever it is that's making trouble. I'll out-wit, out-last, and out-maneuver the creep." She stopped. "Do you think I'm just playing another part? Seems as if that's what I've done most of my life."

"I think this came straight from *you*," he said. "You're writing your own script for this."

"It's about time," she muttered. "And I'll start by changing out of these clammy clothes."

When they got to the house, Jayda ran upstairs and shucked off her wet things, replacing them with beige Chinos and a grass green top.

Did she choose that top because Lee had always complimented her when she wore green?

No, of course not. To prove it, she took it off and donned a blue and beige plaid shirt with half-length sleeves, and then hurried downstairs.

Bug was there. Smoot had apparently let her in, and now they were deep in a game of Monopoly.

"How's it going?" Jayda asked. The board sported a hotel on St. Charles Place and houses on Virginia and States Avenues.

"Bug's ahead," Smoot said. "But if I could just get Ventnor Avenue, I could start putting up houses, too."

"Maybe I should tell Dave Bradbury he needs Ventnor Avenue," Jayda commented.

Smoot squinted at her, obviously puzzled.

Bug didn't look up. "She means Dave wants to put up houses too," she said.

Smoot frowned. "I don't get it."

Jayda ruffled his hair. "Never mind, Smoot. It was a lame joke."

"Yeah," Smoot agreed. Shifting his gaze to Bug he said, "Your turn."

Lee put out his hand to Jayda. "We're not needed here. Let's go somewhere and share those secrets."

Smoot's head snapped up. "What secrets?"

"Pay attention, Smoot," Bug said. "I want to buy the Pennsylvania Railroad from you."

"No deal," Smoot said, and then when Lee and Jayda headed toward the back door, Jayda heard him whisper, "Are they going to kissy face?"

Lee chuckled softy. *"Are* we, Jayda?"

Jayda hit him lightly on the arm. "Don't be a doofus. We're not seventeen anymore. Where does Smoot get ideas like that?"

"I *was* married when he first came to live with me, you know."

Jayda hadn't known, but she didn't want to admit it. It seemed that she'd been outside the loop on everything. Or just plain not interested enough to stay in touch. "Divorced?" she asked as she led him into the Remembering Room.

"Two years now." He was silent for a moment, and then said, "She was mainly interested in being married to a war hero. They made a big deal of me when I left and when I first got home." He rubbed the hook on his left arm. "When I let it be known I didn't want any of that, she decided she didn't want any of me."

"I'm sorry," Jayda said. She had a sudden urge to go to him, wrap her arms around him, and comfort him. *Kissy face* him. Where was that all coming from? She'd chosen to leave him and her feelings for him behind all those years ago.

"Over and done with." He looked around. "I've always liked this room."

"It's a good place to share secrets," she said lightly. "Actually, I just want to bring you up to date on what's happening." She motioned for him to sit on the sofa. "You started me on an odyssey, you know, when you told me to go get my hair done."

He gave her a sheepish look. "Did I say that?"

"You know you did. You wanted me to catch up on things via Velda. I probably would have signed papers and gone back to L.A. if I hadn't gone to her."

"Oh, yeah, I remember. Best way to learn all the news."

"Right," Jayda said. "Now sit back and listen. I want to connect all the dots for you, as Bug says." Perching on the sofa beside him, she told him everything that had happened leading up to Bug's telling her to "talk to the dead" by seeking advice from the records they'd left behind in the wall of drawers. She included her conversation with Aunt Leora, Lucas's visits, the nasty little notes, Belinda's arrival, and Bracken Morehead almost forcing his way into this room to look for some kind of deed. About Jake Sterry probably having covered wagon canvases in his barn. And last but not least, about Ethan and his friends arriving on Friday to start production on a pageant that was to save the old house but that she had no idea for financing any of it.

Lee seemed to be thinking about it all, but what he said was, "You're still tight with Ethan?"

"We're friends," Jayda admitted. "He's very talented. If anybody can stage a production that will raise awareness of the legacy of this old house, it's Ethan."

Lee gave a noncommittal grunt.

Good grief, Jayda thought, *he can't be jealous!* She remembered that he'd been wild with jealousy when they were seventeen and Randy-from-Hollywood had breezed into town to live with an aunt for a while. That had been the summer Jayda and Lee had starred in a community production of *The Music Man*. And *that* had been where Randy got the idea that Jayda should be in his uncle's movies.

"You've got the look plus a great voice," Randy had said. It hadn't been long before he'd started pushing her to go back with him to California and meet Uncle Ralph, the movie producer, who was looking for a fresh-faced, innocent-looking type. For a while she'd resisted, saying she needed time to think about it. He'd countered with that memorable quote from the show. "You don't want to end up with nothing but a lot of empty yesterdays."

That had tipped the scale. She'd gone.

Over and done with, as Lee had said.

"Well, anyway." Jayda had lost the thread of the conversation, if there had been one. "Anyway, there's no money to pay Ethan and Paul and Sal or to pay for scenery and costumes and . . . there's actually no money for anything, so maybe my any-thing-you-can-do-I-can-do-better attitude is all down the tube."

"Have you been up in the attic lately?" Lee asked.

Sometimes it seemed to her that he spoke in non sequiturs. "What does the attic have to do with anything?"

"Scenery," he said. "Costumes. Leora volunteered to store things from the pageants and shows we did after you left. If I'm not wrong, there are probably even costumes up there from *The Music Man*." The corners of his mouth turned down, and Jayda couldn't help but wonder if he was remembering that it was after this show that she'd gone away.

"I guess I do recall she stashed stuff up there," she said. "Maybe the old house can help to save itself."

♦ ♦ ♦

The thing that struck her first was that there was a lot more stuff in the attic than there'd been when she and the cousins had played hide-and-seek there. It had apparently been accumulating since those days. One corner was stacked high with stage flats. She didn't turn them over to see what scenes they depicted. But even if the scenes were wrong, those flats could be repainted to portray whatever Ethan needed. There were two rather flimsy-looking handcarts which would never have carried anything across the plains. But they were substantial enough to haul a few paper-stuffed flour sacks across the front lawn of the house in a pageant.

There were boxes and trunks stacked in the center of the big, open room. Jayda recognized one of them. She and the cousins had pulled old clothes from it to outfit the impromptu shows they put on for the family when they were very young. Actual pioneer clothing, as she remembered. She opened one and for a moment examined the contents to make sure there wasn't one of those nasty circle-and-slash notes lurking inside. Then she took out a shabby blue calico bonnet. She was holding it up to the light when Lee called her. "Come over here, Jayda. I just found our old *Music Man* duds." He held up the red coat he'd worn as Professor Harold Hill. "Here's where I dripped pizza sauce on it after a Saturday matinee. You tried to dab it out with a Kleenex dipped in 7-Up."

It touched her that he remembered the incident, and she smiled at him. "I think you can still fit in that coat. Try it on."

"Naw," he said. "Things have shifted around a little since then."

"Come on," she said, moving forward to take the coat. "Here, I'll help you."

Reluctantly he turned to put his good arm through the sleeve, and then the other one. She pulled it up so that it fit over his shoulders, still broad, still firm. But she felt how thin he was as she smoothed the coat down his back. He'd always been somewhat lanky but was beyond that now. Aunt Leora would have said he was "downright puny thin." But all Jayda said was, "There! I knew it would still fit."

"Little extra baggage in front," he said, pulling it together over his stomach.

"But it will still button." She reached out to show him, but he turned abruptly. "Let's see what else is in that old trunk," he said.

He pulled out a fussy woman's jacket with padded shoulders. "Remember this? Eulalie McKecknie Shinn's costume. Velda Klippert was a hoot in that part."

"Typecasting." Jayda laughed as she remembered Velda as the mayor's wife and her cadre of Grecian Urn performers. Leaning over the trunk, she pulled out another costume. "Well, look at this," she exclaimed. "My Marian the Librarian dress."

It was blue. Two piece. Nipped in at the waist. Skirt cut on the bias so that it flared out a little below the hips. It had fit so well, that dress. She'd felt so—what?—*feminine* wearing it.

Lee gazed at her. "You were much prettier in that dress than Marian was supposed to be," he said softly. Moving closer to her, he took the dress with his good hand and held it against her shoulders, propping one side of it with his hook. "You could still wear it."

Could she? She looked down at it. Then up at him. His eyes were shining, the way they'd done years before when she'd worn that same dress.

She might be able to fit into it, but she could never recapture the fresh innocence of the girl she'd been then—the same fresh innocence Randy had known would be just what his uncle was looking for to make fresh, innocent films. The kind of movies they didn't make anymore.

It had all started out so well. How did she get from there to this worn-down thirty-four-year-old whose only purpose in life was to save an old house from destruction?

She wrapped her arms around the dress and buried her face in it. Here was the past. Here was Lee, her handsome costar from way back then. He was in the same red coat, but now with a hook instead of a hand and angry scars disfiguring the left side of his face.

They were both so very, very changed. She squeezed her eyes shut to hold back threatening tears.

Lee stepped forward and wrapped his arms around her, the dress pressed between them. They stood that way until Jayda pulled back. Just a little. She looked up at him. With the thumb of his good hand, he wiped away a lone tear that had formed and slipped down her cheek. His face was so close. *So* close. She tipped her chin, raising her lips to receive his kiss.

But it didn't happen. Instead, they were jolted apart by a shriek from downstairs. It was Bug's voice, and she sounded frightened.

Chapter Seventeen

JAYDA AND LEE STUMBLED BACK FROM each other, like guilty teenagers caught in a forbidden embrace. Neither said anything as they raced down the stairs to see Smoot looking bewildered as he stared at a small card in his hand. Bug was on her feet, and when she saw Jayda and Lee, she sat down again. "I'm sorry," she said. "I shouldn't have yelled. But another of those . . . ," she hesitated, and then went on, "those *things* showed up." She gestured at the card Smoot held.

"What *things*?" Smoot asked. "What is it?" He was beginning to look scared. "I was supposed to take a Community Chest card, but somebody messed it up." He held the card out to Jayda.

Somebody had indeed messed it up. Someone had drawn a black circle around the words "You inherit $100," and then slashed through the words.

Lee's quick indrawn breath made it hard for Jayda to keep her face calm. "It's okay, Smoot," she said. "Somebody's just playing a game with me. Don't worry about it." She took the card and shoved it into the pocket of her jeans.

"Do I still get the $100?" Smoot asked.

"Sure." Bug picked up a stack of Monopoly money and counted out five twenties, then rolled the dice to take her turn. Her glance at Jayda said that she understood and would do her best to keep Smoot protected from the knowledge of what it was.

Jayda nodded her silent thanks as Bug moved her marker and landed on yellow Marvin Gardens. "I'll buy it," she said, and the game went on.

"Lee," Jayda said, "would you stay here with the kids for a while? I need to go into town and talk to Lucas."

"Sure thing," Lee said. "Maybe I'll even join in the game."

His slight smile told her he wasn't going to forget their interrupted kiss.

◆ ◆ ◆

Lucas snapped a finger against the mutilated card when Jayda handed it to him. "Whoever is doing this means trouble," he said.

"Oh, golly, gosh." Jayda opened her eyes wide as she responded. "Do you really, really think so?"

"No need to be sarcastic," he growled. "Just bring me all of these things you've got. I'll start an evidence file."

Jayda hadn't totally ruled out Lucas as the culprit. He wanted her to sell her property. He stood to gain a lot of money, just like Belinda. He himself could be the circle-and-slasher. "I'll keep the file myself," she said, plucking the card from his fingers and sliding it back into her pocket.

Lucas cleared his throat. "Well. Then. I'll be up to check the premises when I can get away to see if there are anymore notes left in unexpected places."

"You do that," Jayda said, and then added, "Thanks."

Driving back toward the house, she couldn't keep her thoughts from drifting to her and Lee. She hadn't let herself think of him much during the sixteen years she'd been gone. Although he'd never expressed his feelings then, she knew she'd hurt him deeply when she'd chosen Hollywood over him. But now it seemed as if there was still an ember in the ashes of what had once existed between them. She was wondering whether it was wise to stir it up.

As she contemplated this new turn of events, she spied Jake Sterry roosting atop a corral rail by his barn. Emmylu had said she needed to talk to him about the covered wagon frames. She might as well stop right now.

Grizzled was the best word to describe Jake Sterry. Dressed in faded blue bib overalls and sporting whiskers that were somewhere between a beard and four days of not shaving, he looked like a stock character in any Old-West movie. He could have doubled for Festus in *Gunsmoke* reruns. Writers liked to have words of wisdom come from the mouths of old guys like him. Jayda remembered Festus saying things like, "If you learn a thing a day, you come up smart."

Jake watched as she stopped her car and approached where he perched on the rail. A saddled horse stood alongside him.

He'd apparently been riding, but now seemed to be doing nothing except enjoying the warm sun. He looked straight at Jayda. "Howdy again, Jane. Seems right nice to have you around where we can lay eyes on you around every turn. We've missed you since you skipped town with that movie dude. You didn't have much sense then."

"That was sixteen years ago," she said. "I've learned a thing or two."

"Maybe not enough. Not if you're aimin' to save Leora's old shack from the wrecking ball."

Jayda thought about whining some lame excuse about how the house was a historical monument to the fortitude of the pioneers, but she stopped herself. "That's what I'm aimin' to do, Jake," she said firmly.

"Whatcha want to do a tomfool thing like that for?" Jake demanded. "Having a bunch of rich folks move in would rev up the economy here so we can live high on the hog like you do down there in Los Angeles." He pronounced it "Loss Anjelees."

She thought of informing him just how high on the hog she'd been living in Loss Anjelees—somewhere just above the hooves—but decided it would be wasting her breath. Instead, she slipped into his manner of speaking. She'd done enough bit parts in Westerns to do it easily. "Well now, Jake, you might think about what scrambling up that hog would cost. There's always a price to everything, you know. You willin' to trade off green fields and orchards for a houseful of new appliances and a big white Hummer?"

Jake spat into the dirt of the corral. "In a second. I've had enough of grubbin' around in them fields and orchards. I'd gladly give it all up for a 52-inch flat-screen TV and a big, soft La-Z-Boy recliner, and a Jacuzzi out the back door. Might even get me one of them new iPhones that does everything but cook spaghetti."

"Sure," Jayda said. "Then you can download a few hours of Dag Nasty since there won't be any birds to listen to anymore. You can get a Kindle so you carry Shakespeare and Milton right there in your front overall pocket. And you can sign up for Twitter and Facebook and text message anybody in the world to share what you're doing right at this very minute."

Jake squinted at her. "What in the Sam Hill are you talkin' about?"

Jayda hesitated. When she'd mentioned his front overall pocket, she'd looked pointedly at it, and at the two pencil slots alongside it. She was disconcerted to see a felt marker there, the kind with a broad nib that could make wide lines. Just like the ones on the circle-and-slash notes somebody had been leaving.

But there was no way it could have been Jake Sterry. He'd known her ever since she was a small child. He wouldn't do that.

Would he?

Jake was squinting at her. "You okay, Janey?"

"I was just thinking about all the good stuff you're missing out on, Jake."

"You're funnin' me," Jake grumbled. "What you here for anyway? You didn't drop by just to jaw."

Jayda nodded. "You're right. I came to find out if you still have the covered wagon frames and canvases that were used in the last pageant that was done here in town."

Jake eyed her suspiciously. "Maybe I do, and maybe I don't. Whatcha want 'em for?"

"Thought we might do another show."

"Yeah?" Jake squinted at her. "Have anything to do with why you're here?"

"Nah," Jayda said. "I just need an excuse to sing up a storm again, like I used to."

"Sing in church then," Jake stated. "You don't need no covered wagon." He looked up at the old house atop the hill, bathed in the golden afternoon sun. "You're gonna stir people up, ain'tcha? Get 'em to thinkin' about old Asa Jorgensen and how he settled this place and built that house for everybody to look up to and make them want to keep it there so they can be proud of what their ancestors done. That's it, right?"

She was surprised by his astuteness. She resisted the temptation to avoid the truth. "Right," she admitted.

"Won't do no good," Jake said. "Too many folks want the money. Bein' proud of the ancestors don't pay the mortgage."

Jayda straightened her back. "Well, then," she said, "it won't make any difference if we go ahead with the pageant."

Jake gazed at her, seeming to consider her statement. But instead of addressing it, he said, "Guess you know Bracken's back. Wants to make sure he gets his piece of the pie."

"I heard." Jayda noticed that the timbre of her voice changed. "Do you know how he intends to do it?"

Jake smiled slyly. "That's for him to know and you to find

out, Janey-girl. You can dang well plan on him doing all he can to push the sale through. And he has a lot of what you call in-floo-ence."

"Glad you warned me," Jayda said. "It's been nice visiting with you. See you around sometime."

She turned to go but stopped when a shiny silver Lexus pulled up beside the barn. Only one person in town drove that kind of car. Dave Bradbury.

Dust swirled around the car as it stopped and Dave got out. "Glad I spotted you, Jayda," he called. "Got somebody here who wants to meet you."

Dave hurried around the car to assist his passenger, a small man impeccably dressed in suit and tie. He smiled as Dave escorted him over the corral rails.

"Jayda," Dave said. "I'd like you to meet Mr. Yoshida. From Japan. He's the major investor in Summertree Meadows."

Mr. Yoshida bowed slightly from the waist.

Dave gestured toward Jayda. "Mr. Yoshida, this is Jayda Jorgensen. She owns the house and property on top of the hill."

"Ah, Ms. Jorgensen," Mr. Yoshida said. "I am so happy to meet you." Apparently he already knew Jake and exchanged a few pleasantries with him. His English was good, Jayda noted. She wondered what she could say to him, but she needn't have worried because he took over. "Mr. David says you are a movie star," he said.

Mr. David talks too much, Jayda thought. "I was in a few movies a long time ago," she admitted.

Mr. Yoshida nodded. "Were any of them . . . ," he hesitated, and then said, "oaters?"

When she didn't respond, Dave said, "Oat burners. Westerns."

Mr. Yoshida nodded. "Yes. An American friend called them 'oaters.' They were my favorite movies as a child."

She laughed, and he joined in. "I was in a few," she said. "But mine were mostly beach movies."

He grinned broadly. "You were a beach bunny."

"You could say that." Again they laughed together. She liked this charming and friendly man. Which was most certainly what Dave Bradbury wanted her to do. Cute ploy. Now she would have to listen to what he had to say about his plans for her property.

But he said nothing about that. Instead, he said, "Mr. David tells me you have a famous horse."

"I assume he means Old Twister," she said. "He was sort of famous in rodeos when he was younger. Would you like to come up and meet him?"

"Ah, yes," Mr. Yoshida said. "But not today. Mr. David and I are on our way to town for business. Maybe later this week?"

"Call me when you'd like to come," Jayda said.

"When it is time for pleasure," Mr. Yoshida said. With another slight bow, he said, "I'm very happy to meet you," and turned to get into the car.

"Nice guy," Jake commented as he and Jayda watched the shiny car pull out of the yard and speed off down the highway. "He's gonna make all our dreams come true once you sell him your prize property, Jane."

"Don't hold your breath." Jayda turned to go.

She hadn't gone more than three steps when Jake said, "Thought you wanted them covered wagon canvases. They're here in the barn. But it'll take a truck to haul them up to your place."

"I'll make arrangements," Jayda said. She wasn't going to show it, but she liked the old reprobate. When she had been going to leave all those years ago, he'd said she was making a mistake. He said she'd come home eventually, and she'd be like "that there perfessor" said in *The Music Man*, that she'd be "a sadder but wiser girl."

He'd been right.

At the house, she found Smoot and Bug and Lee just finishing their Monopoly game. Smoot had managed to build three hotels on each of the three red properties. Bug landed smack on Kentucky Avenue as she finished a turn.

"Wipe out," she said, handing him all of her money and properties. "You're totally ruthless, Smoot."

"Yeah," he agreed happily and then looked up at Jayda. "That guy called. The one from California. He said it's time to kill the fat calf since he'll be here tomorrow. I told him we don't have any fat calves, just fat chickens."

Jayda laughed and thought Lee would join in. He didn't. His head was down. In an effort to make things light, she said, "Well, then, I'll just have to go to the store and find a fat something else. And you're all invited to the welcome dinner." To tell the truth, she was a little nervous about seeing Ethan again.

Having Smoot and Bug and Lee to dinner would help her get through it. "Will you all come?"

Smoot nodded enthusiastically, and Bug said, "Sure, I'd love to meet your Hollywood friends. Maybe I'll run away with one of them like you did." She grinned to indicate that she was not serious. Or at least not totally.

All Lee said was, "No need to go to the store. I'll bring up a couple of the fat chickens Smoot mentioned."

"Maybe we could have chicken and dumplings," Smoot said. "Aunt Leora made that real good."

Motioning for the kids to follow him, Lee headed for the door. Smoot gathered up his Monopoly game. "Tarzan is still outside, Jayda. He needed to go and hasn't come back yet."

"It's okay, Smoot," she said. "I'll call him."

But she wasn't thinking about Tarzan. She was wondering what effect having Ethan arrive would have on that tiny spark that had flickered in the ashes of her and Lee's old relationship.

Chapter Eighteen

JAYDA WISHED LEE HAD stayed long enough for her to tell him about meeting Mr. Yoshida. And about the black Magic Marker she'd seen in Jake Sterry's overalls. Plus she wanted his reaction to Jake's statement about Bracken Morehead having "in-floo-ence" with the local people, which would keep them from backing her resistance to the Summertree Meadows development company.

But he'd faded away like a deleted file after she'd identified her imminent visitors as her ex-husband and his friends.

Oh, well. She'd go to bed and hope for better things tomorrow.

But first she walked down the hall to the Remembering Room, thinking she might open a few drawers and find a possible story or two for Ethan to work on.

The first thing she saw when she entered the room was the corner of a paper sticking out of one of the upper drawers. She didn't think it had been there before. Another circle-and-slash note? She didn't want to know, but on the other hand, how could she go to bed without knowing? As she reached up to pull the drawer out, she wondered who could have come into the room since the last time she'd been there. How could anybody get past Lee and Smoot and Bug? Was he/she still in the house?

"Tarzan," she called, needing a warm body close by. But then she remembered Smoot had said the dog was still outside.

Her heart thudding, she pulled the paper from the drawer and looked at it. It was a receipt for new kitchen cabinets, dated just four years before. Harmless. No ugly black marks. Just something that had poked up the last time the drawer was shut.

It just went to show how nervous this whole circle-and-slash thing was making her. She hated the perpetrator for making her see threats where there were none.

But she wasn't going to let him stop her. Slamming the drawer shut, she hurried to the back door to call Tarzan, who came bounding toward her from the corral. Folded around his collar was a small, square piece of note paper.

Jayda spent the night tossing and turning and suspecting everybody in her circle of acquaintances of plaguing her with the nasty notes. Who could have got close enough to Tarzan to put one on his collar? Why hadn't he barked? It must have been someone he knew—and trusted.

Finally she slept, but not before she heard the pound of Twister's hooves as he performed in the moonlight—for whoever was there watching him. This time she didn't even try to go see who it was.

The next morning, Jayda found two ready-to-cook chickens

in an iced cooler outside her front door. Even though she knew they were from Lee for the celebration dinner for her upcoming guests, she examined the cooler inside and out for any surprise scraps of paper. There weren't any.

Bringing the cooler inside, she distracted herself from the notes by thinking that the birds were some of the contented hens she'd seen pecking happily in Lee's yard just a few days before. She'd become squeamish since she'd been living in the city. She preferred to eat meat she hadn't met.

She remembered days of the past, when the men of the family sharpened the big knives and then led a home-grown steer or a pig to the slaughtering area by the old wheat granary. They dispatched the animal quickly, then gutted, skinned, and hung the carcass up to cure for twenty-four hours before carving it into meal-sized pieces. When she'd expressed horror about the whole thing, as a child, the men had quoted another family motto. They'd taken pride in producing what went on the dinner table.

But Jayda had never reconciled herself to the fact that the animals she helped feed and raise became food for the family. So why, she wondered, hadn't she become vegetarian? She decided she'd lacked the resolve. Just as she'd lacked the stamina to be like those pioneers. Which was one of the many reasons she'd left to live in the fantasy world of Hollywood—where chickens came wrapped in plastic.

Well, she wasn't going to get bogged down thinking about all that today, or about the threatening notes either. She had company arriving in a few hours. Ethan and Sal and Paul—from

Hollywood—were coming to create a fantasy to save the old house.

She couldn't help but wonder how Lee would react to actually meeting Ethan in person, after his glum expression when she'd spoken of him the night before. Would he really come for dinner? Or would he just send Smoot with Bug?

Whatever will be will be, she muttered. In the meantime, she needed to do something with the chickens. Smoot had suggested chicken stew with dumplings.

Okay, so how does one create chicken stew? Aunt Leora had made it every now and then, but Jayda had never learned how. There must be a recipe around somewhere, she thought.

It was then she remembered Arvilla's 1910 seventh-grade home economics notebook with its collection of recipes. If she was lucky, it would tell her something to do with chickens.

"Let's check it out, Tarzan," she said, leading the way to the Remembering Room.

Tarzan lumbered to his feet. He'd been sleeping ever since she'd fed him earlier. Wherever he'd been, whatever he'd done the night before seemed to have worn him out. Had he gone somewhere with whoever had put the note on his collar?

"I wish you could speak," she said as he followed her to the wall of drawers.

She remembered the one where she'd found the notebook. Second row from the right, about halfway down. Not too high, which made her think Arvilla must not have been very tall if she'd chosen a low drawer to keep her stuff in. Not that it mattered, but she knew Ethan liked to have his actors look something like the person they were playing. He'd probably want to include Arvilla in the pageant. Maybe there were pictures of her somewhere. She'd look for some after she got the dinner under way.

She found the notebook, and sure enough, there was a recipe for chicken and dumplings. It involved cooking the chicken for a long time so the meat could be easily boned and shredded.

"I need a slow cooker," she told Tarzan. In a kitchen cabinet she located a couple of decent-sized Crock-pots. She felt a bit more in charge of things once she had the birds cooking.

Back in the Remembering Room, though, she felt overwhelmed. Where should she begin looking for pictures of her ancestors? Surveying the two hundred drawers, she said, "Arvilla, speak to me."

Tarzan's ears raised. *"Woof,"* he said.

She patted his head. "Not you, dear. Want to go out?"

He knew the word "out." He raced to the back door and happily ran outside when she opened it.

"Don't forget to write," she called after him as she turned to go back to the Remembering Room. And then she turned again, recalling that someone had got too close to Tarzan the night before. She waited in the doorway for the dog to finish his business and then called him back inside, hating herself for being a nervous Nelly—another throwback name she must have learned from her Aunt Leora—but not wanting any harm to come to her faithful friend.

Back at the drawers, she surveyed the entire wall. Where were the family pictures most likely to be? She vaguely remembered having seen albums when she was young, but she hadn't been all that interested in them.

She began pulling out drawers and riffling through them. She did find a couple of pictures, but neither of them was Arvilla. Or at least the one female was nothing like what she pictured Arvilla to be. But what did Jayda know of her beyond the home economics notebook and the brief letter she'd found shortly after she'd arrived?

She looked closely at the pictures. One was an unidentified wedding photo, with the groom seated and the bride standing slightly behind him with her hand on his shoulder. The other picture was of two men standing in front of the house she was in right now. They were dressed in suits and wore hats. They stood a distance apart, but they held something between them, reaching out so that each grasped a corner of it. Some kind of document, Jayda guessed. She flipped the picture over. "Asa Jorgensen," she read. "Ephraim Morehead. On the occasion of the presentation of the deed, April 14, 1915."

She froze. So it was true. There had been a deed, just as Bracken Morehead had said. So perhaps he did, in Jake Sterry's words, own a "piece of the pie."

Jayda's first impulse was to shred the picture and burn it in the fireplace. But she couldn't do that. She was a Jorgensen. Stalwart. Upright. Above all, honest. She'd have to show it to Bracken. They'd have to search for the deed.

But not today. Turning the picture over again, she saw that both faces looked sour and dour. Whatever the "presentation" was, it wasn't friendly. Jamming the photo back into the drawer, she slammed it shut and returned to the kitchen, where the aroma of the slow-cooking chicken was already flavoring the air.

Paul's gaudily painted truck-with-camper-shell drove into the yard just before 5:00 P.M. Jayda caught sight of it through the kitchen window, so she and Tarzan went out to the porch to watch it stop and the three people inside spill out. She'd decided she and the dog would wait there to welcome them rather than rush out for all-around hugs. This was the first time she'd seen Ethan since the divorce became final, and she was reluctant to greet him too enthusiastically.

But Tarzan knew what to do. As soon as he recognized the three people, he leaped off the porch and bulleted toward them, barking joyously. He wasn't a dog to jump up on people, but he crowded close to Ethan, gargling in his throat and twirling his tail. Ethan fell to his knees beside him, wrapping his arms around Tarzan's big brown body and burying his face in his fur.

Jayda gave up on being the cool hostess and vaulted off the porch to join the crowd. Ethan looked up as she came close, and she was touched to see there were tears in his eyes. He gave her a smile. "You can't imagine how I've missed this big hunk of dog flesh," he said, his voice wobbly.

Jayda stopped. Why had she thought his emotion was from seeing *her* again?

"He's missed you, too," she said lightly, then turned to hug her old friends Paul and Sal.

There was time for a tour before the other dinner guests were to arrive at 6:30. Ethan was enthusiastic about everything he saw. Before they went inside the house, he stood back to admire it. "Jayda," he said, "tell me again why you never brought me here. Didn't you know I'd love it?"

She did know. That was why she hadn't brought him to Blackbird. To the family farm. To the old house. She knew it would appeal to his creative, enthusiastic mind and he'd love the whole "we can do it" thing that had kept her family going all these years. Nothing was impossible to Ethan. Ask him to create and stage a pageant in three months, and it would be done. Ask him to carve a home out of a wilderness, and it would have been done—if he'd lived at the time of Asa Jorgensen. Wasn't it that work-yourself-to-death attitude that had driven her away in the first place? So, no, she hadn't brought him here.

"The reason I didn't bring you," she said, "was because I wanted to stay in my fantasy world of memorized lines and set action. All this"—she gestured to indicate the surrounding territory—"meant real action and work and sacrifice. I didn't feel I was up to it."

"And now?" he asked.

"Now?" She gazed around at the valley spread before them with the mountain peaks rising sky-tall in the background. She smiled. "Now the mountains are mine and they're going to stay that way. With your help." She gestured to include the three of them.

"Atta girl." He strode over to wrap her in a familiar hug.

She stood within his embrace long enough to realize she'd spoken the truth. She *could* accomplish this task that had been given her, despite the file of nasty notes. Not without help, but did Asa Jorgensen conquer the wilderness without help?

Sal immediately claimed Aunt Leora's vegetable garden in back of the house. Sal grew tomatoes and peas and peppers in pots on the little balcony of her and Paul's apartment in California. She was almost incoherent with pleasure over the garden. "This is my dreamscape," she said. "Please, may I take care of it while I'm here?"

"It's yours," Jayda said. She'd enjoyed what small amount of work she'd already put into the garden, but she was glad to give it up. Sal was a thin, pale, little thing, but if she wanted to pit herself against all those demanding growing things, it was fine with Jayda. Sal would have done well as a Jorgensen.

A ringing telephone sent Jayda scurrying to answer it. The call was from Dave Bradbury, saying he'd be bringing Mr. Yoshida to the house tomorrow to talk with her.

Jayda thought about the tomorrow she'd intended to fill with getting her visitors acquainted with the territory so they could better envision the pageant they were planning. "Dave," she said, "could you bring him the day after? Tomorrow's pretty booked."

"Tomorrow," Dave stated firmly. "Mr. Yoshida is flying back to Japan in the afternoon."

"Okay, tomorrow," she agreed. "If you don't stay too long."

"Business takes time, Jayda," Dave said smoothly. "Especially business as important as this."

"There is no business," Jayda said. She was getting tired of saying it.

"You invited him up to see the horse," Dave said.

Jayda sighed. "One o'clock, then," she said shortly, thinking she'd like to get lunch over before they came. She wouldn't know what to serve Mr. Yoshida. She had no idea how to make the delicate Japanese foods she'd eaten at restaurants in Los Angeles.

Hanging up, she hurried toward the back door but stopped when she heard her friends' voices filled with consternation in front of the house. Dashing to the front door, she saw immediately what they were concerned about. While they'd all been in the garden, someone had defaced the camper shell of Paul's bright truck with a spray-painted circle and just part of a broad slash, as if the perp had been interrupted while in the midst of the job.

Jayda launched into abject apologies, explaining briefly what it was about, but Paul shrugged it off. "Actually," he said, "it adds a bit of panache to the old wreck, don't you think?" he said.

Ethan and Sal and Paul were settled in their rooms and had a chance to wash up and refresh themselves with cold lemonade on the porch before Lee and Smoot and Bug arrived. Jayda had put Ethan in the Good Morning, Sun room, as Smoot called it. Ethan was a morning person and would welcome being awakened by the bright sunshine. She put the married couple, Sal and Paul, in the west-facing room on the other side of the house because Paul was not a morning person and liked to sleep in.

They had all exclaimed with excitement about the house, admiring the high-ceilinged, spacious rooms. Jayda had to promise an extensive tour before they would stop exploring and get unpacked. While they did so, she escaped to the kitchen where she checked the chicken and dumplings (they were perfect!) and tossed delicate little lettuce leaves and cherry tomatoes from Aunt Leora's garden with a light dressing for a salad. She'd spread the table in mid-afternoon with a golden-brown cloth and the brown pottery dishes she remembered from her childhood, so everything was ready, including homemade ice cream. She'd found that Aunt Leora's old electric freezer still worked, and the recipe was there in her mind from the time she'd been in charge of making ice cream for family gatherings.

Lee and Smoot and Bug arrived right at 6:30, with Smoot in long pants for a change and his stubbly hair newly washed. Lee wore a long-sleeved shirt which didn't conceal his hook hand but covered up the mechanism. Bug had scrubbed the mascara from around her eyes and had her dyed black hair becomingly drawn to the back of her head with a red clasp. All three seemed somewhat subdued about meeting the people from Hollywood.

But Jayda need not have worried. There was a slightly awkward moment when Sal, sitting on Lee's left, suggested they all join hands to say grace. She reached out for his left hand. He hesitated, keeping the hook in his lap. But Sal smiled at him, holding out her own hand. "It's an honor, Lee," she said, and grasped the hook firmly when he brought it up.

Dinner was a roaring success. Everyone was delighted with Jayda's story about finding the recipe for chicken and dumplings in Arvilla's ancient notebook, and she had to bring it to the table for them to exclaim over.

"That was really good," Smoot complimented. "I think Gertie and Darlene are glad they could be part of it."

The California guests looked puzzled.

"The chickens," Lee explained. "I tell Smoot all the time not to name them because they will eventually end up on the table. But he thinks they'd be pleased to give us such pleasure."

Smoot nodded. "They would. They really liked to eat the corn and stuff I gave them, so I know they'd be happy about this." He indicated the pot of stew. "Come over to our house tomorrow and you can meet the others."

Everybody laughed, and Sal, on Smoot's right, gave him a big hug.

When Jayda got up to dish out the dessert, Bug came to hang over her shoulder. "Did Arvilla help you to find her recipe book?" she asked in a low voice. "Were you talking to the wall?"

"Well," Jayda said, "I guess you could say that. I was asking for something to help me with this project I've taken on."

Bug smiled with satisfaction. "The dead have spoken. You'll be using it again."

"Maybe," Jayda said. "By the way, Bug, Smoot told me you'll be going away for a while."

Bug's face lost its smile. "I was. My mom has to—" She didn't finish her sentence, but Jayda remembered Smoot had said something about rehab. Then the smile, or a ghost of it, returned to Bug's face. "But Belinda said I could stay here with her. She and my mom used to be best friends."

"You could have come here, too, Bug," Jayda said, putting the dishes of ice cream on a tray.

"Could I?" Bug said. "I would have liked that." Picking up the tray, she took it to the table and passed out the dishes.

After they'd eaten—and exclaimed over—the ice cream, Jayda took them all to the parlor where Ethan had said he'd give them an impromptu concert of the music he and Sal had already created. Seated at the piano, he began playing a toe-tapping melody that he said was the "preparation for the journey" music. He progressed on to something he called "the wagons and the oxen." Eventually he got to "Wilderness Lullaby," which he said was the only one totally finished. "Sal finished the lyrics on the way up here," he explained. "She'll be doing the script and lyrics."

He began playing softly, and after an intro, Sal sang:

> *"Listen now, my little child, the wilderness is singing;*
> *Singing softly, crooning sweetly, peaceful slumber bringing."*

The music was plaintive, almost sad but sweet, and Jayda saw a tear sliding down Bug's face before she turned away so nobody could see her.

"And now," Ethan said, "Enter the heroine and hero." He played something strong with a fragile under-melody. "This is you, Jayda," he said. "The strong pioneer woman—a blossom in the wilderness who will grace it with her presence while doing all that is necessary to establish a dynasty." He grinned. "Corny, eh?" He finished that music and began something that spoke of power and strength. "And this, Lee, is you," he said. "The leading man, the leader, the eventual patriarch of the clan."

Lee shot up from his seat. "Wait," he said. "What do you mean, that's me?"

Jayda groaned inwardly. Why hadn't she prepared him for this? She hadn't told him that she'd informed Ethan of his singing talents. He and she had been costars in several productions there in Blackbird, and she had just assumed . . .

"My stage days are over." Lee's voice rose with each word. "Can't you see what I look like?" He held up his hook and touched his scarred face with it. "Who would believe me as a leading man?"

He turned to Jayda. "The dinner was delicious, and I thank you for it. Tomorrow I'll get those covered wagon frames from Jake. Let me know what other behind-the-scenes work you'd like me to do."

He whispered something to Smoot and then quickly left the room for the second time in two days. They heard the front door close softly.

Chapter Nineteen

JAYDA'S FIRST IMPULSE WHEN LEE left so abruptly was to run after him. She rose from her seat, but Bug held up a hand. "Let him go," she said. "He's not going to listen to any explanations right now."

"But," Jayda protested, "I want to apologize for—"

Bug shook her head. "It would just make things worse."

Bug was right, of course. But, impulsive as always, Jayda wanted to try to fix it. Rewrite the scene. *Now.*

"Later," Bug said. "He'll feel better then. He doesn't like to be reminded of how changed he is."

Jayda mentally kicked herself for totally ignoring that fact. How was it that Bug, at fourteen, was wiser than she was at thirty-four? She nodded. "Okay, tomorrow."

She wondered if she could sandwich going to see Lee in between taking her guests on an exploratory tour of her property and meeting with Dave Bradbury and Mr. Yoshida.

Smoot settled it for her. "L. G. always feels better after he's been to ther-a-py," he said. "In the afternoon."

"You're right, Smoot." Jayda turned to Ethan and Sal and Paul. "Sorry," she said. She didn't specify what she was apologizing for.

Ethan nodded. "I was the one who blundered into that one."

Jayda shook her head. "Not your fault. We'll work it out." She hoped she could soothe Lee. One thing she knew: it would be practically impossible to find another leading man for the pageant who could be as convincing as he was. A major setback.

"So who's up for a tour of the house?" she asked quickly.

Paul yawned. "Could we do that when I can see again? My eyes have been glued to the highway for the past two days, and I'm ready for sleep."

Jayda whacked her forehead with the heel of her hand. "I forgot what a long drive you've had. You guys go on to bed. Tarzan and I will walk Smoot and Bug home, and then we'll turn in too."

Smoot stood up. "L. G. said Bug would walk me home."

"Okay," Jayda said, "but who will walk Bug home?"

Bug's eyebrows went up. "Who needs to? Jayda, I was finding my own way home long before you came." She put out a hand to Smoot. "Come on, kid, let's brave the things that go bump in the night."

Smoot giggled, and Bug grinned over her shoulder as they got up and left.

Jayda walked to the door with them. Just before they went

out, Bug turned to give Jayda a swift hug. "Thank you," she whispered.

Jayda watched at the door until the two disappeared down the slope of the hill, touched by Bug's fervent thank-you and wondering if it was still safe for the two kids to walk about in the dark, what with the circle-and-slasher lurking around.

◆ ◆ ◆

She awakened the next morning to the sound of someone singing. It was Sal's voice, and it came from Aunt Leora's garden. Opening up the shutters at her window, Jayda saw Sal out there. Water from the small irrigation ditch on the north flowed along the channels between the rows of growing things. Sal carried a short-handled hoe, and every now and then she bent to redirect the water or hack out a weed. Tarzan was with her, splashing through the water and occasionally snapping up a mouthful.

Jayda opened her window and waved. "Hi, early bird," she called. "I'll have breakfast ready in about fifteen minutes."

"Take your time," Sal hollered back. "I'm totally happy here with the radishes and the dog and the water your garden was crying for."

All-too-familiar guilt swept over Jayda. She'd noticed a couple of days before that the plants looked droopy.

"Thanks," she called to Sal. She pulled her head back inside. But Sal was speaking again.

"Tarzan and I had a nice visit with your old horse this morning." Sal waved toward the corral. "Did you know he gallops around his pen in the middle of the night?"

"Yes, I know," Jayda said. She didn't tell Sal that Twister performed only when *somebody* was there to watch. She didn't want to spook her.

After dressing quickly, she hurried downstairs to find Ethan already seated at the piano, scribbling notes on a sheet of music paper. While they'd been married, he'd frequently risen early to work while she tried to sleep. It had always amazed her that he could even *think* so early in the morning. After a late show, she was groggy and useless in the mornings. But he said that was when the juices of creativity flowed best for him.

"Oh, good," he said when he saw her. "Now I can plink out this stuff without waking anybody. Except Paul. But he can sleep through anything."

Propping the music on the piano, he played through it, a happy-sounding melody that was almost familiar. "Sounds a little like 'Sweet Betsy from Pike,'" Jayda said.

Ethan nodded. "A variation. I'm using it for narrative purposes, to move the plot along between scenes. In this part, the people are about to arrive here in the valley." He stopped playing and passed a hand across his chin. "It will be hard to come up with music majestic enough to describe their first glimpse."

It was going to be even harder to come up with a new leading man, Jayda thought. But all she said was, "Maybe it would help to see pictures of the people. There should be a lot of them, either in the Remembering Room or the attic."

"Remembering Room?"

"You'll love it," Jayda said.

"So when do we do the grand tour you promised?"

"Right after breakfast," she said. "We'll try to get it in before my appointment with Dave Bradbury and Mr. Yoshida."

She fixed a big farm breakfast—bacon and eggs and toast—and proved that Paul could sleep through anything *except* the aroma of frying bacon. "It won't be like this every morning," Jayda explained to them all as they sat at the table, "but to do the work here on the farm, you need a good breakfast."

"No complaints," Sal said as they enthusiastically dived in. "Granola and an orange picked fresh from our tree is the usual for Paul and me."

"Took me a long time to break Jayda of the bacon-and-egg habit," Ethan said. "She always said—" He made a *ta-da* gesture toward her, giving her the next line.

She picked it up. "'You can take the girl out of the farm, but you can't take the farm out of the girl.'" She thought about those early days of their marriage when their differences seemed so fun and interesting. "Eat up," she said. "And then we'll do the tour."

They'd already seen most of the upstairs since that was where their bedrooms were, and they'd been in the parlor and dining room the night before. So she took them to the Remembering Room before they went outside. All three stopped in wonder when they saw the wall of drawers. "Two hundred of them," Jayda said. "Full of the history of my family."

"Oh, wow," Ethan breathed. "Jayda, I swear I'll never forgive you for not bringing me here ten years ago. You have all this *family*. You know how much I'd like to have connections with *my* ancestors."

Ethan had been left an orphan when he was a baby and had

been adopted by a family not related to him. He'd had a good life, but she did know he'd always wondered about his birth family, of which he knew very little. The fact that he'd been an orphan, as she was, had been one of the things that had drawn them together, but the difference was that she had all this family history available for the asking.

But she'd rejected it all.

She walked over to the desk and picked up the two photographs she'd found before they'd come. "Here's a start on pictures," she said. She handed him the wedding picture and then the one of Asa Jorgensen and Ephraim Morehead gingerly holding the document between them. The deed. Still another thing she needed to think about: telling Bracken Morehead there really had been a deed. That would only intensify his search for it. More trouble.

Ethan gazed at the photos with delight. "Do you know the stories behind them?"

Jayda shook her head. She'd scarcely even considered that her ancestors *had* stories. They were just people who had lived and died and had nothing to do with her. "But everything must be here in the wall," she said. "Somewhere."

Ethan held up the picture of the bride and groom. "This will be perfect to project on the screen," he said.

"Project?" This was news to Jayda.

Ethan nodded. "We'll have a big screen to one side where we'll project actual pictures. You can imagine how much that will add to the show." He squinted at the photo of the two men. "I'm sure there's some drama behind this one. Definitely no friendship lost between these guys." He passed the pictures on to Sal and Paul, and then waved an arm at the drawers. "So where do we start?"

"Anywhere you want," she said.

The morning yielded a whole stack of pictures, garnered from several drawers. Apparently Asa Jorgensen, or someone in the family, had possessed a camera and had made use of it. There was a faded old picture of the valley looking as pristine as if no man had ever set foot in it. There were pictures of rough log cabins and barns, and finally, the framework of the big house on the hill.

One of the middle drawers on the far left yielded something else—the tarnished military button Jayda had found under the Jonathan apple tree a few days before. She remembered randomly pulling out a drawer and dropping it in. It was Sal who found it.

"Oh-ho," she said. "What's this?"

Jayda told about finding it in the orchard.

Sal took the button over to the window where she held it up to the light, squinting at it with interest. "I'd say it's from a World War I uniform," she said. "Do you know who in your family served in that war?"

Jayda hadn't known when she'd found the button, but since she and Smoot had visited the cemetery, she did know. In her mind she saw again the tombstone with the bronze government marker embedded in it.

"His name was Boyd Jorgensen," she said. "His grave marker says he died in foreign lands on July 17, 1918."

"First World War," Sal murmured, turning the button over and over. "We'll do a tribute to him somewhere in the pageant."

. A lovely thought. Jayda was about to say as much when Ethan held up something he'd pulled from a nearby drawer. "The slinky slasher strikes again," he said. It was a circle-and-slash note, but this one was different, drawn with pencil on faded, brittle school scratch paper. Old looking. As if it had been there a long, long time.

Jayda waited for the little chills she'd felt on the discovery of the other slash notes. But they didn't come. Instead, she snickered. "Maybe it's a message from the dead," she said. "Even my ancestors want me to leave."

She began to laugh then, maybe at the absurdity of it all or maybe because it was just one note too many—the straw that broke the proverbial camel's back. She wished she could tell the Mad Slasher that despite his juvenile notes, despite phantom visitors that made the old horse perform in the night, despite a fake note from the past, despite an old deed that very likely did exist, nothing was going to stop her now from doing her best to save the old house.

Except the fact that Lee refused to take the lead in the pageant. How could she convince him to play Asa Jorgensen, once again conquering the land?

"You know what?" she said, putting the brittle note aside to add to her file later. "I think we should invite some of the old-timers to come see all the pictures we found, since their ancestors are here too. Then we can tell them about the pageant and maybe get them to support us rather than to just wish I'd sell the house."

Sal clapped her hands. "Let's have a luncheon. And we can whip up some of Arvilla's pioneer recipes to get them in the mood."

Jayda felt a little thrill race down her spine as she remembered Bug's words: *You'll be using it again.*

"Let's do posters to advertise it," she said. "After lunch."

Jayda was sawing off slabs from a loaf of Aunt Leora's bread that she'd thawed that morning when Dave and Mr. Yoshida came. Early. There was nothing to do but offer them the grilled cheese sandwiches she was fixing. With Greek olives and thick fingers of dill pickles on the side. Typical heavy American fare. Gross. Jayda remembered the delicate Japanese food she'd loved in Los Angeles.

To her surprise, Mr. Yoshida smacked his lips. "I like American cooking," he said with delight. "Often the mother of my American friend made grilled cheese when I was boy."

As they ate, Paul mentioned that he'd spent a couple of years in Japan, which brought on a discussion of the beauties of that land as they sat around the kitchen table.

"But not as much space," Mr. Yoshida said. "No room for a fine development such as Summertree Meadows. It will be be-yoo-ti-ful." Like Smoot, he broke up the long word into handle-able portions. Jayda found it endearing. She liked Mr. Yoshida.

But she didn't like what he represented. At the end of the meal, he pushed back his chair, saying, "Now I want to see the old horse, please. There is no time for the business of buying the house today."

Jayda shook her head as she pushed back her own chair. "No time for that business any day, Mr. Yoshida. I am not selling my property."

He gave her a wide smile. "We will see. I have given Mr. David Bradbury permission to sweeten the pot, as you say. He has a surprise for you." He got to his feet. "We must hurry. Mr. David shall soon take me to the city to catch my airplane."

Jayda got up and led Mr. Yoshida, Dave Bradbury, and Ethan down the hall to the back door. Sal and Paul said they'd stay behind and clean up the kitchen.

Mr. Yoshida stopped short as they were passing the Remembering Room.

"Oh, my," he said, walking inside to survey the pictures they'd found in the drawers earlier. Paul had propped them on shelves and tables. Looking closely at them, he asked, "Ancestors?"

"Yes," Jayda said.

Mr. Yoshida nodded. "Very nice. Japanese also revere their ancestors. It is a good thing to do."

"I'm just beginning to realize that," Jayda said.

Mr. Yoshida said he'd like to look more at the pictures, but he had a plane to catch, so they continued out to the corral where Dave stood back to make a phone call while Mr. Yoshida went up to the railing. Twister, with people to perform for, put on quite a show, ending up with his stiff-legged rocking horse maneuver that had always thrown the best of the rodeo cowboys. That left him with heaving sides, but still enough energy to parade around the corral, head held high, heavy lips drawn back in a magnificent sneer.

Mr. Yoshida laughed and cheered and recorded it all on his cell phone camera. "I will show this to my grandchildren in Japan," he said. "They are like me when I was boy. They like old Western movies."

"Me, too," Ethan agreed. "I grew up on *Stagecoach* and *High Noon* and *A Man Called Horse*. They don't make them like they used to."

Mr. Yoshida nodded. "Too bad. They showed the spirit of a people."

Jayda wanted to blurt out that they don't make houses like they used to either—durable, beautiful, handcrafted houses that also showed the spirit of a people. No sale, she wanted to emphasize again. No matter what the "surprise" was that Dave Bradbury had for her.

But Mr. Yoshida was shaking Ethan's hand, ready to go. Jayda slipped over to stand beside Dave. "I'm still getting the nasty notes," she said. "You said you were going to see that they stopped."

He frowned. "Jayda, I'm really sorry. I've talked to several people, but nobody has a clue as to who's doing it. Maybe we can set up a watch or something when I get back from seeing Mr. Yoshida off. I'll be staying in the city for a couple of days, but I'll call when I return. Then I'll find time to do something about it."

Jayda felt guilty infringing on his time. "You know what?" she said. "Let's forget the notes. If somebody takes pleasure in littering the landscape with them, let him. We've both got better things to do than figuring out who it is."

"Jayda, I'll do anything I can to help you. You know that." Dave came forward and gave her a brief hug, with the bonus of a whiff of his compelling cologne.

What else was there to say? Jayda wished Mr. Yoshida a pleasant flight, and then watched with Ethan as Dave's silver Lexus rolled away.

"Nice guy, Yoshida," Ethan commented as they watched the car disappear down the hill. "Knows the power of the gentle—but lucrative—sell." He came over to put an arm around Jayda's shoulders. "Ya done good, babe. Stand firm."

She liked the weight of his arm around her. It was so familiar, so natural. She grinned up at him. "Right." Impulsively she reached up and kissed him on the cheek, then slipped out from under his arm and started up the hill. "Let's get those posters about the luncheon done, so we can go hang them downtown," she said.

After which, she reminded herself, she needed to see if Lee was all right.

Chapter Twenty

THE FIVE POSTERS, CREATED MOSTLY by Sal, were colorful and attractive. They showed covered wagons toiling up a hill topped by the ghostly outline of a big house with porches and a tower. Behind the wagons was a valley with high mountains in the distance, readily identifiable as the terrain of Blackbird. A number of people appeared in the scene, and Sal dressed each one with scraps of calico or denim Jayda had found in Aunt Leora's rag bag. In large letters they announced, "Come on up to lunch," along with the necessary information.

The posters brought Jayda and Ethan a lot of attention. People stopped to comment as they were placing them, with permission, in various store windows. Some mentioned the attractiveness of the artwork, others spoke of the advertised occasion. A few talked about the futility of fighting the development company. A group of four high school girls stopped to ask questions about Hollywood.

"Is it as wonderful as it sounds?" one of them asked.

"It's just a town with a lot of movie and TV studios," Ethan told her. "But it can be magical sometimes, in a make-believe kind of way." He leaned closer to her. "I'll tell you a secret."

Her eyes widened.

"There's magic here in Blackbird, too. If you don't believe me, come to lunch on Saturday." He flicked the poster with his hand.

"We'll be there," the girls chorused.

An elderly gentleman patted Jayda on the arm. "Your great-great-grandfather was a fine man," he said. "Old Asa Jorgensen."

She smiled at the man, remembering his face but not his name. "Did you know him?"

"Missed him by about twenty years. But my father talked about him a lot. Said he was someone who made a difference."

He said it in a thin, old voice, but it seemed to Jayda that the words bounced off the storefront they stood by and reverberated up and down the street. Her great-great-grandfather *had made a difference.* Wasn't that what everybody hoped to do? Jayda felt that she'd just acquired a purpose: to make a difference.

She remembered the old man's name now. Wilford Morehead—was he a relative of the Morehead who stood with Asa Jorgensen in the old picture, with the document held between them? A relative of Bracken?

"Mr. Morehead," she said, "do you know anything about a deed saying that the Moreheads own part of the Jorgensen property?"

"Oh, that," he said. "There's supposed to be an old deed to that effect somewhere. But most of us gave up on it long ago."

Jayda was relieved to hear that. "I found a picture of Asa Jorgensen and Ephraim Morehead holding a document."

Wilford nodded. "But nobody knows what happened to it. Don't worry about it, Janey. Everybody has forgotten all about it."

She didn't tell him that not everybody had forgotten about it.

At the turnoff to the Bride's House, Jayda told Ethan she wanted to stop by to see Lee. Ethan said he'd walk back to the house. She had the feeling he didn't want to be in on a visit to Lee. Was it because Lee would not lend his voice to the show? Or was he upset because he knew the two of them, Lee and Jayda, had once meant a lot to each other?

As Ethan got out of the car and headed up the hill, Jayda chided herself for even thinking he might be jealous. That was vanity thinking, that two guys might be fighting over her. Was she as immature as the fifteen-year-olds they'd just been talking to?

She waved as he sprinted up the hill and then turned to the house. "Lee?" The front window blinds were down. When he didn't answer, she knocked on the door, and when he still didn't respond, she reached out to try the knob. The door was not locked. "Lee?" she called again before entering the house.

In the dim light, she saw him slumped in the wing chair by the fireplace.

"Lee?" she said once again. "Are you all right?"

Jayda dropped to her knees beside him, reaching out at the

same time to switch on the table lamp next to his chair. "Lee?" Her heart thumped so hard it made her voice ragged.

He flinched when the light came on, which evened out her breathing a little. "Lee?" she said again.

Slowly he raised his right arm and roofed his eyes with his hand, shading them from the light. Then he lifted the stump of his left arm and reached out as if to take her hand but then dropped it back into his lap.

"Are you all right, Lee?" Jayda asked softly.

"No," he whispered. "No." And after a moment, "Have you heard of phantom limbs, Jayda?"

"Yes, I have." She knelt in front of the chair, looking into his face.

"I dreamed—" he said.

She waited.

"I dreamed I was playing the piano. Like Ethan did last night. The way I used to. A medley from the shows we were in. I heard the music."

Jayda waited quietly.

"My left hand," Lee went on. "The fingers. I could feel them stretching for the octaves and dancing up the scales on the runs." Abruptly, he dropped his right hand from shading his eyes and sat up straight. "Has Smoot come back?"

Jayda glanced into Smoot's bedroom, but the empty feel of the house told her he wasn't there. "No. Where did he go?"

"Bug came by. They went off together." He sat silently for a moment before going on. "Good thing, maybe. Gives me time to figure out how to tell him."

A frisson of apprehension shot through Jayda's body. "Tell him what?"

Lee took a deep breath and let it out. "His dad is coming home from Afghanistan. I had an e-mail from him this morning."

"Coming home?" she asked. "Will he be living here?"

Lee shook his head. "There's nothing for him here. He's career military. His folks live in Minnesota." After another pause, he said, "He's sending airline tickets for Smoot to fly to Minneapolis."

Jayda knelt there, rigid, wondering what that would mean for Lee. For her. And, most of all, for Smoot, who scarcely knew his dad. It explained why Lee was sitting there in the dim room, dreading the future and dreaming of the past.

"Well, maybe—" Jayda began but then stopped. Why speculate about things she wasn't involved in? Clearing her throat, she said, "So you'll be flying with him."

Lee shook his head. "Colonel Chad Ferguson, USMC, says Smoot is old enough to man up and fly by himself. He shouldn't be coddled, Colonel Ferguson says. Chad believes in teaching independence, above all things. Over-protection makes boys weak, he says."

That explained a lot of things, like how Smoot was free to wander where and when he wanted. It had worked okay in Blackbird, but how about a big city like Minneapolis? Jayda's mind scurried about, looking for something she could do. But she had no right to interfere. Smoot wasn't hers.

And he wasn't Lee's.

"Don't get me wrong," Lee said. "Colonel Ferguson is a fine

Marine. He has served well and faithfully. But he hasn't been around since Smoot was about four. Smoot doesn't—" He stopped.

Jayda took his hand in both of hers. "I know."

"I have to tell him," Lee said.

Jayda nodded. "Yes." She stood up, still holding his hand. "Lee, come on up to the house. You need to be with people right now. Smoot and Bug will probably come by there anyway, and Paul could use some help in figuring out how to build a stage extension out from the porch. Do you remember how they did it when we were young and were in a pageant?"

He nodded silently and then stood up beside her, wrapping his arms around her. It seemed like minutes before he drew back. "I remember the extension. I helped build it." He gazed down at her. "You sure Ethan won't mind if I come up?"

She slanted a look at him. "Ethan? Why should he mind?"

A slight smile tipped a corner of Lee's mouth. "Jayda, you never were all that good at reading people without a script. Ethan resents me."

Jayda shook her head. "I'm sure you're mistaken. Why on earth would he resent you?"

With his good hand, Lee cupped her cheek. "Because, Jayda, he knows I love you too."

It was the "too" that slammed into Jayda's brain. It took her a while to herd her thoughts. Finally, she said, "Lee, Ethan and I are divorced. *Divorced*. And he knows you and I were just *friends*. *Best* friends back in the old days when we starred together in the shows. Back when we were a duo. Lee and Jane."

185

Lee looked away. "Maybe *you* thought it was just friendship, Jayda. But when I was Petruchio, I *loved* you as Katherine. When I was Harold Hill, I *loved* you as Marian the Librarian."

His face said it had been *her* he'd loved, not the fictional characters. But how could he? When she was seventeen and eighteen, she had *been* the characters she played. She hadn't had an identity of her own. Had he seen behind it all to a real person?

If he had loved her then, she hadn't recognized it. He'd never given her any sign, other than those kisses under the Jonathan apple tree, when she thought they were just goofing around. He'd never *said* he loved her, except as a line in a show. So she'd looked upon her feelings for him as a hopeless crush, and when Randy from Hollywood had shown up offering to make her fantasies come true, she'd thought *that* was love and had followed him to California.

Lee took his hand away from her face. "Give me a few minutes to clean up, and we'll go."

The moment when she should have told him how she'd felt was gone. She'd muffed her lines. She listened to the sound of water from the bathroom, wondering if it would have made any difference sixteen years ago if she'd known he loved her. Would she have gone to Hollywood anyway? Or would they have married and produced a brood of cute kids like Emmylu and Nathan did—with maybe a boy like Smoot? Or maybe they would have gone off to realize their dreams of performing professionally, together. Maybe Lee wouldn't have gone to Iraq then. He wouldn't have lost his arm.

But there was no good in what-ifs. The past was cemented in, as unchangeable as all that family history in the wall of drawers. Only an hour ago she thought she'd discovered a purpose, a *destination*: to make a difference, as old Asa Jorgensen had done. But he'd had a map that showed the way through the wilderness, and she didn't.

When they got to the house, Tarzan came to greet them, wagging his tail effusively as if he'd wondered where Jayda had gone. From the house came the sound of Ethan pounding out one of his just-composed songs for the show.

Paul was in front of the house, making sketches on a pad. "I've brought Lee to help," Jayda said. "He remembers how the stage extension was done before."

Relief showed on Paul's face. "Bless you, Lee. I've been worrying how to get the supports just right where the land slopes away."

Jayda was glad that Paul truly needed Lee's help. It would keep Lee from thinking about how to tell Smoot he was going away, at least for a little while.

She climbed the porch steps just as Ethan came out. "Oh, good," he said. "You're here. That music I was playing, that's Maren's song—your song—when you first see where your new home will be. You're thinking about how it will be someday, but right now it's just a bare hill."

"Sounds good, Ethan. I'll be honored to sing it." She saw that he'd spotted Lee. His eyes narrowed just a little, but rather than comment, he went on telling her about the music. "While you sing," he said, "we'll project the pictures we found this morning on a big screen. That will make the entire scene more authentic."

She nodded. "That would be good. But what fairy godmother is going to wave her wand and change a few pumpkins into a big screen and other equipment? Aunt Leora left some money for me to use, but not enough for that kind of thing."

Ethan waved a hand. "Where's your faith, Jayda? We'll find a way when we need it."

That was so typical. Ethan's attitude had always been that whatever they needed—money, for instance—would show up when it was crisis time. He'd liked to quote a line from the movie *Field of Dreams*: "If you build it, they will come."

And things had usually worked out. Ethan would get an unexpected assignment for some background music in a new movie, or she would land the lead in a dinner theater show. They'd survived from one crisis to the next. But she'd found it difficult to live that way. Another factor contributing to the divorce.

She noticed Ethan staring at a truck coming up the hill. "Well," he said, "that's obviously not your buddy Dave Bradbury coming back to talk."

Obviously. The faded and dented truck held two people inside. It drove around the circular driveway in front of the porch and came to a stop. The passenger got out, waving to the trio on the porch. Belinda. This time in a magenta silk pantsuit, molded to her body. Blonde hair piled high and elaborately curled.

"Wow," Ethan breathed. "Who's the babe? Can we put her in the pageant? Maybe the hostess at a high-class saloon?"

"Bite your tongue," Jayda whispered. "No saloons in this pageant. And that lady is my cousin Belinda."

"Maybe that's why you never brought me here," Ethan said with a grin. "She's *hot*. How about the dude? Perfect for a villain."

Jayda watched the driver step from the car. "He's *trouble*," she said. "His name is Bracken Morehead."

"Morehead," Ethan said softly as they approached. "As in the other party in that old picture you showed us of your great-great-grandfather with the paper between them? Holding on as if it were frying their fingers?"

"Right. His great-great-grandson." Moving forward, she said, "Belinda. How nice to see you again."

Belinda gave her a dazzling smile that included Ethan. "Hello, Jayda. Why don't you introduce me to your friend?"

Jayda did the intros, watching Ethan's eyes light up as he shook Belinda's offered hand. She remembered a long time ago, when she'd been just a small girl, Belinda had been in a local production of *Li'l Abner,* playing the part of Stupefyin' Jones. The male characters in the show had gone catatonic whenever Stupefyin' showed up. It still happened. Even to Ethan, who was used to Hollywood beauties, and even though Belinda was at least a dozen years older than he.

Jayda turned toward Belinda's companion. "Hello, Bracken," she said.

He acknowledged her greeting with a terse nod. "Jane," he said.

She could see he was making an effort to be civil, probably prompted by Belinda.

"I was just talking to Uncle Wilford," he said. "He mentioned that you found a picture I'd be interested in seeing."

"It doesn't prove anything," Jayda said.

"It proves there was a deed," Bracken insisted.

"You can't tell it's a deed."

"You can't prove it's not." Bracken marched across the porch. "I'm going to take a look at it. Now. And then I'm going to go through every drawer on that wall. It's in there somewhere."

Jayda ran around him and positioned herself in the doorway so he couldn't get by. "Not now, you're not," she said. "I'll make a copy of the picture for you, and then we'll set up an appointment for you to come back and we'll both start going through the drawers. But you're not going in there today."

He scowled. "Who's going to stop me?"

Ethan stepped up beside her. "Cool it, cowboy. The lady says later."

The two men were almost the same height, but Bracken was beefier. Jayda was impressed that Ethan would stand up to the bigger man. The two of them glared belligerently at each other.

"Look," Jayda said. "I'll make a copy of the picture right now, and you can come back when it's more convenient to talk about it."

"I'm going in there right now," Bracken said loudly.

Down the slope, Lee and Paul stopped talking and started up the hill, apparently alerted by the rising voices.

Bracken glanced at them. "Hurry up with that picture," he snarled.

While Ethan guarded the door, Jayda dashed inside to the computer printer and quickly ran off a copy of the old picture.

When she handed it to Bracken, she said, "Now, I'd appreciate it if you'd leave."

Bracken scrutinized the photograph and then turned to go. "I'll be back," he said. He gave an angry motion with his head to Belinda, expecting her to follow him, but she waved him off.

"There's a party goin' on here, Bracken. I'm gonna stay a bit."

Ethan nodded as they all watched Bracken go. "Like I said, he'll make a great villain. Typecasting."

♦ ♦ ♦

Jayda watched Bracken's wreck of a truck rattle down the road a bit and then come to a dust-swirling stop. Bracken got out at the same time Twister trotted into view, followed by Bug and Smoot, who held a bridle. "Twister," Smoot hollered. "Stop."

Twister, his head held arrogantly high, ignored him.

Tarzan, apparently surprised that the horse was loose, came over to stand by Jayda, pressing against her leg as she watched Bracken stride over to Smoot and grab the bridle. "Let me handle this," he said loud enough for Jayda and the others to hear. "Him and me have an old score to settle."

The horse, obviously tired by now, allowed Bracken to catch up, slip the bridle over his head, and then climb onto his back. Bracken was considerably heavier now than he'd been when he and Twister had been adversaries, and it took more effort to get aboard, but he made it. Yanking the reins, he kicked the old horse in the ribs. "Back to prison, you old sidewinder," he growled.

Twister took two steps forward before launching into the

maneuver that had gained him his name. He twisted, he cork-screwed, he cycloned. He piled Bracken, right in front of a very appreciative audience who had come closer to watch.

Bracken didn't wait long enough for anybody to comment. He picked himself up, stalked to his truck, and roared off.

Jayda put her hand up to her face to hide a grin, but it was no use. She snickered and then exploded into full laughter, and so did everyone else. Even Lee guffawed, and Tarzan ran around in circles, barking happily.

Smoot giggled with delight. He hurried over to scoop up the reins and pat the old horse. "I love this guy," he said. "If I come talk to him every day, maybe he'll let me ride him in the pageant."

"I'll write special music for him," Ethan said.

Jayda watched Lee's face sober and then crumple. She knew he was thinking that now was the time to tell Smoot that he wasn't even going to be there for the pageant.

Chapter Twenty-One

SMOOT ACCEPTED THE NEWS ABOUT his father coming home stoically, without comment, except to say, "Is he coming here to live with us?"

"No, buddy." Lee knelt down to be on eye level with the boy. "You're going to Minneapolis to meet him. How about that! Your first airplane ride!"

When Smoot remained silent, Ethan said, "Oh, wow, Smoot, how fun will that be!" Paul, too, made a falsely jovial remark that was meant to fill up air space when he obviously didn't know what else to say. Smoot stood stiffly, still hanging on to Twister's bridle. But then the corners of his mouth turned down and he began blinking rapidly. Jayda's newly discovered motherly instinct told her to leap forward, enfold him in her arms, and let him howl out his unhappiness. But she hesitated too long, worried about what Colonel Ferguson might say about such behavior. It was Belinda who leaped forward, followed closely by Bug.

They surrounded Smoot with their arms, and Tarzan wiggled in among the three of them.

"It's all right, darlin'," Belinda said softly. "Let it all out."

And Bug said, "Remember last year, Smoot, when I had to go live with my grandma for a while? I bawled my eyes out."

He looked up at her, apparently remembering, and tried to smile. But then he broke down, and with a loud bellow he pressed his face against Belinda and wept all over her pretty magenta shirt. Belinda laid her cheek against the top of his head, crooning, "There, there, Smootie. There, there."

Throughout it all, Smoot hung on to Twister's bridle as if it were the only anchor he had left. Later, when he'd stopped crying—after everyone had assured him how fine it would be to see his dad, after he'd been patted and petted and soothed—his first concern was to get the old horse back where it belonged.

"He doesn't see so good anymore," Smoot said. "He might fall in a ditch and break his leg. He needs to be back in his corral."

Lee took his free hand. "It's time for us to go home anyway. We need to send an e-mail to your dad."

"I have to go too," Bug said.

They started out after Smoot had been hugged by "the Hollywoodies," as he called them. Jayda and Tarzan joined the little caravan as far as the barn.

As they walked along, Jayda wondered anxiously if Twister had been released by the tormentor who had been harassing her ever since she came. The plague of circle-and-slash notes seemed to have ceased. Was he going on to bigger and nastier pranks now?

"Did you see anybody near the barn when you and Smoot were there earlier?" she asked Bug. "Do you have any idea who could have let Twister out?"

Before Bug could answer, Smoot said in a tiny voice, "Maybe it was me. I was in the corral while you got his hay, Bug. Maybe I didn't do the latch right when I went out."

Lee looked at him sharply. "You were in the corral?"

Smoot nodded. "I go in there a lot. Twister wouldn't hurt anybody he likes. I know he would let me ride him if I was here a while longer."

Lee stopped, facing him. "Smoot, promise me you won't be trying to ride him. Look what he did to Bracken."

Smoot put his chin up. "My dad would let me do it. He's always telling me to man up and do things that make me afraid. Besides, Twister would never buck me off. I'm nice to him."

Jayda had never seen him defy Lee. It was a side of him she didn't even know existed.

Lee seemed a bit flummoxed by it. Putting an arm around Smoot's shoulders, he said, "Well, buddy, as long as you're here, I'm in charge, and I say no trying to ride Twister."

Smoot pulled away. "You're not the boss of me," he muttered.

He'd already begun to change. Was this the kind of boy he would become when he went to live with his dad?

To cool things down, Jayda said, "Smoot, I've been thinking. This party we're planning for next Saturday, when lots of people will come to lunch and hear Ethan's music—how about we make it a great big fantabulous farewell party just for you?"

It took Smoot a moment to change gears. But then he said, "Can we have homemade ice cream and Aunt Leora's buried-in-chocolate three-layer killer cake?"

"Done," Jayda said, and for the first time since Lee had broken the news to him, Smoot smiled.

When Jayda got back to the house, she found Ethan giving Belinda a private concert, playing all the tunes he'd composed so far. Belinda sat on the big blue-flowered wing chair at the side of the piano. Paul was on the sofa with Sal perched very close to her husband, practically on his lap. Wives tended to stake out their territory in the presence of Belinda.

When Ethan played and sang the comedy song to be sung by the spinster Arvilla, Belinda laughed, that tinkly little sound that had captivated everybody in sight ever since she was three years old. Three *months* old, very likely. "I could do that part, Ethan," she said. "I'm quite good at comedy."

He beamed at her. "Nobody would believe you as a spinster."

"I could convince them, darlin'," she said.

Oh, yuck, Jayda thought, watching Ethan adore her with his eyes. "That would be quite an acting job, darlin'," he said.

He almost went down for the count in the smile she gave him before she looked up at Jayda. "Is Smoot okay?" she asked.

"As good as can be expected," Jayda said. "Thanks to you. Letting him cry it out was the right thing to do, Belinda."

"I've had experience," Belinda said. "I raised two kids, you know."

Jayda tended to forget that. The twins, Ross and Rose, were in college now. She hadn't seen them for years. They'd been nice kids, well-behaved and polite, the last time she'd seen them. Belinda had been a good mother.

And then she had the thought, a good mother who probably needs tuition money, now that she was divorced again and on her own. Maybe she was the one who'd been leaving the notes.

"You know what?" Belinda said. "I'd like to hear all about what you're planning. I'll help in any way I can. Even if I can't be Arvilla." She sent another dazzling smile Ethan's way.

He turned around on the piano bench to face her. "Okay, here's the skinny." And he told all about the pageant they were planning. And how Jayda hoped it would convince the towns-people that the house was a gift from the past that should be preserved as a symbol of what they'd been and who they were because of it. He explained how they planned to project the early pictures they'd found onto a huge screen.

Belinda applauded when he finished. "And of course Jayda will have the leading part," she exclaimed. "We can advertise her as coming home to star in the production. Blackbird's own Hollywood star."

Jayda didn't miss the "we." Belinda was already including herself in the plans. Jayda was uneasy that Belinda now knew what the plans were, although that was silly. If everybody in town didn't already know what she and her Hollywood friends were planning, they would after the luncheon and party on Saturday. Besides, Belinda seemed sincere in her enthusiasm for the project. Maybe it was time to trust her.

Jayda forced a small laugh. "A *faded* star," she said. "Let's not get carried away, Belinda."

"You always were too modest," Belinda said. "You've got to promote yourself more, Jayda. I'm excited about your project." Her glance took in all of them: Jayda, Ethan, Paul, and Sal. "And I'm offering my services as wardrobe mistress for your cast of thousands. I worked for a while as assistant to the wardrobe mistress at a Broadway theater in New York. I'll make your pioneers look so authentic the audience will practically taste the lumpy mush they had for breakfast while on the trail."

"That's really nice, Belinda," Jayda said. "But we have no budget to speak of. There's no money to buy fabric for costumes."

"We don't need money," Belinda said. "I'll charm everybody into letting me dig through their attics."

"You're the girl who can do it," Ethan said enthusiastically.

Jayda could see that his dazzlement with her beauty had turned into genuine admiration. She had to admit, Belinda was a class act. And having someone take over the costuming was a positive step forward.

"Lee and I were in the attic here, last week," Jayda said. "Seems that Aunt Leora saved costumes from those pageants we had in the past. We even found our duds from when we played Professor Hill and Marian the Librarian in high school."

Belinda's face brightened. "Lee has such a great voice. Of course he'll be the male lead, right?"

Her words brought back the painful scene the evening Lee had been there to dinner. How he had stormed out of the house after declaring there was no way he'd ever appear on a stage again, mutilated the way he was.

"He says no." Quickly, Jayda changed the subject. "Do you want to look in the attic here right now and see what you can find?"

Belinda glanced at her wristwatch. "I have to go." She got to her feet. "I'll come back in a couple of days."

Ethan stood up beside her. "You're not leaving, are you?"

"Have to," she said.

She didn't say why. Jayda couldn't help wondering if it was because she'd found out what she'd come there to learn.

With a Queen Elizabeth wave of a hand, Belinda tippy-tapped to the door. "Ta-ta, little darlin's," she trilled as she went out.

Ethan took a step forward. "Could we give you a lift some-where?"

"I'm good," Belinda called back over her shoulder. "But you're a sweetie for asking."

As they all watched, she daintily descended the porch stairs. Just as she got to ground level, Bracken's truck pulled up and she got in. Perfect timing. Planned, Jayda thought.

Ethan bounded down the stairs, watching the truck until it disappeared down the hill. Then he slowly came back up on the porch.

"We've been had, little darlin's," he said.

Jayda snorted. "Welcome to Belindaland. Don't worry about it. You're not the first to fall under her charms, nor the last."

Ethan stared at where the truck was now just a puff of dust.

"I spilled my guts. I told her everything. She knows now that we're only grasping at straws with this pageant. How's that going to hold back the developers? We have no big-time artillery to fight them."

"What I want to know," Sal said as she sat down on the porch swing, "is why she would so blatantly demonstrate where her loyalty is. I mean, why didn't she at least sneak around the corner to get into that guy's truck?"

Jayda shrugged. "Look, guys, Belinda is Belinda. And she'd have found out what we're doing when we start auditions anyway. So what ammunition have we given her that she can use?"

What indeed? Jayda wasn't as easy about the situation as she pretended. Belinda had always been able to see chinks in someone's armor when nobody else knew they were there. But how *could* she use the information they'd so eagerly handed over to her?

After a long silence, Sal stood up. "I'm going to go for a walk and find some snakes to bite."

"I'll join you," Jayda said. "You guys want to come?"

Ethan walked toward the door and opened it to go inside. "I think I'll sit down and compose some Cruella de Vil music while the emotion is hot. I've just added a villainess to the show."

"Okay," Jayda said, and then called, "Tarzan! Walk!"

Even as she said it, she felt an emptiness. Tarzan hadn't come back to the house with her. He had flopped down near the corral once Twister was inside, as if he planned to stand guard. Smoot had hugged him fiercely before he, Lee, and Bug had gone down the hill.

He should have come home by now.

Jayda hurried out to the front porch. "Tarzan?" she called.

There was no response. No big mound of brown fur trundling eagerly across the lawn, tail wagging. It was totally unlike him not to come.

"Tarzan?" she called, louder.

Sal and Ethan came up alongside her. "When did you last see him?" Ethan asked.

"At the barn," Jayda said.

"Let's go see if he's still there," Sal said.

He wasn't. Old Twister peered at the anxious threesome and then began his stiff routine, sneering, trotting around the corral, occasionally flinging out his back legs.

Jayda was getting panicky. If they didn't find him, what would that do to Smoot? To lose the only home he knew and then lose the dog he loved.

What would it do to *her*?

Chapter Twenty-Two

Jayda could feel her palms sweating. She rubbed them against her jeans. "Maybe he decided to follow Smoot and Lee. I'll bet that's where he is."

Sal and Ethan immediately started down the hill. "Does he go there alone?" Sal asked.

"Never has before." Jayda tried to keep her voice even. "But that's not to say he didn't try it today." Of course that's where he'd be. Nobody had been paying enough attention, so he'd gone looking for his pal Smoot.

But he didn't come bursting out of Lee's house when they approached—jogging now, in a hurry to find the dog.

Smoot and Lee came out, however, and Smoot's face bunched up with alarm when Jayda asked if they'd seen Tarzan since they left the barn.

"No," Smoot said. "Is he lost?"

"Oh, no. He's just wandered off somewhere to be by himself."

Jayda heard the false note in her voice, and so, apparently, did Lee.

"Well, buddy," he said to Smoot, "let's go help find that rascal. Do you think he's playing hide-and-seek with us?"

"No." Smoot's face was serious. "He doesn't know how. Maybe somebody stole him." He ran down the pathway to the road. "Tarzan!" he hollered.

"Lee," Jayda said in a low voice, "will you drive down to the highway and see if—"

He nodded, silently understanding that she was saying maybe Tarzan had been hit by a car.

"I'll go with him," Ethan said solemnly. "He'll drive, I'll look."

His voice was as ragged as hers. In her total concern for herself and for Smoot, she had forgotten that this had been Ethan's dog too. She prayed silently that they wouldn't find Tarzan's body along the road. She remembered how a dog her cousin Lucas had had when he was young had been hit by a car and had died alone in the dusty weeds. Lucas had carried him home, crying into his bloody fur.

"The rest of us will go back to the house," Jayda said. "Maybe he'll be there with Paul by now."

Jayda, Smoot, and Sal cut up through the pasture and orchard, calling the dog's name in unison, like the chorus of a Greek tragedy.

By the time they reached the house, they had to face the fact that Tarzan was truly gone. Smoot crumpled. Jayda led him to the porch swing and sat, pulling his head onto her shoulder.

He didn't cry. In a thin voice he said, "If somebody took him, I have to stay here till he comes back." Jayda realized that Smoot felt he couldn't go live with his dad until the dog was home.

"I know, Smoot," she said. "I know."

It wouldn't have been hard for someone to take the dog. All anyone would have had to do was stop their car, open the door, and the trusting dog would have willingly jumped in. Who in Blackbird, where everyone knew everyone else, would do that? But everyone *didn't* know everyone else. Not anymore. There were all the new people in the new houses. Things had changed since she'd lived here.

On the other hand, she couldn't blame the new people just because they were new.

Her thoughts were interrupted by the arrival of Lee's old truck. He and Ethan got out, grim-faced, but with the news that they hadn't found a dead dog on the road.

Ethan came over to touch Jayda's shoulder. "Are you okay?" he whispered.

She wasn't, but for Smoot's benefit she said, "Yes. We'll find him."

Ethan squeezed into the space left on the swing and put his arm around both her and Smoot. She knew he was hurting, too. He loved Tarzan as much as she did. Reaching out, she put her hand on his, wishing fervently she could roll back time to when he and she and Tarzan had been all together in their little Hollywood apartment.

The entire group sat or stood on the porch, glumly watching the sun set, until Lee said, "I'm going into town and ask around."

He was heading for his truck when they all saw Dave Bradbury's Lexus coming up the hill. It passed the barn and came to a stop in front of the house. Dave got out and opened the back door to release an overexcited Tarzan. The dog leaped up the stairs and raced toward Jayda, Ethan, and Smoot, who stood up to welcome him. He jumped up on them, whining and gargling in his throat as if trying to tell them something. He barked and wriggled and licked faces. Smoot hugged him fiercely.

Dave came up on the porch. "Found him about four miles down the road," he said. "Figured you wouldn't want him off by himself like that, so I brought him home."

Jayda wordlessly flung her arms around him, burying her face in the space between his ear and shoulder. Enemy or not, right now he was her hero.

She stayed plastered up against him, breathing in the scent of his cologne, which now seemed more comforting than compelling, long enough to regain control of her emotions, and then leaned back. "Four miles away?" she repeated. "Did you see any cars nearby? Somebody who might have dumped him out?"

Dave shook his head. "All I saw was one tired and thirsty dog. It seemed to me he'd been walking for quite a while. I had a bottle of water, so I poured some into my hands, and he really lapped it up."

Dave was smiling and apparently enjoying her close

proximity. His arms were tight around her. Jayda pulled away, saying, "I wonder—"

Jayda didn't finish her sentence that maybe Belinda and Bracken were the culprits who had taken Tarzan for a ride. She had no evidence of that. The fact that she suspected Belinda's twittery visit had been a set-up job was not enough. The way Bracken's truck had arrived to pick her up at exactly the moment Belinda left was suspicious but not incriminating. Even Bracken's ugly behavior didn't mean he'd do harm to the dog. And luckily, it appeared that no harm had come to Tarzan.

"You wonder what?" Dave prompted.

"I wonder if it's some kind of warning," she said limply. She stepped away from Dave and dropped down beside Smoot to hug Tarzan again. He smelled of weeds and dust.

Ethan knelt beside her. "Who would be that rotten, to take a dog far from home and let him loose?"

"I don't know," she said. "I'm just happy he's home."

"So am I, babe." Ethan reached out a hand to cup her cheek. The familiar gesture brought a lump to her throat.

She got to her feet. "Hey, let's celebrate the return of the lost. I'll make root beer floats."

While everyone slurped the floats and Tarzan chewed a Milkbone treat, Dave drew Jayda aside. "I'm guessing the dog-napper was the guy who's been harassing you," he said so only she could hear. "I think he's letting you know he's upping the ante."

Jayda nodded. "That crossed my mind. But there was no note on his collar this time. No circle-and-slash."

"He's apparently gone past that," Dave said. "That was grade-school stuff. Now he seems to be going for threats that'll really spook you."

Jayda considered that, shivering a little. "I'm not going to cave in, not even after this. There's too much at stake." Although with Smoot leaving, she had to admit to herself that some of the motivation for keeping the area pristine would be gone.

Dave put his hands on both her arms, above the elbow. "Promise me you'll call me if you see anything out of the ordinary."

"I will, Dave. I will."

As he turned to leave, he said, "I'll be in touch later, Jayda. We need to set up an appointment so I can explain Mr. Yoshida's new terms. They're good. You'll be tempted. Beyond endurance, I hope."

He smiled again, that wide, white-toothed smile that crinkled his eyes, and Jayda couldn't help but remember the feel of his circling arms, the whiff of his cologne. "I won't be," she said. But she couldn't refuse to meet with him. She was beholden to him now, as Aunt Leora used to say, for bringing Tarzan home. "But I'm willing to talk about it. Not until next week, though. This week we're getting ready for the luncheon and Smoot's farewell. A lot of people will be coming."

His smile faded, replaced by a look of concern. "Is that a good idea? I mean, having people all over the place? What if your villain decides to sabotage the affair?"

She hadn't really thought of that. "Well," she said, "if he

makes a move while there are so many people here, maybe some-body will catch him at it."

After Dave left, Sal sidled up to Jayda. "I heard what he said about meeting to talk about Mr. Yoshida's offer. Want reinforce-ments so you won't weaken?"

"Thanks, Sal," she said, "but I think I can handle it. Don't you trust my sales resistance?"

"What *I* don't trust is Dave Bradbury," Sal said.

"Dave?" That surprised Jayda. "But he just brought Tarzan home."

"Maybe he took him in the first place. Maybe he's the mad circle-and-slasher. Think about it, Jayda. He has a lot to gain if you sell to Mr. Yoshida."

"He's just doing his job." Jayda didn't want to put Dave on the list of suspects, along with Lucas and Belinda and Bracken and Jake Sterry and who knew who else?

But she had to admit, he *was* a possibility.

Chapter Twenty-Three

JAYDA THAWED SEVERAL OF AUNT Leora's food packages to feed everyone after the root beer floats were finished. Smoot sat the whole time with one arm wrapped around Tarzan, handing him more bits of food than he ate himself. At the end of the meal, he announced that he was staying the night. "To watch over Tarzan," he said. "To make sure no one steals him again."

"We wouldn't let that happen, Smoot," Ethan said. "There are a lot of us here to guard him."

Smoot eyed him. "There were a lot of you here when he got tooken away."

After a quick glance at Lee, who gave a nod of assent, Jayda said, "Tarzan would be happy to have you stay, Smoot. But your favorite room isn't available, you know. Ethan is staying in the Good Morning, Sun room now."

"I know," he said. "But there are lots of rooms I like. Except the Remembering Room."

Jayda recalled he'd said that on the first day he'd come to visit her. He'd said that was where Aunt Leora talked to dead people. It wasn't any wonder he didn't want to sleep in a "haunted" room.

"So which one do you pick?" she asked.

He seemed to be thinking, and then without looking up, said, "The Remembering Room, so I can tell my dad I slept there alone. Except I'm going to have Tarzan stay with me. My dad'll say I was brave to face my fear."

Jayda felt as if her heart would break for the boy. She'd acted the emotions of a broken heart before, onstage. And maybe even a couple of times in real life, like when Ethan had suggested they end their marriage, and more recently a few days ago, when she'd learned how much Lee had loved her all those years ago. But she'd never experienced heartbreak to this depth as she watched a seven-year-old boy deal with his father's expectations. A boy whom she'd come to regard as almost a son. A boy who was teaching her what family was all about.

She wanted to bawl out, "Oh, Smoot, you don't have to do that!" But she didn't. She told herself once again that he wasn't hers, and if this was what Colonel Chad Ferguson demanded of his son, she had to abide by it. Maybe that's the way brave men came about.

So what she said was, "Okay, Smoot. Let's go pick some sheets and blankets to make a bed on the sofa in that room."

He shook his head. "Aunt Leora has some sleeping bags in the attic. I'll get one of them. That's more like a soldier."

"I'll go with you to get it," Lee said.

"I can do it myself." Smoot headed for the stairs, with Jayda and Lee following. "Come on, Tarzan." Halfway to the landing he turned and said, "I can tuck myself in, too, so you can go home, L. G."

Lee put his arm around Jayda as they both watched Smoot continue up the stairs, his step resolute, his eyes straight ahead. Lee didn't say anything and neither did she, but his arm tightened around her as Smoot disappeared from view, and then he turned just enough to embrace her fully, his ragged breath warm on her cheek. She wasn't sure how long they stood that way before he dropped his arms and, with a whispered "I'll be back in the morning," left the house.

♦ ♦ ♦

The next morning, Jayda rose early after a night of sleeplessness interspersed with nightmares, in which she searched for something she couldn't quite identify. She'd originally intended to start the day by going through as many of the drawers in the Remembering Room as she could, intent on skidding away from the reality of Smoot leaving. Her plan had been to pull out all pictures and letters and anything else having to do with members of the community other than the Jorgensens. She wanted to put them on display for the party on Saturday, to show how closely the town was tied to the old house. She needed to find more pioneer recipes, too, that she and Sal could prepare for the luncheon.

But she didn't want to disturb Smoot in the Remembering Room before he was ready to get up. So she went to the living room where Ethan already sat the piano. He'd been playing softly, probably so he wouldn't disturb those who were still sleeping.

"I've got 'Maren's Song,'" he said triumphantly. "It's written just for you."

Maren. That was the part Jayda was to play in the pageant. Maren Jorgensen, young wife of Asa. According to Sal's script, based on some translated pages from an old diary she'd found in the wall of drawers, Maren had been homesick for the flat, green land of Denmark and the people she'd left behind. As the covered wagon company toiled across the brown mountains on the way to establish a new home, she'd wondered if the sacrifice was more than she could bear.

Ethan thrust some scribbled music and words into Jayda's hands, and then turned back to the piano. The song was written in a minor key that made it plaintive and lonely. Jayda could feel the young wife yearning for familiar scenes and family she might not ever see again. Then there was a segue into a major chord, with Asa's voice joining Maren's, and the music soared as they sang of their hopes for a new life in the mountains of the west. Jayda could almost hear Lee's voice blending with hers, could feel his arms around her and his breath warm on her face, the way it had been last night before he broke away and hurried off into the darkness.

Although Lee would not be doing Asa's part, Jayda knew that she could easily sink into the character of Maren. Or was it more accurate to say "escape"? That was her best thing, losing herself inside a character. *Being* that person. But this time she couldn't fully escape. The emotions of her real life overwhelmed those of the character she was to play. She couldn't get away from them.

Jayda remembered the day Ethan had wondered if he could do the music to match the mountains. "You're almost there," Jayda said when she finished the song. "It's really nice."

He nodded. "Yes, it is!"

They were back to familiar territory. Jayda grinned. "Modesty is still your big thing, I see."

"Yeah." He grinned back unapologetically, his eyes alight with enthusiasm. "The music came to me about 2:00 A.M. after the stuff with Smoot."

Jayda remembered that he always worked better when something stirred his emotions. So at least some modicum of good had come out of the "stuff with Smoot," as Ethan put it.

Smoot was wearing some kind of military jacket when he finally appeared. "I wanted to stay asleep," he said, "but Tarzan needed to go out."

So he, too, had probably spent a restless night, there in the room where Aunt Leora talked to the dead.

"If you want to, you can go back and catch another forty winks," Jayda said. "Breakfast will be a little late." In fact, everybody might have to fend for themselves that morning. She didn't feel like fixing anything. Nothing sounded good.

Smoot echoed her own thoughts when he said, "I'm not hungry." He hitched the much-too-big jacket up around his shoulders.

The jacket looked old and a bit ratty. The brass buttons were tarnished. At first Jayda thought it was something from World

War II, but when she looked closer, she decided it was World War I vintage. Probably belonged to a long-ago Jorgensen who'd served in that conflict. Very likely to Sgt. Boyd Jorgensen, who'd been killed in that war.

When Smoot came closer to see what Ethan was scribbling on the music paper, Jayda asked, "Where'd you find that neat jacket?"

Smoot pulled it closer around him. "In a trunk in the attic. Aunt Leora let me and Bug play with the stuff up there sometimes. This is my favorite thing."

The buttons were familiar. It took Jayda a long minute to remember where she'd recently seen a similar button. Then she knew. They were the same as the one she'd found in the dirt and grass under the Jonathan apple tree. But it couldn't have come from that jacket. All of its buttons were in place. To make sure, she called Smoot over to give him a hug and then turned back the button side to see awkward stitches securing the next-to-the-top one. As if someone inept at attaching buttons had done the best he could to bring himself back to inspection order.

So the button from the orchard *had* come from this jacket.

Jayda squelched a little shiver of . . . apprehension, was it? But why? Boyd Jorgensen must have lost a button from his uniform the last time he was home. And she had found it, all these decades later. What could that information have to do with anything?

Could it somehow be connected with the perpetrator of the circle-and-slash notes?

Just to make sure the buttons were the same, she went to the

Remembering Room and got the one she'd put into a drawer. It matched the other buttons perfectly.

But so what? She didn't know if she was supposed to be connecting these random dots in her life, or if they were all destined to be just that—random.

Jayda took the button back to the drawer and began looking for more pictures she could use on Saturday.

♦ ♦ ♦

The rest of the week was filled with activity aimed toward the pioneer luncheon and farewell party for Smoot on Saturday. Sal helped Smoot create attractive flyers, which the two of them took downtown to tell people the double purpose of the party. She kept the boy occupied during the next few days helping her bake cookies from recipes in Arvilla's old home economics notebook and pulling up new little carrots to put in the old-fashioned stew from the same book, as well as other busy tasks. He worked steadily, with Tarzan at his side at all times.

Bug was there every day too, taking care of whatever task needed doing.

And then Jayda spent an entire afternoon braiding whatever June grass in the orchard wasn't already done. She adorned each braid with a yellow ribbon like the ones on the trees where Smoot and Lee lived, symbols of the wish for the military people to come home. She said her ribbons were meant for Smoot.

Lee came up the hill each morning to help Jayda scan and copy all of the things she'd found in the drawers—handwritten letters from various people in town, school pictures and other snapshots, documents of awards not only to Jorgensen children but to others in town as well. She had decided not to let the originals leave the property. As she searched the material in the drawers, Jayda watched for more circle-and-slash notes like the one they'd found earlier, but none showed up. Neither did the deed Bracken was so eager to find.

As a background beat to all the activity was Paul's sawing and hammering and drilling as he built the stage extension out from the south porch. He said it would be ready for people to walk on by the weekend.

◆ ◆ ◆

The party on Saturday was even better than their expectations. More people came than they'd had reason to hope for. Jayda suspected that many came just to meet the "Hollywoodies," as Smoot called them, but at least they were there. Everybody made a fuss over Smoot, and Ethan did his part by playing a stirring medley of military songs while a group of high school boys carried Smoot on their shoulders at the head of a whole parade of young people.

The food Sal and Jayda had prepared was eaten with pleasure, with many remarks about how the pioneers must not have had it so bad after all. The townsfolk swarmed around the displayed memorabilia, exclaiming with delight when they found something from their own ancestors.

The culmination of events was Ethan's concert of songs from the upcoming pageant. He passed out words for the chorus parts, and Jayda was surprised by the good voices she heard.

The girl whose voice had impressed her at church was there. Her name was Caitlin, Jayda learned. Ethan picked her to sight-read one of the solos, complimenting her when she finished.

At the end of his demonstration, he said, "Tryouts next Saturday. You all better come back!"

It was a fine day altogether, marred only by the realization that Smoot would be leaving in two days. But they still had Sunday to enjoy together. Lee, at Smoot's request, accompanied Jayda and the boy to church. Following the service, they all went to the cemetery, where Smoot said a tearful good-bye to his mother. After lunch at the house, Smoot said he had one more place to visit. He took Jayda and Lee up the many stairs to the round room at the top of the tower.

On the way, he showed them the scars on the walls from a time the tower had caught fire in a lightning storm and would have burned, he said, if the townspeople hadn't come to save it. Aunt Leora had told him the story, he said. Jayda remembered the drawing of the quilt block showing the tower on fire. Someone had chosen to commemorate it that way. She'd look for more information in the wall of drawers, she decided.

Smoot told stories about other spots along the way, stories Jayda had heard when she was young but which hadn't meant all that much to her. Stories of the strong people who had lived there. "Aunt Leora told me," he repeated.

Aunt Leora had told her too. But the seeds had fallen on barren ground. Smoot was more deserving of carrying on the Jorgensen heritage than she was, Jayda decided, even though he wasn't related.

"This is my best place," Smoot said when they got to the round tower room and stood gazing out of the window. He took the hands of both Jayda and Lee, grasping them tightly. He looked up at Lee, then to Jayda, and lastly, down to include Tarzan. "I wish—" he began but didn't complete the thought.

"I wish so, too, Smoot," Jayda said under her breath.

When Smoot went over to press his nose against the window to take a last look, Jayda moved closer to Lee. "Go with him," she whispered.

He gave her a questioning look.

"To Minneapolis," she said. "He's only seven years old."

He nodded slowly. "I had the same thought."

"Do it," she told him.

Since it was Smoot's last night in Blackbird, and since he wanted it so much, Jayda let Smoot take Tarzan to his and Lee's home. She would wonder later if what happened the next day could have been prevented if the dog had been there to bark.

Chapter Twenty-Four

WHEN LEE AND SMOOT BROUGHT Tarzan home on Monday morning, they both wore wide grins. "L. G.'s going with me on the airplane," Smoot said, clinging tightly to Lee's hand.

Lee nodded. "It's been a long time since I saw his dad. I need to get reacquainted. After all, he was my sister's husband."

"That's wonderful," Jayda said. "You'll have a fine trip together."

"Yeah!" Smoot said.

Jayda knew Lee had invented the "get reacquainted" story so he wouldn't have to tell Smoot he was too young to travel alone. Smoot probably wouldn't have accepted that. He would lose face in his dad's eyes that way, and that was the last thing he wanted to do. But if Lee was going for a visit, that was okay.

They didn't stay long. Smoot spent a long moment hugging Tarzan, and then Jayda. Lee embraced Jayda, too, holding her close, and then giving her a lingering kiss that made Smoot giggle. It brought back a flood of memories from those days when she hadn't realized he was kissing *Jane* rather than just extending their stage romances. She felt herself sinking into it, wishing it didn't have to end.

Before he released her, Lee put his mouth close to her ear and said, "Thanks for pushing me to go. I may stay there a few days."

And then they were gone—Smoot bouncing with excitement now, a very different boy than the one who'd been sunk in a hopeless pit since he'd heard the news that he had to leave.

After Lee's truck rolled down the hill, Jayda walked around the side of the house to talk with Paul, who was erecting the railing along the edge of the porch extension today. "I'm relieved that nobody fell off on Saturday," he said. "But I guess Sal's warning signs kept them away."

He grinned as he flicked a thumb at the calamity posters Sal had made for that purpose.

"Good thing," Jayda said. "Where *is* Sal?"

"In her garden patch," Paul said. "Where else? You're going to have to pry her out of there when it's time for us to leave."

"Guess you can't leave, then," Jayda commented as she headed for the garden at the back of the house. She wished she knew how to make it possible for them to stay. But she didn't even know if it was possible that *she* could stay.

Sal was in the garden, tending to the growing things she loved so much. "I'm having the time of my life. I've been up for ages," she said when Jayda rounded the corner of the house. "I printed out a batch of flyers about the tryouts that we can distribute downtown later. We might as well strike while the iron is in the fire, to mix a metaphor. Judging from the enthusiasm of the crowd last Saturday, we'll get a good response."

Jayda smiled, although her heart wasn't in it. "I hope so. Maybe I'll take the flyers downtown right now. As Aunt Leora used to say, 'If you have a hill to climb, waitin' won't make it any smaller.'"

Sal laughed. Straightening up, she said, "You don't know how lucky you are, Jayda, to have grown up with all the beauty of the world and a homegrown philosopher too."

"I'm just beginning to realize it," Jayda said. She was going to say more, but her cell phone in her pocket alerted her to a call. It was Dave Bradbury. "I'll be by to pick you up in five minutes," he said. "We're having breakfast at the Back Porch. And I won't take no for an answer. Mr. Yoshida is getting itchy for an answer to his new terms."

"I can drive down into town," Jayda said. "I have errands to run anyway."

Dave sighed. "You're afraid to ride in my car with me."

"How did you guess?" Jayda said.

Dave chuckled. "Okay, I'll see you at the Back Porch."

Jayda hung up and turned to Sal. "I'll be having breakfast with Dave Bradbury, in case you need to get in touch."

"Breakfast with the Barracuda," Sal said. "Nice title for a mystery movie."

Jayda nodded. "But he did bring Tarzan home last week when someone took him," she said. For her, that made up for any flaws he might have.

Dave Bradbury was waiting for her when she got to the Back Porch, the cozy little café on Main Street. He'd chosen a table by the big bay window in front. She wasn't entirely sure of his motives, but she suspected he wanted to play to the townspeople, to show them that whether they favored the sale of the Jorgensen land or not, he was being aboveboard in his dealings with her.

"Hi," Dave said as she approached. Leaping from his chair, he pulled one out for her. She couldn't help but notice his cologne again. He placed her chair close to his own, but she hitched it away a few inches when he turned to signal to Rella Mae, who ran the café, that they were ready for menus.

While they waited for her to come, Dave gave Jayda one of his gorgeous smiles and said, "That was a great send-off you had for Smoot on Saturday. I'm sure it gave him some pleasant memories to think about on his lonely journey today."

"It won't be so lonely, after all." She told him about Lee deciding to escort Smoot to Minneapolis. She didn't mention her part in it.

"I'm glad to hear that," Dave said. "Smoot's a great kid."

Something about the look on his face prompted Jayda to ask, "Do you have children, Dave?"

He nodded. "Two. Marissa and Todd. They live with their mother. We're divorced. I wish I saw them more than I do."

He pulled his wallet from a back pocket and took out a picture of the two kids, smiling proudly as he pointed them out. Jayda noted that he obviously loved them.

"And you?" he asked. "Do you have any?"

She shook her head, wondering if she should tell him how

Ethan had wanted to wait until they could afford to buy a house, which never happened, and then the marriage broke up. She was saved from saying anything by the arrival of Rella Mae, who handed them attractive flower-decorated menus. "Well, hi there, Jane," she said cordially. "Nice party last Saturday."

As she spoke, she ran her hands familiarly over Dave's shoulders, giving them a slight massage. "And how is Mr. Dave this morning? I suppose you're having the usual?"

Jayda wondered if the performance was for her benefit, to tell her that Dave was staked-out territory. She remembered Aunt Leora had written years ago that Rella Mae's husband had skipped town, leaving her with four kids and no means of support. But skinny little Rella Mae had surprised everybody by being an excellent cook and quite an entrepreneur when she opened the café.

Dave twisted around to look up at her—and maybe, Jayda thought, to get out from under her roaming hands. "You know Rella Mae, don't you, Jayda?"

"We were in high school together," Jayda said cordially and with a bright smile. "Good to see you again, Rella Mae."

"Likewise," Rella Mae said. "Isn't it great what Dave is doing for our little town? Bringing in all the new people? I tell you, it's really pepping up the economy, which we could all use. And it will be even better when they start building on your old place, Jane."

Mentally, Jayda crossed off the Back Porch as a possible place to leave a stack of Sal's tryout flyers about the pageant auditions.

"I think I *will* have the usual, Rella Mae," Dave was saying. "How about you, Jayda?"

"I forgot you call yourself Jayda now," Rella Mae said. "Fancy new name to go with living in Beverly Hills?"

Jayda didn't bother to tell her that she'd lived a long way from Beverly Hills. All she said was, "I'll take what Dave's having."

Dave's breakfast turned out to be the "pioneer breakfast." Two eggs, wheat toast, hash browns, and a small dish of fresh raspberries—far more food than Jayda was used to eating for breakfast, but appropriate. She'd need the strength of the pioneers to keep the pageant trekking along the trail.

It wasn't until the end of the meal that Dave brought out the papers containing details of Mr. Yoshida's new offer for her property.

"Jayda," he said as he spread the papers before her. "The way the real estate market is—and probably will be for a while—you'll never see another offer like this. This project has become Mr. Yoshida's dream, and he's willing to go top dollar. Even beyond, as you'll see from these figures."

The figures were indeed impressive. And Mr. Yoshida was willing to make some concessions as to where to put parking lots. The old orchard would remain intact. The barn would stay, although a big part of the pasture would grow houses rather than grass.

But Mr. Yoshida had decided the house had to go after all. "The spot where it stands is too much the crowning glory of the whole development," Dave said.

"For the millionth time, no deal," Jayda said.

"Jayda, Jayda," Dave chided, "almost everybody in town is pushing for this sale. How can you go against them? What will you do with the old house? What good is it to you?" He leaned closer, so close that she either had to stop breathing or go ahead and inhale the scent of his cologne. "Jayda, what would you do here in this little town? Sit there in the old house like the empress on the hill until it crumbles around you?"

"I'll sit there just like Maren Jorgensen did," Jayda murmured, which brought a puzzled look to Dave's face.

She didn't get a chance to explain who Maren was because her cell phone rang for a second time that morning. It was Ethan. "Jayda!" he shouted. "You'd better come home! Something has happened!"

Jayda started to ask what, but then realized that they had lost their connection. She tried to call Ethan back two more times, but there was no answer. She rose to her feet. Dave stood up, too, his face concerned. "Something wrong?"

She scooped her purse from the empty chair beside her. "I have to go back to the house. Thanks for breakfast."

"I'll go with you." Dave pulled out his wallet and dropped bills on the table.

"Whatever you wish." That was a bit abrupt, but her heart was thudding so hard she couldn't think. Ethan had sounded scared. She hurried out of the café, with Dave close behind. "I'll drive," he said. "We'll pick your car up later."

Obediently she followed him to his car. Her hands trembled. She probably wouldn't be the best driver in the world at the moment. She tried not to think about what might have happened. Had Lee and Smoot had an accident? Had something happened to Tarzan?

When they got to the house, they saw two cars parked in front. One was Lucas's Hummer. The other was Belinda's sleek little lavender BMW convertible, this time with the top up. A cluster of people stood on the hill where the stage extension had jutted out. It no longer jutted. A big portion of it had collapsed onto the slope. About eight feet below, a person lay sprawled on the grass just beyond the splintered wood. Sal, Belinda, and Ethan crouched alongside.

Jayda gasped and then ran forward. "What happened?"

It was Bracken who answered. "City boy doesn't know squat about building a platform," he said.

She took the time to glare at him. "City boy has been building platforms on movie sets for fifteen years," she said before hurrying over to the fallen Paul. He didn't even open his eyes as she knelt down. He just lay there moaning. One of his legs was twisted at an odd angle.

"I'm so sorry," Jayda whispered. "What happened?"

"Later," Ethan said.

There wasn't much she could do. Sal sat by Paul's head, murmuring to him and wiping his forehead with a white handkerchief. Belinda was busy adjusting an afghan somebody must have brought from the house. "We called 9-1-1," she said. "The paramedics will be here soon."

Lucas, who'd been barking orders of some kind on his cell phone, came over and helped Jayda to her feet. "Heck of a deal," he said. "Appears he was carrying two-by-fours over to the edge when it collapsed," he said. "Bracken was helping him, but he was far enough back, and he didn't fall off."

Bracken was helping him? The "far enough back" comment made Jayda look at Bracken with suspicion. Had he known the stage was going to collapse?

"Kind of puts a crimp in your plans," Lucas commented. He was about to say more when they heard a siren, and everybody looked up to watch the approaching paramedic truck.

The paramedics were swift and efficient. After checking Paul over, they cut off his pant leg and wrapped his leg to a splint. Then they unloaded a folding gurney from their truck. They strapped him to it and lifted it inside.

"There's not room for you, ma'am," one of them said to Sal, who tried to get in behind him. "We're taking him to the medical center in the city. You can rejoin him there."

Then they were gone, siren wailing again.

"I'll drive you to the hospital, Sal," Dave said. "And Jayda, you come, too, so you can be with her."

"Thank you," Sal whispered. Her face, which had gained a little color from being in the sun for her gardening, was so pale now that it looked ashen. Ethan had an arm around her thin shoulders, helping her to the car. "He'll be all right," he said.

Dave settled Sal in the front seat and opened a back door for Jayda before getting behind the wheel and speeding off down the hill.

Jayda leaned back against the soft leather, grateful that Dave had been there to take charge. She was no good in emergencies.

What had ever made her think she could follow through with this pageant and save the old house?

To add to the drama, lightning flashed from the dark clouds in the west as they barreled down the highway. Was it her ancestors telling her to give it up and let the old house drift into the past as they had done? She really couldn't see any alternative. They couldn't do the show as planned without Paul.

Chapter Twenty-Five

THE SKY WAS DARK WHEN THEY left the hospital, even though it was early afternoon. The thunderstorm that had been brewing when they'd arrived rumbled all around them as Dave drove Jayda, Sal, and a groggy, sedated Paul home. Jayda was grateful that Dave had waited with her and Sal while Paul's leg was set and a cast put on his leg. She was sure he had a stack of business to take care of back at the Summertree Meadows development office, but he'd stayed—comforting Sal, sweet-talking nurses out of information about Paul's condition, insisting they go to the cafeteria for lunch at noon.

Flashes of lightning backlit the old house as they came over the hill that overlooked Blackbird, making it seem to Jayda like a movie scene of people returning to a haunted house, where the audience is forewarned that there are explosive episodes yet to come. Watching, she felt something build up inside her, as if feeding off the energy of the lightning flashes. The next time Paul moaned, she knew what it was. Rage. Towering rage. She knew in her heart that this had not been an accident caused by careless construction. Something had made the platform fall, and it had been done by the same person who had left the notes for her and taken Tarzan. Of that she was sure. But someone had been hurt now. This was more than taking a bewildered dog away from his home just to worry and scare her. This time a *person* had been *injured*.

Jayda was not unfamiliar with hot anger, but she had never felt it to this extent, not to where it boiled up inside her, threatening to spill over like water bubbling up in a pot on the stove. Should she speak, now, in the car? It would probably be better to wait until they looked over the "crime scene" to determine what had been done to cause the incident. And find out if there were any clues as to who had done it.

While Jayda pondered, Sal said, "It must have been like this the night of the fire."

"Do you know about the fire?" Jayda turned to look at Sal in the backseat. When Sal nodded, Jayda said, "Tell me about it."

"Jayda, old buddy," Sal said, "you're going to have to spend more time in the Remembering Room, reading your own family history. Didn't you know there was a fire?"

"Well, yes, I sort of did," Jayda admitted. "And Smoot pointed out a few charred timbers the other night that mark where it was."

Smoot. Her heart dropped a notch as she thought about him, about the fact that they wouldn't be enjoying his happy presence anymore. At least he wasn't facing this transition alone.

Jayda twisted around to look more directly at Sal, who sat against the back door of the car, cradling Paul's head, gently stroking his forehead, soothing him each time they went over a bump in the road and he moaned. "Did you find some information about it in the wall of drawers?"

Sal nodded. "I did. The tower caught fire in a thunderstorm, much like this one. I've been thinking about making it the climax of the pageant. The way the residents of Blackbird all came together to save the house was pretty dramatic. Seems appropriate for the situation right now. Ethan could write us some fire music, I'm sure."

Jayda tried a small grin. "So you're planning to set the tower ablaze again?"

"Simulated, dear girl," Sal said. "Paul's had experience with pyrotechnics. Remember, he helped with the fireworks displays at the Hollywood Bowl for several summers."

Jayda's grin disappeared. "But Paul's not in any shape to do anything anymore."

Paul raised himself to a half-sitting position. "Yes, I am." That seemed to be about all he could manage, and he slumped back against Sal, who helped him to get more comfortable, adjusting his leg, covered by the heavy plaster cast, to a slightly different angle before she continued. "It was right after the house was finished, and no one was living in it yet. The town was new, and there was no organized fire department. In one journal, Asa described the flaming tower as looking like a gigantic candle from where he and his family were living at the time. He was sure he was going to lose the house." Sal spoke softly, using her storyteller voice.

"So what happened?" Dave said. He seemed as mesmerized by the story as Jayda was.

"In his words, 'the rain descended and so did the towns-people.' That's a direct quote," Sal said.

In a musing voice, Dave said, "'And the rain descended, and the floods came, and the winds blew and beat upon that house; and it fell not: for it was founded upon a rock.'"

It always surprised Jayda when Dave quoted the Bible. It revealed a side of him that wasn't generally apparent.

"When the rain came," Sal continued, "Asa took it as a sign that his house would stand. Metaphorically, as well as physically, I take it. It was a great comfort to him because the whole property was in dispute at the time, with Ephraim Morehead trying to prove he had laid claim to it first. Asa was of the opinion that Morehead saw an opportunity during the thunderstorm and set the house afire himself."

"Ephraim was Bracken's great-great grandfather," Jayda said. The thought came to her that Bracken might try a repeat performance of the fire, and as they drove up the final hill, she looked at the house for any sign of smoke. "You're right, Sal," she said. "I really do need to spend time reading the family history." And, she thought to herself, she'd better do it fast before Bracken turned up the deed that, according to the photo she'd found, really had existed. She needed to be prepared.

Dave parked beside Lucas's Hummer, which was still there alongside Belinda's little car. As they started to get out, the rain began pelting down. It seemed as if buckets were being poured upon them. Dave got on one side of Paul and Sal was on the other to get him up the stairs, but then the door burst open and Lucas, accompanied by Bracken, with Belinda tapping along behind, was there to help hoist Paul inside.

"Thanks, guys," Paul said in a rough voice. "You'll forgive me if I don't sit down for a visit."

"We're hauling you right upstairs," Lucas ordered. "And I recommend you stay there for at least a week."

"No way," Paul protested. "We need that stage extension repaired as soon as possible. They gave me a walker at the hospital. I'll be up and about tomorrow."

"So you gonna hammer the nails with your cast?" Lucas said. "The supports all have to be redone. Somebody sawed a couple of them clean in two."

Jayda's anger flared again. "Any clues as to who might have done it? Footprints or anything?"

Lucas shook his head. "It's all grass under there, you know. Nothing that would hold a footprint. No clues whatsoever. I've put caution tape all around the perimeter until it can be secured again."

He was definitely in his cop mode, Jayda thought. And he'd done what needed to be done.

Dave stayed long enough to see that Paul was comfortably settled—not upstairs, but in the Remembering Room on the ground floor. "If Smoot could stay in there with the ghosts, so can I," Paul said. He chose a sofa to sleep on, and Sal said she'd stay beside him on a reclining chair.

Jayda walked Dave to the door when he left. "I'll round up some volunteers to clean up the mess and rebuild," he told her. "I'll come, too, unless the sky has fallen at the office. Which I better go check on now."

Jayda threw her arms around him. "I don't know what we would have done if you hadn't been here," she said. "Thank you, Dave. Thank you."

He hugged her back, tight, for just the appropriate length of time. Then he ran out into the rain and was gone.

Jayda stepped onto the porch, which was sheltered from the downpour, looking around to see if the person who'd caused the stage extension to collapse might have left another of his ugly little notes. But he was apparently far past that now, for she found nothing in the entire porch area. Maybe there was something underneath the extension, taped to a support. Perhaps to the one that had been sawed in two. But Lucas said he'd examined the supports. He hadn't mentioned any notes.

Yet Lucas was still on Jayda's list of possible suspects.

And Bracken. Who else? Jayda knew Paul and Sal didn't trust Dave, but she wasn't going to put him on her suspect list unless she saw some evidence. Not after what he'd just done for them.

There could be any number of angry townspeople who could have sabotaged Paul's work. And injured him. Intentionally or not.

In frustration, Jayda stood at the top of the porch stairs and bellowed her rage into the rain-filled darkness. The skies responded with a brilliant flash of lightning and a clap of thunder.

"Wow," somebody said, "you really get results."

It was Ethan, slogging across the lawn in the rain. He climbed the stairs and grinned at Jayda, rain dripping from his clothing.

"It's not funny, Ethan," she said. "And by the way, where have you been?"

He shrugged. "Didn't see any point in pacing the floor wringing my hands while you were at the hospital. How's Paul?"

She told him, and then said, "I didn't hear where it was you were in all this rain."

He gazed off in the direction from which he'd come. "Looking for inspiration for the finale to the show. You might say I was communing with the dead." He looked at her puzzled face. "I was at the cemetery. It was quite an experience in the midst of a thunderstorm." He went inside, and in a moment, Jayda heard crashing chords from the piano, music full of energy and power.

Jayda was not surprised. During their years together, Ethan had often disappeared when he needed inspiration, driving off to the ocean, or to a clanking factory, or sometimes to the busy LAX airport. Anywhere the energy was high.

She could use a little inspiration and energizing herself.

Marching into the house, she went to stand in the curve of the piano and held up her hand. "Ethan," she said, "take me back to the cemetery."

The storm was retreating by the time they walked out past the barn, where the old horse watched from the doorway, and up the hill beyond, past the rain-swollen brook and through the stand of quaking aspen to the family graveyard. They hadn't bothered to bring umbrellas, so now Jayda was as wet as Ethan, which wasn't a problem in the warm air.

On the way, Jayda told him about the trip to and from the hospital and how Dave had been such a help. She told him she hoped old Asa Jorgensen was communicating tonight because she meant to demand that he tell how to fight this thing that was going on. She was prepared to listen, she said.

"You don't listen," Ethan said. "You *feel*. That's how old Asa will come through."

But Jayda felt nothing as they walked through the rows of dead Jorgensens. A random flash of lightning lit up the tall obelisk that marked old Asa's grave, but he didn't speak to her, or convey any guidance of what she needed to do. She realized that wasn't the way it was done, anyway.

"Open yourself up, Jayda," Ethan said softly. "It's a two-way thing, you know, like a radio. The receiver has to work as well as the transmitter."

Jayda walked up to the monument and let her fingers follow the carved-out words: Asa Jorgensen. Born. Died.

"Asa," she whispered. "What should I do?"

She waited.

Nothing.

She made her way to the more modest stone that marked her parents' graves. She looked at the names. Then she walked around to the back. Lucas had been true to his word. He'd had the ugly black circle-and-slash sandblasted, or whatever. It was gone. There was just the name: Jane, beloved daughter.

Jane. Who had given up on her life when she was four.

"Is it time to give up on the house?" she whispered.

She had no sooner spoken than a last flash of lightning from the weakening storm lit up her name. Jane. A plain, strong name for a descendant of the Jorgensens who'd wrested a home from the wilderness. Not Jayda, who took on the name of whatever character was scripted for her and acted accordingly. She faintly remembered the small, determined girl she'd been before her parents were killed—the girl who'd been called Miss Tornado because of the way she whirled across the landscape. That was before her name had been chiseled on the cold stone, convincing her that her parents had taken her with them, leaving behind an empty shell that she eventually filled with fictional characters.

Had old Asa spoken in the lightning flash? Was it time to be Jane again? Was that what her great-great-grandfather would have told her if he truly could speak with her? Would he say that she should channel her anger into activity?

Would he say that the blood of her stalwart progenitors was there in her veins as surely as their history was in the wall of drawers?

"Ethan!" she called.

"Yo." His voice came from somewhere in the corridor of Jorgensen graves.

"It's time to get on with it," she called. "Hurry!"

He was by her side before the word had died away.

"Time's a-wasting," she said. "I've got to go through the drawers until I unravel the mystery of the deed. I need to talk to Belinda about costumes, and ask Velda Klippert if she'll be our show hairdresser. I have to find wagons to go with the covers we got from Jake Sterry. I want to find out if there's a sound truck in town that we can use to advertise the show. I—"

She stopped when Ethan took her by the shoulders and stared into her face. "Whoa," he said. "Is this really Jayda I'm hearing? Jayda, who never did anything without a script?"

"This is Jane," she said firmly. "And I'm writing my own script from now on."

Chapter Twenty-Six

JAYDA LAUGHED INTO THE DARKENING afternoon as she and Ethan ran hand in hand through the rain back to the house. Ethan glanced at her curiously, but he didn't ask about her obvious change of mood, for which she was grateful. How could she explain how it felt to be Jane again? It was like slipping on a familiar but scarcely used dress when the one she'd been wearing had grown threadbare and constricting. Nothing had changed, really. Paul's leg was still broken. Smoot was still gone. The house was still in jeopardy. But she'd realized that her family—Aunt Leora and Uncle Len and the others—had not meant to consign her to her parents' grave when they'd had her name chiseled on the back of their tombstone. Quite the contrary. They'd meant to show that she was part of the vast clan of Jorgensens, heiress to whatever that meant, part of the long chain of family that went back uncounted generations, and eternally bound to them all, especially to the two who had given her birth—Thomas and Diane.

No, she couldn't explain it yet to Ethan, bereft, as he was, of family ties. And she wouldn't be changing her name. She'd remain as Jayda to those who knew her that way. But underneath, *she* knew she was Jane.

Although Lucas's Hummer was gone, Belinda and Bracken were still at the house when Jayda and Ethan got there. They were together in the kitchen, Belinda bent over a page of Arvilla's old seventh-grade recipe book and Bracken stirring something in a pot on the stove. Jayda didn't know yet whether they were involved in the harassment that had been going on, but she knew she had to make peace with Bracken on one count, anyway. After all, the entire game plan might be subject to change if his claim was true.

"Bracken," she said, "I'm sorry I haven't gotten back to you earlier about the deed. How about we talk about it after I change out of my wet clothes?"

He gave her a bewildered look, apparently not at all prepared for this nonhostile Jayda.

"We can at least pool what we know about it," she said. "And then tomorrow when Paul is awake in the Remembering Room, we can start going through the drawers to see what we can find."

Bracken stared at her blankly, but Belinda straightened up and said, "Splendid idea. Go for it, Bracken."

Still he didn't say anything, but his look changed to one of speculation, as if he were wondering what Jayda was up to. While he stood silent, Belinda said, "I brought a backseat full of clothing I've rounded up that can be used for costumes. I thought it would be nice to dress up some of the people who come to the audition on Saturday, just to get them in the spirit. And Bracken and I are trying out some recipes that we might use for refreshments."

"Good thinking," Jayda said. "By the way, Belinda, I want to thank you for taking in Bug so she doesn't have to leave town."

"I'm glad to have her," Belinda said. "I guess I didn't use up all my motherly instincts raising my two kids. She can use a whole truckload of mothering."

Jayda was touched. "She seems to enjoy helping with the pageant."

"About time that girl enjoyed something," Belinda said. "She has more problems than Twister has sneers. Her self-esteem is lower than an angleworm's belly." She paused to give Jayda a warm look. "Actually, it's you who should be thanked. You've taken her in as part of the family. She says you understand her, even down to braiding the June grass."

Jayda contemplated that as she started up the stairs to shuck off her soggy clothes. Was it possible she'd made a difference in Bug's life? She wasn't sure, but what she *was* sure of was that Belinda had. She really didn't want to keep mistrusting Belinda. But that didn't let Bracken off the hook.

Halfway to the staircase, she turned and called, "What is it you're cooking up for Saturday?"

Belinda chuckled. "I wondered when you'd get around to asking. Remember the rhubarb pudding Aunt Leora used to make? The one with the Danish name that she said couldn't be pronounced unless you were a native speaker? And the big white cookies?"

Jayda nodded.

"I found the recipes in Arvilla's notebook," Belinda said. "Bracken is doing the pudding and I'm figuring out what we need for the cookies."

Jayda's taste buds leaped to attention. She's forgotten those items from her past. "Cool!" she said.

In the background she heard Ethan's crashing chords on the piano and knew that some things, at least, were going right. The refreshments were a fine idea. And Ethan's music, inspired in part by the thunderstorm, was powerful and stirring.

♦ ♦ ♦

The first thing Bracken said when Jayda came back downstairs in dry clothes was, "That old picture you found is evidence that there is a deed, you know."

"At least there *was* a deed," she amended. "I'm not disputing that, Bracken. But in order for you to claim any property, we have to find it and make sure it's valid."

"Well, what do you think I've been trying to do?" His rugged face reddened, making the old scar across his cheek stand out more.

Jayda put up both hands, palms outward in a placating gesture. "Okay, okay, I know. Let's not get into another argument." She cleared her throat. "Bracken, you told me a few days ago about trying to find the deed under the Jonathan apple tree. What was that all about?"

He glared at her, his lips pressed together as if holding back a harsh answer, but then he seemed to reconsider. He then said,

"Can we sit down for a minute and I'll tell you what I know? Then maybe you can do the same for me."

Sitting down together helped to turn down the pressure-cooker atmosphere. Bracken started with an explanation about how it had become like a legend in his family that part of the Jorgensen land rightfully belonged to the Moreheads. His great-great-grandfather Ephraim had bought the land from a man who'd arrived in the valley ahead of the Jorgensen company.

"I wonder why there isn't a record of it, then?" Jayda asked. "There should be a copy of it in the county records, shouldn't there? Maybe your relative never officially filed for the land."

"Somebody could have taken it *out* of the records and destroyed it," Bracken said ominously.

"Maybe," Jayda admitted. "But I wonder what happened to the copy in the picture?"

Bracken shrugged. "I've thought all along it was in that wall of drawers."

"But what does digging under the apple tree have to do with it?" Jayda asked.

The obstinate look Bracken had worn since they started talking faded. "It's kind of a funny thing. Somehow down through the years another rumor got started that said somebody buried the deed under that tree. I was just checking it out. I didn't find anything."

Jayda thought of the military button from Boyd Jorgensen's coat that she'd found under the Jonathan apple tree. What kind of connection were they going to find?

They didn't get a chance to go through the drawers the next

day because Dave Bradbury, true to his word, sent a contingent of three men to help clean up the wreckage of Paul's stage extension and rebuild it. The only trouble was, they were *young* men. Teenagers, to be exact. Big. Football-player size. Strong backs that made short order of the clean-up work. But not too swift when it came to reconstructing the supports and adding the railing.

Paul hobbled outside with the aid of Sal and his walker as soon as he heard the commotion on the porch. He talked the young men into hauling him down the slope and installing him on a rather unstable chair there so he could give instructions about sawing and hammering. The guys tried to follow his directions, and one of them said something about having taken shop at school. Paul could see that these willing young men were simply not up to constructing something as complicated as the criss-cross support system under the extension.

Jayda could tell by his face that Paul was in considerable pain. "We don't have to have the stage completed by Saturday," Jayda told him. "Give yourself another day to rest up."

He wasn't too hard to convince. He allowed the boys to take him back inside the house, and soon Sal reported him as sleeping again.

Jayda thanked the boys and said that they could go home for now, but that they should for sure come back for the auditions on Saturday.

"Got a part for a mule?" the red-haired one asked with a snort. "If you need braying to be done, I'm your man. But Travis, here—" He flicked a thumb at one of his companions. "He's had the lead in our high school musicals for a couple of years. This year he played Curly in *Oklahoma*."

Travis grinned shyly. He was a tall boy, blond, with an open, sunburned face, probably from working in the fields. He reminded Jayda of Lee at seventeen. "So you'll be coming to audition, right?" she asked.

"Yeah," he said. She half expected him to scuff his toe in the dirt, a typical gesture of a shy cowboy in the Western movies she'd been in.

Gazing at him, Jayda hoped that if he was a good enough actor to make people believe he could head up a company of pioneers, he could play the part of Asa Jorgensen.

But not opposite her. He was too young.

No. She was too old.

Before she could think further along that line, Dave Bradbury's car glided up the hill. And Dave was there, taking over, directing the boys as to what needed to be done, and how.

"I started out in construction," he explained to Jayda. "So don't worry about the supports being done right."

And they were. Even she could see that when they were finished. The intricate pattern of two-by-fours underneath the stage was undeniably sturdy and firm—as long as the perpetrator of previous crimes did not saw them in half again. Lucas had promised to get some men to help her keep watch on the house and the yard so that no more vandalism could be done. Jayda was still a little nervous about it all, but in the grand tradition of show business that "the show must go on," she looked forward to Saturday.

♦ ♦ ♦

She was surprised at how many people showed up for the auditions, a lot of them young. Travis and his companions confessed they had rigged up a sound truck with equipment from the high school and had traversed the neighborhoods of Blackbird advertising the event. Jayda smiled to herself about that. What young girl would be able to resist the invitation of those three guys to come and work with them on a show? Jayda took special note that Caitlin came. Her voice had impressed Jayda when it rang out over the congregation in church and then again when Ethan had asked her to sight-read a solo the previous Saturday. An intriguing thought began percolating in Jayda's mind.

Several large families came, hoping to make it a fun summer activity. Emmylu was there with her brood, accompanied by her husband, Nate, a fine-looking fellow who could easily have played the part of Asa—except that he couldn't sing. He volunteered to assist with the lights and sound.

Even a few people who hoped to see the house sold came to be in the show. "It'll be a right fittin' good-bye to the old place," Jake Sterry declared.

Ethan was an excellent majordomo, directing the crowd and delighting them all with spontaneous bursts of the music he'd composed for the pageant. At one point, he handed out copies of one of the group songs, and in ten minutes he had the crowd sounding as if they'd rehearsed for weeks.

"You're all in!" he hollered when they finished a run-through. "Show up next Saturday and we'll start you off along the trail."

Sal distributed copies of the rehearsal schedule, and those who were to be in only the group numbers left for home, but not before they enjoyed the refreshments Bracken and Belinda had made. Everyone exclaimed over them. Several of the older folks said the rhubarb pudding and cookies were "just like Grandma used to make."

When it was time for the individual part auditions, Ethan started off with the minor roles for which several people qualified. Ethan whispered to her that he was going to write in a couple more parts, especially one for Jake Sterry, who would be typecast as a grizzled old cowboy.

When it came to the part of Asa—the leader, the empire builder, the stalwart pioneer—only one person tried out. Travis. Ethan asked him to sing a couple of songs, and Travis chose "The Impossible Dream" from *The Man of La Mancha*, and "Oh, What a Beautiful Morning" from *Oklahoma*. When the boy stood up to sing, his shyness fell away, and he *was* Don Quixote. He *was* Curly. And when Ethan handed him the scribbled music for "Wilderness Song," he *was* Asa.

"Jayda," Ethan said, "I want you to sing the 'Wagons Rolling' duet with him." He handed each of them some sheets of music.

Jayda remembered her earlier thoughts that she was too old to play opposite Travis. Perhaps Jayda would have gone ahead and done the duet, but Jane voiced a better idea. "May I make a suggestion?" she said. "I'd like to hear Caitlin sing with Travis."

Caitlin confidently came up and took the sheet music. As

they sang, it became clear to everyone, even Ethan, that the stars of the show were now cast.

"Just like you and Lee used to be together," Jake Sterry whispered in Jayda's ear when the two young people finished the duet.

He was right. Memories swarmed through Jayda's head of her and Lee together. She remembered how excited she'd been about singing with him again in this production and what profound sorrow she'd felt when he'd refused to be in it.

But they'd had their day. It had been wonderful—but now it was time for these two new stars. She must give up the lovely songs Ethan had written for her. *Maybe he could write in a mother part for me,* Jayda thought.

But he didn't have a chance to do that. After everyone had gone home, Ethan came to Jayda, his eyes shining. "I waited until the auditions were over to tell you," he said. "My manager called early this morning. He's nailed a really great assignment for me. I'll be scoring a major movie."

Jayda held her breath. She knew he had more to tell.

He did.

"They're waiting for me, babe," he said. "I'll be leaving Monday morning."

Chapter Twenty-Seven

JAYDA REFLECTED LATER THAT IT was a good thing she had found her true identity before Ethan went back to California. With her previous penchant for hiding behind whatever fictional character she was playing and her need for a script, the Jayda she had been in California would have freaked about having to take over as director of the pageant. But she'd had years of professional work. She'd worked with a number of creative directors. She'd learned what worked and what didn't. Now it was time to pass that knowledge on to others and push the show forward to performance. She could do it.

Besides, there was no fictional character to hide behind, no script, now that she wouldn't be playing the part of Maren.

Of course, there was still the possibility that she could convince Lee to direct the show, once he got back from Minneapolis. She hadn't heard a word from him or Smoot since they had left. Perhaps no news was good news. Her hope was that Smoot was adjusting so well to being with his dad that there was nothing to report.

"Sal can play the music," Ethan had told her. "It's all finished. She can read my scratchings as well as I can. And Paul is already getting back to the production stuff." Jayda knew he referred to the pages of notes and sketches Paul had been making while he was recuperating with his broken leg. He had also been busy locating fireworks he could use to stage the fake fire for the finale. He was almost back up to full speed.

Jayda didn't even try to coax Ethan to stay. She knew him too well for that. He was ready to throw himself totally into this new assignment, just as he had leaped wholeheartedly into the pageant idea. It would fill his world for as long as it took to complete.

She drove him to the airport in the city, with Tarzan in the backseat for company on the way home. Ethan gave her a lingering kiss at the curb when they parted and whispered that whatever had made the difference in her in the past few weeks, he liked it. She wasn't sure what he whispered to the dog as he hugged him fiercely and stroked his fur. But what she did know was that he was already hearing the new music he would begin putting to paper as soon as he was seated on the airplane.

She also knew that there would never be any reconciliation between the two of them, and in a way, she was relieved.

◆　◆　◆

Before she tried to sort out the chaos that Ethan's leaving had created, Jayda decided to get things settled with Bracken.

She'd promised they'd go through the drawers looking for clues about the old deed, so that's what they started to do on the day after Ethan's departure. They cleared off a desk in the Remembering Room and brought drawers to it. Jayda was surprised that Bracken went about it methodically, not just ripping the contents of the wall of drawers apart without thought, as she'd first suspected he'd do. Instead he suggested that since their first clue of the deed was 1910, as recorded on the back of the old photograph, they should try to locate papers close to that date, before and after. As they removed items from drawers, he filed them neatly into a stack of manila folders he'd brought with him, labeling each one as he proceeded. When she complimented him on his approach to the search, he gave her a smile that was a mix of sarcasm and humor, the first smile of any kind she'd seen on his face. "I've worked in a library since a devil bronc ended my rodeo career." He touched his back to indicate where the injury was. "Amazing what even an old cowpoke can learn when he's sidelined."

While they worked together, with Tarzan snoring on a rug nearby, Sal scanned the music Ethan had left, and Belinda put together costumes from clothing she'd gathered from around the town and from a thrift store she'd visited in the city. In the attic she'd discovered a stash of specially designed items from previous productions as well as an old churn and a galvanized washtub complete with scrub board. Perfect for props, she said.

Velda Klippert brought over a collection of wigs as well as sketches of hairdos of the latter part of the nineteenth century. Emmylu presented Jayda with a stack of pioneer sunbonnets for women and girls. "I stitched them up between flipping pancakes and reading bedtime stories," she said. "Let me know what else I can do."

Bug was frequently there at the house, lonesome for Smoot but happy to be helpful. She was an odd little thing, but creative and smart, and a treasure to Paul in his lighting and sound set-ups. Jayda hoped she knew how appreciated she was and she made her feel welcome at any hour of the day.

Things were humming along, and Jayda would have been happy except for the absence of Lee and Smoot. She hadn't seen a circle-and-slash note since Paul's accident. Maybe that person realized he or she had pushed too far that time—that it hadn't been a harmless prank to scare her. Or maybe he'd given up.

Or maybe, as Dave Bradbury had said, the perp was building up to a grand finale, like the show itself. That made Jayda hold her breath when she thought about it. So she didn't think about it.

Dave hadn't pushed her any further about examining the new renderings Mr. Yoshida had approved. He told her Mr. Yoshida himself would explain his latest offer since he was coming from Japan again very shortly.

The search through the wall of drawers didn't yield anything having to do with the deed in the first couple of days, but Jayda found several things of interest. There was a stack of carefully prepared family group records that someone had put together. They listed names like Jens Jorgensen and Bodel Larsdatter with information such as their birthplace (Stokkemarke, Maribo, Denmark), their marriage date (26 April 1863), and that Jens was a carpenter, information Jayda had already learned.

They'd emigrated to America, sailing on the ship *Wisconsin* from Liverpool, England, on 27 June 1877. They brought with them a son, Asa, born 27 July 1868, in Denmark, later gaining United States citizenship along with his parents. And even later leading a group of pioneers to settle Blackbird.

Asa. Great-great-grandfather Asa.

Jayda felt goose bumps rise on her arms. Suddenly old Asa was real, not just a name on the tall monument in the cemetery.

"Bracken," she said, "look at this."

Since it had nothing to do with his family nor with the deed, Bracken wasn't all that interested. But he did glance over it and then say, "You might be interested in this, too." He handed her a folder that contained several pages of handwriting. In Danish. Jayda didn't recognize any of the words except the name at the top: Bodel Larsdatter Jorgensen. Asa's mother. Another of the vast army of ancestors to whom Jayda was connected, whose blood she carried. Whose legacy she must carry on. This apparently was her journal. In Danish.

Two sentences of the text were underlined in red. Jayda stared at the foreign words.

Jeg har engang sagt, at der ikke fandtes noget smukkere end mit hjemland Danmark. Det var for jeg havde set bjergene.

This was the language her ancestors had brought with them from the old country. She wished she could have heard their voices speak it.

An arrow pointed to the edge of the paper where there was apparently a translation of the Danish sentence:

I once said that nothing could be more beautiful than my homeland Denmark. I had not seen the mountains then.

Again Jayda's arms sprouted goose bumps. Here was what Ethan had been looking for. A summation of the emotions of the people they would portray in the pageant. A finale. A culmination. The arrival in the valley. It had meant so much to those travelers to get to their destination, to find that it was good. They had settled down here, right here! And they'd established families, who had in turn established families, who in turn—it went on and on. And their descendants were now scattered all over the country, leaving the old homestead behind. There were probably many who had never set foot in Blackbird. Why should they care about what happened to the old house?

But Aunt Leora had cared, and she'd guessed accurately that Jayda, who'd pulled away both physically and emotionally, would care. The burden of preservation had funneled down to her.

No, not the burden. The *privilege*.

She wondered if Ethan could put all *that* in a final chorus for the show. Quickly she moved to the computer where she scanned in the page and sent it on to him in California.

By Friday, Bracken and Jayda still had not found anything to do with the old deed. Bracken gave up for the day, saying he'd continue the search the next week. Before he left, he asked Jayda if she minded that he was trying to make friends with the old horse out in the corral. "We've been adversaries long enough," he said. "People will probably be interested in his story when they come to the pageant, so I'd like to get him ready."

"I don't mind, if Twister is willing," she said. "I'm not sure you *can* make friends with him, though."

"I've made friends with you, haven't I?" Bracken asked. "Well, sort of. It couldn't be any harder than that." With the first genuine grin she'd seen him give anybody, he went out, leaving her wondering what he was up to. Grin or no, she still didn't fully trust him and knew she couldn't until the problem of the deed was settled.

After Bracken left, she went back to look through a few more drawers. She was rewarded with the discovery of a brittle old flyer—she recalled reading that they'd been called "broadsides" back then—advertising homesteads in "a valley as beautiful as the eye can take in." Some of the printing was totally faded out, but there was a name handwritten in one corner. "Ephraim Morehead," it said.

Maybe this will have something to do with the deed, Jayda mused. Jayda pulled a folder from Bracken's stack, but before she could label it, the phone rang. She picked it up. "Hello," she said.

There was silence on the other end. Thinking it must be a telemarketer, she was about to hang up when a voice, disguised by some kind of device said, "Don't relax too much, Jayda. The best is yet to come."

She slammed down the receiver, causing Tarzan to leap to his feet in confusion. "Let's go find Paul and Sal," she said to him.

Then she remembered that Paul and Sal had gone to the city in quest of the pyrotechnic stuff he'd need for the show's finale. She was alone there, with Tarzan.

Nervously she looked out of the kitchen window. Everything seemed peaceful outside, but inside her chest her heart thundered. She tried to calm herself, but the voice, tinny and otherworldly, had spooked her.

With her hand on Tarzan's collar, she led him back to the Remembering Room, feeling safer there with that army of ancestors.

"Asa," she said. "What should I do?"

In answer, there was a soft knock at the front door.

Chapter Twenty-Eight

TARZAN STIFFENED AT THE SOUND of the knock. He stood at full alert, ears lifted, tail at half-mast, and gave one sharp bark. Then both he and Jayda froze, listening for whatever might come next.

There was another rap at the door, followed by a faint voice calling, "Jayda." Or that's what it sounded like. Jayda wasn't sure and she remained motionless, but Tarzan raced down the hall and across the living room, barking joyously, wagging his tail, leaping up to scratch on the door.

It was obviously someone he knew. Had Ethan changed his mind and come back?

Jayda hurried to the door and flung it open, thinking as she did that perhaps she shouldn't trust Tarzan so much as to open up right after she'd been threatened.

Smoot stood there on the porch, much the same as he'd been the first time she'd seen him, wearing a smile so broad it almost wrapped around his head.

"Jayda!" he sang out, launching himself into her arms. He still wore the oversized World War I uniform jacket he'd put on when he'd learned he had to leave. His security blanket, obviously. Sergeant Boyd Jorgensen's jacket, still reeking of mothballs after all those decades in the old trunk.

She squeezed him fiercely, lowering her head to press her cheek against his stubbly buzz cut. "Oh, Smoot!" she whispered. "Oh, Smoot, I'm so happy to see you."

"Me, too," Smoot said, and then let go of her to wrap himself around Tarzan, who was whining and pawing his leg.

Jayda looked up at Lee, standing behind Smoot, whose grin was as wide as the boy's. "We're home, Jayda," he said. "For good."

He stepped forward, and the kiss he gave her was better than any stage smooch they'd ever exchanged. She clung to him, not wanting to let go.

"Come in," she said when she could breathe. "Tell me how this miracle came about."

Smoot raised his head from Tarzan. "My dad loves me so much he gave me up," he said.

Jayda could tell there'd been explanations that had tried to get down to Smoot's level of understanding. She looked again at Lee, who nodded, the smile still splitting his face. "Colonel Chad Ferguson is an okay guy," he said softly.

Smoot got to his feet. "I'm hungry," he announced. "Are there any more of Aunt Leora's little thingies of food?"

Fortunately, there were. Just enough, with one to spare. As Jayda zapped the "little thingies" in the microwave, she made a mental note to simmer up a big pot of soup and freeze it in the little plastic containers that had held Aunt Leora's. They had become part of a familiar ritual that drew people together. This, she realized, was how family traditions came about.

As they ate, Lee told her all that had transpired since he and Smoot had left. There wasn't a whole lot to tell. Colonel Chad Ferguson had actually cried when he saw his son for the first time in three years, Lee said. Smoot had hugged his dad, the way Belinda had hugged Smoot when he'd cried at learning he was to go away, and said, "It's all right to cry, Dad." They'd had a fine week and a half, the three of them, including visits to Smoot's ailing grandparents. It had all been good, the only dark cloud hanging over them being the fact that Smoot would be staying there permanently. But then Colonel Ferguson had said they needed to talk.

"He said his new assignment would demand that he travel a lot, including overseas again," Lee told Jayda. "He decided it would be hard on Smoot not to have a permanent home, especially since he talked incessantly about Blackbird and Tarzan and Twister and you and the old house and Bug and all the rest."

"What's in-cess-ant-ly?" Smoot asked.

Lee gave him a little punch on the arm. "It means you filled up all the air space," he said.

Smoot grinned.

"He asked if I'd like to become Smoot's permanent legal guardian."

Jayda's hands flew to her mouth, and then she said kiddingly, with a wink toward Smoot, "And of course you told him that was impossible." She then reached out and gave Lee's good arm a squeeze before grabbing Smoot and hugging him tightly.

When they had settled down again and Smoot had plopped on the floor to play with Tarzan, it was Jayda's turn to tell what had been going on there at home. Paul's broken leg, Ethan's leaving, Bracken's search for the old deed.

"We saw Bracken at the corral when we came up the hill," Lee said. "He had Twister saddled and bridled and was leading him around the corral. What's that all about?"

"He's making friends with his old archenemy," Jayda said. "He's been decent since I've been working with him to find some clue of the deed. He told me the family story he grew up with."

"Which is?"

Jayda retold the story of the phantom deed. "The only new thing to come out is a family legend that says it might be buried under the Jonathan apple tree in the orchard. And I guess there was some sort of a fight between my relative, Boyd Jorgensen, and his, Jim Morehead, during their last furloughs before going overseas with the army in World War I, back in 1918."

"Likely story," Lee scoffed.

"Maybe it's true," Jayda said. She told about finding the military button from Boyd's army jacket there under the tree. Calling Smoot over, she showed Lee where a button had been sewn on. "I'm hoping we might find a letter from Boyd in the wall of drawers that will say something about it."

Smoot, whom Jayda had thought wasn't even paying attention to what they'd been saying, said, "I know where there are some letters from that guy." Unbuttoning the breast pocket of the old jacket he wore, he pulled out a small packet of letters and handed them to Jayda. "The name in the corner is the same as the one on the headstone in the graveyard," he said. "I sounded it out—Boy-duh."

He was right. There were three letters. The return address on them said "Sgt. Boyd Jorgensen" with an overseas military address.

As Jayda held them, Lee said, "Smoot, how come you didn't show us those letters before?"

Smoot lowered his head and looked up through his lashes. "I liked having a secret that only I knew about," he said.

"It's all right, Smoot," Jayda told him. "We didn't know they might be important. Until now."

She looked at the letters, and another connection slipped gently into place. This was her kin, this young man who had gone away to war and returned in a coffin. But his life had impacted his family, right down to this day, right down to this minute as she held what were very likely his last letters. She pictured his mother, going through the trunk the army had sent a few months after his death. She saw her caressing the uniform and slipping the letters into the pocket before she packed it all away in the attic.

"Are you going to read them?" Lee asked softly.

In answer, she slid the first one out of its brittle envelope. It was dated two weeks before Boyd died in battle, in July 1918.

Dear Family,

*I can't tell you where I am, only that we crossed the
ocean safely.*

It went on to mention a few friends and to say how bad the
food was. The next letter said more about the food, and then
down a few paragraphs it said,

*I guess I should tell you, Jim and I settled the problem
of that deed. We decided after our fight under the apple tree
that it was time to stop letting it tear our families apart,
what with all the other fighting going on in the world. We
think it was fake, anyway. We never could find mention of
the selling company on the broadside Jim's family has that
advertises the property as being available. So we buried the
deed under the Jonathan apple tree and hope it never again
sees the light of day. If Jim chooses to tell you anything further, it's all right with me. But I'm hoping you all just let it
go.*

"I have to show this to Bracken," Jayda said.

♦　♦　♦

Bracken was still leading Twister around the corral when
Jayda and Lee went to meet him, Smoot and Tarzan having
stayed behind to go up to the tower room and gaze out at the
world Smoot loved and was so happy to return to. Bracken was
none too happy to read the fate of the old deed. Jayda knew he
had hoped to find it somewhere, intact.

Bracken's familiar scowl bunched up his face, and he slapped the letter back into Jayda's hand. "I'll find that deed even if I have to dig up the entire tree," he growled. "It's not fake. Just wait and see."

"Bracken," Jayda said, "it's been over ninety years since they buried it. There won't be anything left by now."

"Wait and see," Bracken snarled. "Wait and see."

Jerking Twister's bridle reins, he deposited the old horse back in the corral, then went into the barn, emerging a few moments later with a shovel and heading for the orchard.

"Let him dig," Lee said. "Maybe he'll work off his anger."

But Jayda was afraid. The words of the phone threat came back to her: *Don't relax too much, Jayda. The best is yet to come.* If Bracken was the perpetrator, he was full of so much rage that he might do something drastic even if he didn't find the deed. When she told Lee about the threat, he said, "We'll get Lucas to come up for the rehearsal on Saturday and make sure there are plenty of guys on alert."

◆ ◆ ◆

Later that evening, Jayda asked Lee if he would help with the pageant. "I know you don't want to be in it, but I really need your help in directing it," she said. "You know how to do pretty much all the stuff Ethan was going to do. Since you've been teaching music at the college, you probably have had experience with that kind of thing."

"You've had more experience than I have, Jayda," Lee said. "*Professional* experience. I'll be happy to be the producer and take care of troop movements and logistics and all that, but you'll be the director."

Jayda started to argue, but Lee was immovable. "It's your show," he insisted.

◆ ◆ ◆

The next day, Jayda was beyond stressed. And right in the middle of the preparations for the first rehearsal, Dave Bradbury and Mr. Yoshida arrived on the scene. Dave Bradbury brought him up to the house.

"Mr. David tells me that you are doing a show to honor your ancestors," Mr. Yoshida said. "This is a good thing. I would be honored to be present to watch."

And watch he did. He observed Belinda costume people as they arrived. She was amazing. With scarves and hats and the old clothes she'd gathered together, she outfitted the entire company so that they looked like pioneers struggling along a dusty trail.

Mr. Yoshida watched Paul hobble around with Bug's help to set up a small fireworks show behind the tower room, a preliminary to the "burning of the tower" which he'd stage for the finale of the pageant. The advertised promise of fireworks brought an enthusiastic cast who looked forward to entertainment at the end of the rehearsal.

He watched Lee giving instructions as to how to attach the frames and canvas coverings he'd gotten from Jake Sterry to the wagons loaned by three local farmers, who also had brought their teams of horses.

He watched Sal go through the music with various groups while Jayda took the principals off to another area to read lines.

Jayda noticed that Mr. Yoshida was captivated as he watched a subdued Bracken lead a docile Twister around the yard, well away from the cast members. Bracken still hadn't said anything to Jayda. She wondered if his digging had come to anything.

Mr. Yoshida seemed as excited about all that was going on as Smoot, who had asked permission to take Tarzan to the tower room to watch the proceedings from high above the crowd.

Which was why Smoot was there when the tower burst into flames, following a dozen or so loud pops. For just a moment everybody thought it was part of the fireworks demonstration, but then Paul bellowed that it wasn't time for that as he headed toward the back of the house, swinging his crutches wildly to move faster. Then they heard Smoot screaming from the tower balcony. "Help!" he screeched. "There's fire—!"

Before he finished the sentence, he disappeared from view as if an unseen hand had yanked him back out of sight.

Chapter Twenty-Nine

FOR A MOMENT JAYDA FELT HERSELF swept along with the crowd that headed to the back of the house where there was a door leading to the tower. She caught a glimpse of Lee fumbling with his cell phone in his only hand and yelling for someone to call 9-1-1 before he, too, bounded off toward the tower. Paul gestured wildly toward where he'd set up his fireworks and screamed at the top of his lungs, but the only words Jayda could make out were "fire extinguishers."

Let others take care of those things, she thought. She had to get to Smoot. He was in danger. The majority of the crowd seemed intent on the same thing, with Bug in the lead. Bug raced ahead of everyone, inside and up the stairs, and then came back quickly, reporting that there was nobody in the tower room. Just fire.

So where *was* Smoot?

Finally Jayda broke away from the press of people and

headed toward the back door. She could get to the tower from inside the house, too. She wanted to check on it herself. But she heard Tarzan barking as soon as she entered the house. Running down the hall toward the sound, she figured out soon enough that it came from the Remembering Room. Praying that Smoot would be there with the dog, she flung open the door. But it was obvious he wasn't there. Tarzan burst from the room and headed toward the front of the house, bulleting through the open door and off toward the barn. Jayda followed, the acrid smell of smoke stinging her nose as she caught sight of two figures, one tall, one short, disappearing into the gathering darkness in that direction. The short one, obviously Smoot, seemed to be struggling but was being yanked along by the other. Jayda couldn't tell who the tall one was. He wore a dark hoodie, apparently to cover his identity.

Jayda could see right away that she was too far behind to catch up, although Tarzan was making headway. But she wasn't as fast as the dog. Smoot and his captor had by now veered to the right just past the barn and were on the narrow road that ran along the edge of the ravine and up the hill to the cemetery. Jayda knew she couldn't catch up to them. She was already winded. It would take too much time to run back to the house, get her car keys, and drive up the hill. Smoot needed her *now*.

It was then she caught sight of Twister, saddled and bridled, his reins tied to a corral rail, his ears pricked forward curiously. As she ran toward him, her suspicion that Bracken was the perp grew to certainty. This was part of his plan, to have the horse ready after he set the tower on fire. In the confusion he would escape to the barn, leap onto the horse, and then as the house blazed, he would come riding innocently into the scene. Everybody had seen him working with Twister earlier. They wouldn't suspect that he'd set the fire. Or any of the other things he'd done.

Jayda bolted forward, untied Twister's reins, and then hesitated for a heartbeat. She hadn't ridden a horse for years, except for brief scenes in a couple of Western movies. He could pile her off and break her neck.

But Smoot needed her. And Jayda had ridden horses throughout her childhood. She vaulted into the saddle and felt Twister bunch up beneath her. Turning his head, he gave her a brief look, drawing back his thick lips in his familiar sneer.

"Please, Twister," she whispered. Patting his neck gently, she pulled on the reins to aim his head at the cemetery and then tapped her heels against his sides. "Let's go," she said firmly.

Twister blasted off at a full gallop, covering the ground at a clip Jayda wouldn't have believed he was capable of. Maybe he could see Tarzan. Maybe his fading old eyes could even see Bracken and Smoot. At any rate, he got the idea he was to follow. Within a few yards he was winded, but he kept going, gulping air, his big hoofs pounding steadily. "I'm sorry, Twister," Jayda whispered, "but there's so much at stake."

Not the house. Let it burn. It wasn't worth the price of letting Smoot be hurt by an unscrupulous monster. Jayda could see Bracken's full plan now. Burn the house. Mr. Yoshida would still pay top dollar for the land.

But what about the deed? Bracken wouldn't get a penny without the deed. Was it possible he'd found it somehow still preserved out there under the Jonathan apple tree? He'd still have to prove it was valid.

All of these thoughts spiraled through Jayda's mind as she and Twister entered the cemetery. Up ahead she saw Tarzan, stopped now, bristling, as he faced Asa Jorgensen's tall tombstone. Bracken must have taken refuge behind it and was holding Smoot hostage there.

"Just a little farther," Jayda whispered to Twister. The horse, stumbling now from his exertions, kept plodding onward. A few graves away from Asa's monument, she slid from his back. She must approach Bracken carefully. Desperate as he was, he might do something drastic if she barged in too forcefully.

Tarzan didn't even twitch from his bristling stance as she crept forward. "Bracken," she said sternly. "It's all over. Give it up. Let Smoot go."

There was the sound of a small scuffle as if Smoot tried to escape. But there was no spoken reply.

Jayda inched closer, close enough to touch the cold, hard stone, close enough to smell sweat—*and the unmistakable scent of Dave Bradbury's cologne.*

The shock of realization drove her forward, determined to snatch Smoot from his captor. Dave was largely an unknown entity. She had no idea what he was capable of. Plunging around the edge of the monument, she stared down at Dave as he crouched at its base, the hoodie still partially covering his face, his hand firmly over Smoot's mouth. He stood up when he saw her, dragging Smoot up with him. "It wasn't supposed to be like this, Jayda," he said.

"Let. Smoot. Go." Jayda said through gritted teeth.

"I can't," Dave said almost mournfully. "I'd lose all my bargaining power if I let him go."

"You have no bargaining power, Dave," she said. "It's all over for you. You've dug your own grave by the damage you've caused already. Don't make it worse by—" She stopped, not wanting to frighten Smoot by saying how Dave could make it worse. Taking a deep breath to calm herself, she said, "Why, Dave?"

He gave a derisive laugh. "Don't be naïve, Jayda. You know why. Mr. Yoshida offered me a *very* handsome commission if I could make the package deal of the house and all the surrounding land."

"For money, Dave? I would have thought better of you." She was hoping to distract him long enough to figure out how to get Smoot out of his clutches. Tarzan was ready to attack. But the man would be sure to thrust Smoot forward to ward off the dog. "Stay, Tarzan," she whispered.

Dave shifted his stance just a little, seemingly to get a better grip on Smoot, as he clamped his hand tighter around the boy's mouth. "I need that money," he said. "My divorce wiped me out. I never intended to hurt anybody, Jayda. I thought I could scare you away easily—you, a city girl who spent her time in fantasy land."

Now it was Smoot's turn to shift his position just a little, as if he were relieving a cramp. Then, without warning, he bit Dave's hand and at the same time delivered a hard backward kick to his shins.

When Dave jerked his hand away, Smoot twisted out of his grasp, hollering, "Tarzan! Get 'im!"

Tarzan lunged forward, but Dave slipped away, careening toward Twister, clambering into the saddle, and kicking the horse viciously in the ribs. Then it was all over before it started. Without even looking around, Twister performed his signature maneuver, tossing Dave ignominiously against Asa Jorgensen's tombstone, where he slumped for the few minutes it took Lee to puff the last few steps up the hill. Seeming to swell to twice his size, Lee stood over Dave—angry, menacing, and, despite his disability, fully capable of restraining the man if necessary.

Jayda reached for Smoot, gathering him in close, protecting him with a mother's instincts to sacrifice herself if necessary. Smoot shivered, his breath catching in his throat, and she murmured softly to him. "There, there," she crooned. "There, there." The age-old comfort words of generations of mothers.

They all remained that way, in tableau, until Lucas and Bracken and a couple of other men arrived in Lucas's Hummer. With a minimum of words Lucas asked if everyone was all right and then, with the help of Bracken and a few others, handcuffed Dave and assisted him into the backseat of the car. A man got in on either side of Dave. Bracken, before he got into the front seat, hurriedly caressed Twister's grizzled face and gave Jayda a salute that had the aspects of an apology.

As the Hummer rolled down the hill, Lee came over to surround Jayda and Smoot with his arms. None of them said anything, but there was no need for words. Jayda was certain, in the few moments they stood wrapped around one another with Tarzan nosing up to be part of them, that they all realized they were a family.

Old Twister, although trembling from his exertions, seemed none the worse for his participation in Smoot's rescue when Jayda, Lee, and Smoot led him down the hill to his corral. Smoot rubbed the old horse down thoroughly while Lee and Jayda gave him water and a special treat of oats. When they left to return to the house, he hung his head over the top rail and snapped his yellow teeth at Tarzan.

He would be fine.

The fire was out by now, thanks to the volunteer fire department and the efforts of the pageant cast. It had been confined to the top room, and the witch-hat roof had partially collapsed. But the house would stand.

Mr. Yoshida offered abject apologies for Dave's crimes. "It's not your fault," Jayda assured him. "But you can give up on trying to persuade me to sell."

He gave her an enigmatic smile. "Maybe," he said. "You will not mind if I 'hang around,' as you say, for more rehearsals? This was a very good true-life Western movie where the good guys catch the bad guy."

◆ ◆ ◆

Six weeks later, the pageant, titled *Seeing the Mountains*, was a huge success. With Jayda directing and Lee overseeing the general details, it went off without a hitch, playing to overflowing crowds both weekends of its performance. People came from as far away as the city, having been attracted, no doubt, by tales of the real-life drama that had gone on there.

The cast was amazing, so filled with enthusiasm and Ethan's

music that they brought the crowd to its feet every night. And it was obvious to Jayda that the two young stars, Travis and Caitlin, would be playing together in future productions, following in her and Lee's footsteps.

It was gratifying to Jayda to hear people from the audience and cast alike asking if they could do another show next year. She couldn't answer them. Although the show was such a success, the fate of the house was still uncertain.

Mr. Yoshida stayed the whole six weeks, coming to every rehearsal. He was there after the final wrap-up when the closing night audience had gone home. He was there when Sal dissolved in tears, saying she was sorry it was over. "I don't want it to end," she wept. She gazed all around, taking in the house, the garden, the soft night, and especially the people there with her.

"It doesn't have to end," Mr. Yoshida said. "I have a new idea for this old house."

Jayda took in breath to once again say, "No deal," but Mr. Yoshida put up a hand to hold it back.

"This is a new idea," he repeated. "A school of arts. You have the faculty already." He gestured to include all of them who had worked on the pageant. "Perhaps your friend Ethan, too. Do a new show every summer. Teach all year long. It will be the crowning glory of Summertree Meadows Estates." He smiled broadly. "And it is complete with an old Western horse. And ancestors. It is very good to honor ancestors."

"But I still won't sell," Jayda said.

"You do not have to," Mr. Yoshida said. "You own the house. You are like your ancestor, Asa Jorgensen. You draw people together. You lead them to a better place. You make a difference. I will present this new idea to our investors. But I must know if you like this idea."

Jayda nodded enthusiastically. "I like it very much, Mr. Yoshida."

"It will take much work to make this a success." He smiled broadly and then said, "One more thing. We will need a new generation to come along to carry on this good work." He looked pointedly at Jayda and Lee. "Do you think so too?"

Jayda was breathless. As Aunt Leora had said, things had worked out. Or at least there was a good possibility they would. Like her ancestors who had kept the wagons rolling through the wilderness, she had kept slogging toward a goal. And what a journey this was promising to be!

"I think so too, Mr. Yoshida." She put out a hand to draw in Smoot and then she moved closer to Lee, who gazed down at her with shining eyes. "If the pioneers could do it," she said, "so can we."

About the Author

Lael Littke is the author of more than forty books in both the national and LDS markets, including three women's novels co-authored with Carroll Morris and Nancy Anderson: *Almost Sisters, Three Tickets to Peoria,* and *Surprise Packages.* A native of Mink Creek, Idaho, she graduated from Utah State University and did further studies in writing at City College of New York, Pasadena City College, and UCLA. She lives in Pasadena, California.